You are about to experience
the most paralyzing terror
ever unleashed ... the final
hour of evil. One step beyond
the very boundaries of belief...
it has already begun.

THE DISCOVERY

She moved to the basement, telling herself to remain calm. A sound. Movement. Somewhere ahead. Or was it her imagination? No. More sounds. Maybe another woman. Someone else trying to beat the rush to the machines. She stopped, listened, looked around.

There was no one there.

"Hello," she said as she moved slowly past the janitor's dressing room.

A slight echo. But no answer.

"Is anyone here?"

Breathing. Waiting. And no reply.

Her legs seemed incapable of feeling, paralyzed. She walked down the corridor and stopped. There was a dark blotch in front of the compactor room. Strangely, it seemed to be expanding.

Moving closer, she leaned over. It was blood—a trickle coming from under the door. She wanted to run for the elevator. But could she? Someone was certainly hurt, possibly caught in the compactor.

She jiggled the knob and opened the door; it was black inside.

"Is anyone in here?"

No reply. She fumbled for the light switch and flicked it on.

She looked ahead.

Then she screamed, her lungs seared by a blast of hot air, her skin shriveled on her body.

THE GUARDIAN

JEFFREY KONVITZ

BANTAM BOOKS
TORONTO · NEW YORK · LONDON

THE GUARDIAN
A Bantam Book / January 1979

ISBN 0–553–12390–4

Published simultaneously in the United States and Canada

Bantam Books are published by Bantam Books, Inc. Its trade-
mark, consisting of the words "Bantam Books" and the por-
trayal of a bantam, is Registered in U.S. Patent and Trademark
Office and in other countries. Marca Registrada. Bantam
Books, Inc., 666 Fifth Avenue, New York, New York 10019.

PRINTED IN THE UNITED STATES OF AMERICA

To Victoria
who lived through it.

And to Rufus
who edited Chapter 27.

PROLOGUE

November 1963

Dr. Martin Abrams carefully packed his handmade pipe, lit the tobacco, and glanced into the file on the right side of his desk. "How do you feel?" he asked, constricting his heavy brown eyebrows.

"Feel?" the patient responded blankly, deep in the well of a trance.

Abrams noted the patient's discomfort. "You're relaxed, aren't you?"

"Yes," the patient replied unsurely. "Very relaxed."

"That's good."

Silence.

Then: "I want to talk about your mother," Abrams said.

The patient started to squirm. "I don't remember my mother."

"Yes, you do. You remember everything. Tell me about her."

Hesitating, the patient described the woman, and their relationship.

Abrams nodded. "Okay," he said, jotting notes. "Now tell me how she died."

The patient exploded in terror. "I . . . don't remember."

"You do. Tell me!"

"She died. . . . A long time ago."

"How?"

"Cancer."

"That's not the truth. Tell me how she died!"

1

"Cancer. Melanoma. I went to see her in the hospital. She was in tremendous pain."

"Is that all?"

The patient rambled on, then stopped, sweating.

Abrams relit his pipe and clenched his teeth tightly on the stem. "How did she die?" he demanded once more.

The patient looked wildly around the room.

"How?"

"They brought her back from the hospital. One morning her nurse was sick and couldn't come in, and Mother was in more pain than ever. She said that if I loved her, I would help her to die. I cried. Then I turned off her support machines and went to school. When I got home, she was dead."

"How did you feel about this?"

"Guilty."

"And what did you do about your guilt?"

"I don't remember."

"You do! Tell me!"

Agony. Confusion. Then: "I couldn't live with it."

"So . . ."

"I tried to kill myself."

Satisfied, Abrams probed deeper, quickly compiling a dozen pages of impressions. Then, concluding the session, he broke the trance. Within seconds the patient was lucid.

Abrams gave the patient some coffee. "I want to ask you some questions," he said.

The patient nodded.

"How did your mother die?"

"Cancer."

"Wasn't she murdered?"

"Murdered? Are you crazy?"

"Me? No. And neither are you."

The patient laughed.

The psychiatrist shook his head. "I want to ask you something else."

"Okay."

"Did you ever try to kill yourself?"

"No. Absolutely not."

"Are you sure?"

"Yes."

"All right. That's good."

The patient smiled and heaved a sigh of relief.

Abrams sat back in the chair and dumped the burned tobacco from his pipe into the wastepaper basket. He closed his notebook and nodded, all the while marveling at the most extraordinary case of repression he had ever seen.

December 1966

Arthur Seligson stepped out of the IRT station on Bleecker and Lafayette streets, convinced he had done the right thing by leaving the apartment. In the morning, Sue would have forgotten the argument and he could return home after having had a night on the town. Anyway, their relationship was becoming a drag; he was sick and tired of her bitching, and if she couldn't live with the fact that he was bisexual and enlightened enough to choose an occasional male companion while still preserving their relationship, she could pack her bags.

He turned down Houston, walked toward the East Village, and entered a club called the Soiree. He had never been there, but everyone in the gay underground was familiar with the place, if only by reputation. The club wasn't very large. In fact, it was too small to hold the crowd already inside. There was a bar near the door, a dance floor beyond, and a raised stage in the rear, occupied by four black musicians and two transvestite dancers. The decor was unexciting, but few of the people in the place were there for the view, and even if they were, the lights were so low and the smoke and haze so dense that very little was visible in any direction anyway.

He checked his coat, approached the bar, leaned toward the bartender, and ordered a scotch on the rocks. He waited until the bartender had delivered the drink, then took the last available seat and looked around, studying the faces. This was a different part of town. A different crowd. A more open way of life than he had ever encountered. It excited him.

He took off his mohair sweater and draped it over the top of the chair. The cotton shirt underneath was already drenched with perspiration. He asked for a glass of water, carefully tended the scotch, then reached toward a dish of pretzels and grabbed a handful. The man next to him smiled; he smiled back.

The man was attractive, blond, about his own age and very thin. He was dressed smartly in a black Italian knit sweater over white dress shirt and skintight jeans, embroidered on the pocket.

"Howya doing?" the man asked.

"Pretty good," Arthur replied.

"My name's Jack. Jack Cooper."

"Arthur Seligson."

Jack smiled a set of flashy teeth and sipped from his glass of bourbon. "Haven't seen you here before."

Arthur liked the sound of Jack's voice—soft, clear, distinct, feminine. "I know. This is the first time."

Behind them, the jazz combo finished the set and left the stage. Celebrating the silence, Arthur downed his drink and protested as Jack bought him another.

"You from around here?" Jack asked, moving his seat closer.

"No, Yonkers. Grew up there. Went to school in Buffalo. Came back to Columbia for graduate work, and that's where I am now, occasionally going to class and working part-time at Bloomingdale's."

"You live alone?"

"No."

"Just a roommate?"

"No . . . a girlfriend."

"Then you're really cheating tonight."

"No. . . . There are no secrets. I am what I am and she knows it."

"But it's not easy."

"Not easy at all."

Jack smiled, motioned to the bartender, and pointed to their glasses.

"And what about you?" Arthur asked as he watched the bartender fill his glass for the third time.

"I study literature at the New School and work here part-time."

"Doing what?"

"Mostly tending bar. I've lived in the Village about four years and worked most all the joints. I came in from Cincinnati. To be an actor. Didn't do very well, though. I did a commercial for a soft drink I'd never heard of, a couple of voice-overs that never ran, and six weeks as the Wall in a touring company of *The Fantasticks*. Pretty good, huh? Six weeks onstage without a word. Now, that's acting. But what the hell. I wasn't much of an actor, though I couldn't admit it to myself at the time."

Arthur nodded reassuringly.

Jack pulled out a pack of Pall Malls and lit a cigarette. "What are you going to do when you get out of school?"

Arthur shook his head. "I don't know. I guess I've become a professional student. Diplomas and honors make great decorations but don't teach you a damn about making a buck. And selling widgets at Bloomingdale's is not a career. So . . . I'll just take some more classes till they either throw me out or I marry a rich man's daughter."

"Or son?" Jack asked.

Arthur grinned. "Or son."

Laughing, Jack placed his arm around Arthur's shoulder. "You got a good head. And a good smile. I like you."

Arthur sipped from his drink. "The feeling's mutual."

Jack held out the pack of cigarettes. "Smoke?"

Arthur shook his head. "No," he said as he hic-cuped. Christ, he was loaded. "Never touch the stuff."

Jack put the pack away. "I might as well ask," he said.

"What?"

"When did you come out?"

"In college," Arthur answered without hesitation. "During my senior year. On a vacation . . . a ski trip. I went to Stowe, Vermont, and met a guy from the University of New Hampshire. He was a good skier and I'd never skied before. So he started to teach me, and we hung out for a week chasing broads but not doing too well. The last two nights we stayed in his hotel room and got drunk. And on the last night it hap-pened."

"Did you feel guilty?"

"Not a bit." Arthur paused as Jack laughed and continued to sip his drink. "And you?"

Jack lifted his brow archly. "I'm an old hand. Started when I was fifteen with a marine who was sta-tioned at a base outside of Lexington, Kentucky. And that was some noisy affair. My mom caught us in the hay one night when she was supposed to be out of town. Boy, did she flip out. Thank God my old man had died a year before or he would have cut my throat. As it was, my mom almost did. She was tough. She kept asking me why, and I told her if she were a boy and had an old lady like her beating on her every day, she would have grabbed onto the first cock that came along and held on for life. Well . . . she didn't think too much of my reasoning, so she beat the crap out of me every night for a month until I got the hell out of there . . . took the first bus I could find to parts east . . . Philadelphia, to be exact . . . and then here. Haven't seen her since. I heard that the shock of having a fag for a son blew her mind and she just flipped out. But I never checked, 'cause I don't give a damn. She wasn't much of a mother to start with."

Arthur digested the chronology. "Have you been with a woman since?"

Jack shook his head.

They continued to talk and drink through another set, until Jack looked at his watch and grabbed Arthur's hand.

"You going home to your lady tonight?" he asked.

"I hope not," Arthur replied.

"My place is only a couple of blocks away. Why don't we get a bottle of wine and go back there? It's quiet. We can talk. I'll light the fireplace, turn on some good music and whatever."

"Sounds good," Arthur said.

They stood and maneuvered to the exit. As they waited for their coats, a short, stocky man in a Moroccan djellaba grabbed Jack and hugged him.

"Charlie Kellerman," Jack said. "Arthur Seligson."

Kellerman embraced Arthur, then looked to Jack. "You leaving?"

"Yes. I'll come in at twelve tomorrow. And I'll work tomorrow night, but not on bar." He glanced at Arthur and grabbed Kellerman by the throat. "We should only have a piece of this joint. This queen is getting rich."

Kellerman laughed, then put his arm around Arthur's waist. "You spending the night with this creep?"

Arthur just smiled.

Kellerman drew deeply on a cigarette. "I give him my highest recommendation. But watch yourself, I might get jealous."

They all laughed. The hatchecker handed them their coats. Kellerman hugged Jack once again, gave Arthur's arm a tight squeeze, cocked his head once more, and brazenly kissed the air.

"Don't do anything I wouldn't do," he cautioned.

Jack laughed. "You're the corniest bastard I ever met."

Kellerman smirked, dragged on the cigarette again, and retreated into the crowd.

Jack called after him and placed his arm through Arthur's.

"Ready?"

"Ready."

They looked at each other, smiled, then left the club.

November 1978

As the tires spun hopelessly into the mud, Annie Thompson cringed and looked through the side window, straining to make out the edge of the roadbed. Other than her reflection, she could see almost nothing, and that made the ordeal so much worse. And God, she looked terrible, her eyes bloodshot, her face almost colorless.

Bobby Joe Mason gripped the wheel of the Volvo sedan, rammed his foot against the accelerator once more, and grabbed Annie's arm to keep her from being thrown forward. "At this angle, it's a bitch," he said, recapturing her attention. He looked up the summit road toward the ridge of the Adirondack peak and repeated through tightly gritted teeth, "A goddamn bitch!"

"We really know how to pick a week, don't we?" she mumbled, shaking her head and listening to the pounding of the rain on the roof.

"What the hell," he said.

The tires continued to spin, kicking up mud into the shears of the gale that had unexpectedly exploded out of Canada less than an hour before, catching them twenty miles from nowhere, unprepared and ill-advised, the weather report having predicted sunshine and warm days right through the Thanksgiving weekend.

Annie jumped in the seat, banging her knee on the dash, startled by the crash of a branch on the nearly obscured windshield. Bobby laughed, then reached back for a parka.

11

"Slide behind the wheel. I'm going to push. . . . When I yell 'gas,' press the accelerator to the floor and hold it there."

"Do you think it will work?"

"It better. Or else we're going to have to back down the entire road to the highway."

She grimaced in frustration. "Oh, great."

He snapped open the door, jumped out, slid to the trunk, braced himself, and breathing deeply, shook his head to shed the water trickling over his face. Above him the sky was black. Ahead, the apex of the road was shielded by an advancing mist that crept down the incline between the thick crop of mountain trees.

He wiped each of his hands, noticing that the flesh had already turned white from the biting cold. "Hit the gas!" he screamed.

She pressed the acccelerator. Mud shot up in his face. The wheels slid wildly from side to side, trying to bite into the ground.

"Keep going," he yelled, rocking the car again and again, until it finally shot forward and settled into the roadbed, the engine racing.

He sloshed up to the front door and jumped inside. "Let's get out of here," he said, gasping for breath.

Annie leaned over and wiped the mud off his face. "We did it!" she cried triumphantly.

Smiling, Bobby gunned the car up the road and crossed the crest of the peak, turning through a short expanse of dense wood into a parking area that fronted a two-story pine cabin and formed a proscenium for a natural amphitheater of trees.

"It looks the same," she cried happily.

He leaned over and kissed her gently on the cheek. "I told you it would."

She wrapped her arms around his neck and buried her head in his heavy wool sweater.

"Come on," he said, pushing her away. He rubbed his hands together to crack off the dried mud and then buttoned the parka. "I'll get the bags. You take the food."

"Okay," she said.

They collected the bags and packages and carried them up a short stone path to the porch, where he took a set of keys from his pocket and opened the door. Then they pulled the bags inside, turned on the lights, locked the door, and threw their coats on the over-stuffed sofa that stood in the middle of the floor, facing an old stone hearth.

The interior of the cabin was exactly as they remembered it. Heavy beams overhead. Furniture well laid out. Kitchen to the right. Staircase on the left, leading to the twin bedrooms on the second floor.

"I'll put the food away," she said.

He nodded and moved toward the woodshed door.

She popped into the kitchen and inspected the cabinets and appliances. Most of the shelves were empty, except for a jar of paprika, a canister of sugar, and several containers of seasonings. The potbelly stove seemed in good condition, but the icebox smelled from disuse. She left it open while she put the contents of the bags away.

"There's no wood in the shed," Bobby called, his voice nearly obscured by the wind.

She looked over her shoulder. "The agent said the wood was in the downstairs bin."

"I'll check."

She listened. The basement door creaked open. She heard footsteps on the basement staircase, some rustling below, followed by more footsteps, this time on the way up. Then silence.

"Hey!"

She turned.

He smiled, his arms loaded with logs. "Thing's filled to the top."

"Good," she said. "Now, start the fire and get that sweater off or you'll catch pneumonia."

He walked out of the kitchen as she pounded her arms with her hands, trying to keep warm; she was stiff, achy, racked by the discomfort that comes from cold dampness and biting wind. Yet she was unbelievably happy. They were alone together at the cabin just as they had been a year ago, two weeks after meeting at the start of the fall semester at college. It had all seemed so daring then, since both of them had been on their own, away from home, for so short a time, but now it seemed . . . well, just perfect, the culmination of a year together, sharing, laughing, crying, knowing each other as neither had ever known a person before.

Annie walked to the kitchen entrance, watched him toy with the paper and wood in the hearth, then walked up behind him, knelt, and threw her arms around his neck. "How you doing?" she asked in a whisper.

"Almost there," Bobby replied as he placed the last log on the pile, struck a match, and touched it to the newspaper.

She reached over his shoulder, grabbed the bellows, and handed it to him, kissing his ear almost as an afterthought.

He touched her hand. "I love you," he said softly.

The paper ignited. He fanned the flames until the underside of the wood started to smolder.

She tightened her grip on his body and pressed close. "Let's make love," she said.

He smiled. "It's colder than hell."

"It'll warm up. And we'll do it here in front of the fireplace."

"What if someone looks in the window?"

"Who?"

"Someone."

"If someone's up here on the mountain in this weather, he deserves every bit of entertainment we can offer."

They laughed. He pushed her over on the rug, kissed her softly, then pulled back in reaction to a violent gust of wind. He glanced at each of the windows to assure himself that no one was there, then turned, facing the fire.

She slowly unbuttoned his shirt, ran her tongue up his chest, removed his pants, stood, took off her own clothes slowly, suggestively, her pink body slithering through the dance of the fire's flames, then lay down beside him again, pressing her small firm breasts against his chest.

"Promise me something?" she asked, staring up at him with round green eyes that shone like lanterns.

"What?"

"That you'll never leave me. Or let me go. Or stop loving me."

He smiled. "I promise."

She laid her head on his shoulder. The patter of rain relaxed her. So did his warm, soft body. If it poured all week, it might prove a godsend. They could lie together like this for hour after hour, isolated from the world. In fact, she wished that they might never leave, that everything could remain just as it was at that moment. She felt his hand between her legs, rubbing slowly. She wanted him . . . so much. But she was tired. And the pounding of the rain seemed to be moving far away, retreating like the muffled sound of a drumroll.

Within moments she was asleep.

The last of the fire's live embers died into ash as Annie opened her eyes and yawned. The room was cold, and except for the assault of the storm, unnaturally quiet. She reached out for Bobby's body, but felt only the coarse hairs of the animal-skin rug. She looked around the room. The lights were out, and she was alone. Shivering, she put on her pants and blouse. The sleeve buttons in place, she sifted through the embers of the hearth with the poker. The remains gave off almost no heat. She must have been asleep at least five hours, and since they had fallen out at about ten o'clock, it had to be near three in the morning. A quick glance at the total darkness outside the cabin windows assured her that she was probably right.

She was angry. The bastard had gone upstairs to bed, leaving her alone, cold and naked on the living-room floor.

She stood and turned the switch on the table lamp; nothing. She tried the ceiling lights; dead too. The main fuse must have blown.

She walked carefully through the darkness to the staircase and began to climb, the wood squeaking loudly beneath her feet. Stepping onto the top landing, she flicked on the hall switch—again no lights—and poked her head into the master bedroom. It was empty, as were the second bedroom and both bathrooms.

Something was wrong; she could feel it. Her stomach churned into a knot, as a cold perspiration began to dampen her skin.

Running down the staircase, she moved quickly to the door and grabbed for the peg where Bobby had put the house and car keys; the peg was empty.

"Bobby," she yelled, almost in tears.

No response. Only the continued beating of the storm. And an almost audible sense of stalking terror.

She threw open the door. A chill blast of wind struck her face. She walked out and glanced over the porch railing. The mist had now spread everywhere, and she could barely see the car. Stepping down into the mud, she slowly maneuvered along the path and threw open the car door. The key wasn't there. And no sign of Bobby. She opened the glove compartment, took out a flashlight, turned it on, and looked toward the trail over the hood. Glancing downward, she gasped. The hood was partially open; ends of wires extended from inside, over the fender to the ground.

Terrifyingly aware that there was no telephone and no way down the mountain in the storm, she ran back to the cabin, slammed and locked the cabin door behind her, and panned the flashlight carefully over the room, examining the corners, looking for movement. Apart from the shadow of her own body, there was nothing.

The cabin was unbearably cold, and she was wet. She had to get the fire started again.

She ran to the basement entrance, opened the door, and looked down the rickety staircase, the flashlight beam dancing from step to step. She called Bobby's name as she descended. No answer.

The basement was a storage area. Toward the rear were several old couches and love seats piled on top of each other. Cardboard boxes were stacked in the corners, filled with utensils and broken bits of furniture. The woodbin was underneath the staircase, nestled next to the side foundation.

Laying the flashlight on the floor, she grabbed the top of the bin; it was jammed. She fought it, prying it up, until the hinges snapped and the lid opened. She felt for the logs; the bin seemed empty. But Bobby had said it was filled!

She picked up the flashlight and aimed it inside. Bobby was in the bin, jammed into the corner, one eye open, staring, his throat slashed, his body dismembered.

She screamed into the cold damp air. Then everything went blank as she ran up the stairs, crying, clutching at the walls and banister, the beam of the light ricocheting wildly off the walls. She stumbled over the top step, dropped the flashlight, and careened into the couch, falling to the floor. Struggling to her feet, she reached for the door, throwing it open.

She stopped, frozen in place, so terrified that the cry that erupted from her throat was silent, a funnel of air.

A man was standing on the porch, the sleeves of his shirt covered with blood. He was old, short, emaciated, his sunken eyes black and cold. The hair on his head was dirty, strewn wildly around his shoulders and against a crusty face covered with several days' growth of beard.

He stepped inside and croaked a horrible, demented laugh.

She screamed and stepped back.

"Shut up!" he commanded gruffly.

She grabbed the table lamp and threw it. As the lamp cord whipped across his face, his eyes exploded with anger.

Turning wildly, she raced for the staircase and threw herself upward, falling flat on her face. She looked up; two teenage boys were hulking over her, laughing, holding knives in their hands.

"God," she cried. "Help me."

The boys started down the steps. She fell backward, over and over, reaching the living-room floor on her side, half delirious.

The old man grabbed her by the hair. The boys ripped off her blouse and pants. She kicked for their groins as the old man grabbed her breasts, pressed the knife to her throat, and slapped her repeatedly.

"Beg for your life!" he said.

"Please," she cried. "Rape me, do anything, but don't kill me."

They all laughed—insane, maniacal, piercing.

She quieted, moving her stare quickly from one to another. Then she pushed past the old man and ran to the front door. It was locked. She turned, watched the men move slowly toward her through the shadows, then jumped through the front window, landing facedown, cut all over, pieces of glass buried in her body. She pulled herself to her feet and ran across the parking area to the woods, stumbling frantically through the underbrush. Behind her the men were calling to her, barking death. She started toward the main road. She could hear them getting closer. She could feel blood pouring from her body. But she could see almost nothing . . . nothing except a soft light in the distance that suddenly appeared as she climbed over a low rock wall and slid down the other side.

The light seemed to be close by, beyond a few trees and on the other side of the road. Yet, as far as she could remember, there was nothing there.

The pounding of feet interrupted her stupor. She looked over her shoulder. The three men were on top of the rocks, staring down, oblivious of the pelting rain. She started to run again, faster, through the branches, toward the light, which seemed to grow brighter, then wane. Yet that was probably an illusion, a figment of her imagination. Maybe there was no light, only a diabolical trick of nature's elements, a mirage born of desperation. If only this *was* a dream, she thought to herself as she stumbled forward, a nightmare that would end as she opened her eyes. Bobby would be next to her, sleeping. The fire would be burning. The room would be warm and safe. If only! She screamed as the old man called her name. How did he know it?

She ran into a small gully and squinted in the direction of the light. Yes, she could see it, no more than a hundred feet away. She pushed forward, aware of the men walking calmly close behind, delighting in her agony.

Brushing aside some branches, she entered a clearing. Standing across from her was a figure in a nun's habit, surrounded by a strange aura of light. The nun's eyes, bulging and swollen, were covered by hideous white cataracts. Her skin was wrinkled and cracked like dried clay, her lips blue and thin. Her hair was dead, stringy and broken, laid over a waxen complexion. She was breathing slowly. Her hands clutched a gold crucifix.

Annie approached the nun and fell at her feet. Behind her, the men raced into the clearing and stopped. Seeing the nun, the two boys retreated and disappeared. But the old man remained. He dropped his knife, moved closer, and began to shake.

"The Lord's cunt," he screamed.

Annie cringed; his voice ripped at her. She looked at the man, then the nun.

The old man pointed. "I name thee damned, Sister Therese," he said. "And your rejoicing should be considered. Your penance is nearly served." He stepped closer. "Then shall the minions of hell o'erstep these bounds. I, Charles Chazen, declare the moment at hand!"

Annie buried her head at the nun's feet as the ground erupted, shaking, pulses of light battering her senses. Her body hurt, her ears pounded, her head throbbed. Everything started to turn. She cried. And screamed. And tore at herself.

And suddenly there was silence. She looked up. A light sprinkle of rain hit her face. The nun was gone; so was the man who had called himself Charles Chazen. At her feet lay his knife.

She picked it up, dragged herself to the edge of the clearing, and looked out blankly, seeing nothing.

A tear dropped down her cheek. And she was frozen, like a statue in a park.

March 1979

The hour hand of the clock on the outside wall of the Banco di Roma stuttered toward midnight as a black Mercedes limousine pulled out of an alley onto the Via del Tritone and turned west, heading toward the Vatican behind a Carabiniere van.

In the rear of the limousine Monsignor Guglielmo Franchino scanned the passing streets. His face was taut, though expressive; his hands, topped by tufts of white curly hair, lay in his lap, wrapped tightly around two large manila files. He was a big man with a ruddy complexion, the angular features of the northern provinces, and a commanding, insular expression reflecting the years of lonely hours he had devoted to ecclesiastical history under the auspices of Cardinal Luigi Reggiani of the Holy Office and Sacred College.

The limousine passed below Trinità dei Monti, curled through Piazza dei Popolo, crossed the Tiber into St. Peter's Square and stopped in front of the pontifical residence. Within minutes another limousine pulled behind. Franchino sat silently, his animated eyes tethered ahead. The door of the other car opened. Footsteps approached. Cardinal Reggiani appeared and smiled graciously.

Franchino climbed out of the limousine; he and Reggiani embraced.

"I was afraid you had not gotten my summons," Reggiani said as they entered the building.

"It came just as I returned from Lake Como," Franchino replied, smiling.

Reggiani cleared his throat and popped a medicated lozenge into his mouth. "You have the files?"

"Yes." Franchino held them up.

"And Sister Angelina?"

"I will contact her tomorrow."

They reached an imposing door at the crest of a long corridor. Reggiani pressed the bell. Seconds later the door opened and the Pope's secretary invited them inside.

The Pope, a small, unprepossessing man with very Latin features, was seated behind a fourteenth-century Neapolitan desk. He rose as the secretary closed the chamber door. Franchino and Reggiani greeted him, then stood back as he repositioned himself in the desk chair.

"I will pray for you, my son," he said, staring at Franchino.

"Your Holiness," Franchino replied, bowing.

There was silence. Submerged in thought, the Pope beckoned toward Franchino, indicating the files.

Franchino handed him the first. "The background of Sister Therese/Allison Parker," he declared, his voice not far above a whisper.

The Pope read the material and gave it back.

"The successor," Franchino said, handing over the second.

The Pope read this more carefully, expressed his satisfaction, then placed the file on the desk and sat back, waiting.

The secretary opened a corner cabinet and withdrew a volume of writings covered with a sheepskin binding etched with Florentine figures. He opened the volume, placed it next to the file, and left the room, closing the door. The Pope placed a pince-nez on his nose and began to read.

Franchino braced his body for the long hours ahead. He had been through this before, having read the

words himself during the death watch over his predecessor, Monsignor Wilkins. Intuitively he knew which
passages were important and which would spark that
dread feeling of anticipation for the upcoming confrontation with Charles Chazen. Remaining immobile,
he gradually edged into a stupor until recalled by the
Pope's detail of Uriel's charge to the angel Gabriel:

> Gabriel, to thee thy course by lot hath given
> Charge and strict watch that to this happy place
> No evil thing approach or enter in.

> This day came to my sphere
> A spirit alien from Heaven
> One of the banished crew
> Hath ventured from the deep
> Him thy care must be to find.

He watched the dance of images that grew like
pristine paintings from his imagination. He could hear
Gabriel's voice ordering the seraphim to Eden's bower,
where they would find Satan at Eve's ear. And he could
perceive the image of Satan, who, once ejected, would
return as a mist by night to drag man to his eventual
fall.

The Pope detailed the fall of man, described how
God sent his Son to judge them, then continued reading, his voice drying and cracking, his face sagging
from fatigue. Outside the small window, Franchino
could see the first hint of daylight as the Pope recounted
Satan's return to Purgatory, where he charged his minions to follow him to the new world.

> I call ye, and declare ye now, returned,
> Successful beyond hope, to lead ye forth
> Triumphant out of this infernal pit
> Abominable, accursed, the house of woe,
> And dungeon of our tyrant:

Franchino felt a crawl of sweat ooze over his body
as he flashed to those moments, fifteen years earlier,

when Satan had tried to emerge from the bowels of Hell. He looked at Reggiani. The Cardinal's eyes were closed, his face serene. The Pope's words seemed to fall on Reggiani's ears like music. Of course, Reggiani had never faced Charles Chazen. Franchino had!

By noon the Pope had completed most of the text. They had been standing for twelve hours. Finally the Pope lifted the manuscript and recited the Almighty's charge to his children. Since man had transgressed, perverting Eden, then man would be given the task of guarding against the approach of Satan . . . just as Gabriel had been charged by Uriel. And all such Sentinels would be chosen for their iniquity—attempted suicides—not only to guard the Kingdom of the Lord, but to sit penance for their sins and thus save themselves from damnation:

> No longer in Paradise shall man dwell
> Eject them, Son
> And know ye that Satan, swearing his return
> Shall be their charge
> That their issue, conceived in sin
> Shall be chosen for sin
> To sit and watch for Satan's return and
> Thus incur my eternal forgiveness
> To cleanse their souls by eternal penance
> To sit as Sentinels

The Pope placed the volume on the desk and indicated the chamber door. Franchino opened it. The secretary reentered.

Franchino and Reggiani kissed the Pope's ring. Without a word they turned and walked out, their footsteps echoing into silence.

Monsignor Franchino's car turned off the autostrada and continued along a two-lane road into the wooded foothills of the Apennines. Seated behind the driver, Franchino prayed to himself, eyes closed, head tilted back, mind oblivious to the occasional farmhouse or cluster of stucco homes that sped by the windows. It was eleven o'clock. They had been traveling for two hours, having left Rome while the last hint of daylight still trickled over the horizon to the west of the city.

"*Signore* . . ." the driver suddenly said, breaking the long silence. He slowed the limousine and indicated a sign that read PONTE NORTE.

Franchino glanced at the fork in the road and pointed toward the right. The driver started the car up a steep incline.

"The road becomes very narrow," Franchino cautioned. "Be careful."

The driver veered the car from the cliff side; nodding approvingly, Franchino reached for a cabinet attached to the rear of the front seat, pulled out the files, and glanced quickly through the contents. Suddenly he jerked forward and grabbed his chest. A sharp pain dug into his side. His throat constricted; his breathing tightened. Panicked, he reached back into the cabinet for a vial containing blue tablets of nitroglycerin, and popping one out, placed it under his tongue and swallowed. He waited. The attack of angina began to subside. He breathed deeply, replaced the vial, and noted the time of onset of the fourth angina attack that week.

The tension was debilitating him; God grant that he survive it.

"*Signore* . . ." the driver yelled once again, pointing.

Franchino held his chest a moment longer, then put on a pair of spectacles to get a better view of the Montressa Abbey, now in sight on the plateau above.

"Pull up to the east entrance," Franchino commanded as he buttoned his frock.

"*Si, signore.*"

The driver gunned the car up a final rise and into the abbey driveway.

Franchino grabbed the files, opened the car door, and stepped out. Looking up, he noted that all the windows were dark except for one on the second floor.

"I won't be long," he said.

He walked through the abbey gate into a courtyard, then climbed the main staircase to the first landing; a figure was waiting in the darkness halfway down the corridor.

"Sister Angelina," he said as he stopped.

"Franchino," Angelina replied.

Franchino smiled. Angelina's unintimidated voice had lost none of its authority during the past fifteen years . . . but had it really been that long since New York?

He stepped forward as she moved into the sweep of the moon's presence. Embracing her, he examined her dull gray eyes. She looked old, her skin furrowed, her lips chapped. A hint of gray hair declared itself along the edge of her habit. The hands that held his sleeve were discolored and callused. But there was a solemnity on her face that he envied. Her soul had worn her temporal deprivations well.

"Did you hear the car?" he asked.

She nodded. "I have followed your progress since the Ponte Norte."

"As ever, you are most observant, Sister."

"As you are, Father . . . or you would not be here."

He raised his brow grimly.

"Come," she said, taking his hand. "There is brewed tea inside. A warm fire. And very discreet walls."

"I am grateful for your hospitality."

Angelina led Franchino to her chamber and quickly poured two cups of tea, placing both on a bare table in the center of the Spartan room. He sat and opened the files. She stoked the logs in the fireplace, commented on how well he looked, then joined him.

"It has been a long time," she said, sipping from a ceramic teacup.

"Yes . . . very long," he replied. "You've been well?"

"Well enough. My gout has bothered me. And I have suffered periodic disabilities. But I've been happy. And I've found peace. If there is more that one can hope for, my poor senses have proven inadequate in the search."

"I am happy for you, Sister."

"And you, Father? Where have you been? What have the years brought you?"

"I've spent most of my time in Rome. At the Vatican." Franchino's expression suddenly deepened. "And the rest in New York."

"How is Sister Therese?" Angelina asked.

Franchino darted a glance at the files. "She is well."

"May God have mercy on her."

"And protect her."

Angelina stared. "You've come a long way to find me. Though there is affection between us, your face tells me this visit is not one of hospitality."

Franchino fidgeted. "Cardinal Reggiani sends his blessings."

She nodded. "What does he want of me?"

"Your devotion. Your love. Your help."

"And you?"

"I ask the same."

She stood, walked to the window, and looked out at the night. "It is peaceful here. This is where I belong."

"The Sentinel has served her penance. She has been touched by the hand of God. Her vigil is nearly ended."

She turned back to him. "Chazen will not wait. Chazen will bring death."

"There is always death."

"Yes, I know . . . but I came to this place to put everything behind me. . . . It was my impression—our agreement—that my impersonation of the rental agent was to be my sole contribution."

Franchino nodded. "Yes. And I can't fault you if

you resist. One confrontation is enough to ask of anyone. But without you, our trial would have been impossible. Allison Parker might never have preserved her soul as Sister Therese. The line of succession might have been broken. . . . You have searched your soul for strength once before. And can do it again."

Angelina covered her face with her hands, praying, then looked up and leaned against the wall. "This time . . . I can't."

Franchino stood, grabbed the files, and thrust them at her. "You must!"

He stepped back, intercepting the glow of the kerosene table lamp. She waited, then slowly thumbed through the pages. He could see the doubts and terrors in her eyes. Yet she was engrossed. And he was convinced he could rely on her.

She walked to the table, placed the files facedown, and looked at him.

"Can I refuse?" she asked.

He clasped his hands together, emitting a small, breathy sigh. "Yes."

"And what would you think of me?"

"I would think that you have weakened in your devotion to Christ. But I would understand and forgive you."

"And if I say yes?"

"I would think you a fool. But I would bless you."

He swallowed a mouthful of tea and waited. Five minutes. Ten.

"I will come," she finally said.

He embraced her once more.

"What would you have me do?" she asked as she sat on her cot.

"You are to go to New York and take residence at the Archdiocese. There you are to do nothing until I arrive."

She smiled almost imperceptibly. "I almost forgot how persuasive you can be, Monsignor Franchino."

"It is not I who did the persuading. But you. I can

find nothing in your heart that is not already there. I am a simple man. Not a god."

"A simple man . . . but a strong one!"

He walked to her and placed his hand under her chin. Lifting her head, he stared deep into her eyes, then nodded, convinced that they had done the right thing by calling on her services once more.

"Will I return with you to Rome?" she asked.

"No," he replied with a reassuring smile. "I'll return by myself. On Tuesday I'll send a car for you."

Nodding, she patted out the wrinkles on the cot and spoke wistfully. "I have not left these grounds in fifteen years. I had hoped I might remain here till my death, devoting myself to Christ. I had hoped that I might earn his forgiveness for my sins. But I knew that one day you would seek me out. Even on the most restful of nights, when the air of the mountains drifted lightly over the abbey and the creaking of the foundation and apportments wove together into a lullaby, I sensed that it would not last. That I would have to leave the place that I had fled to for salvation. The place where I had found what I had longed to find."

Franchino looked at his watch. "I must leave. You need not walk me out."

"But I will."

He assisted her up and followed her into the corridor.

"Do you make use of any of the other rooms?" he asked as they started down the staircase.

"Only the room next to me, and the chapel. There are many chambers in the abbey that I have never even entered."

They turned out of the courtyard to the limousine.

The driver was outside the car, leaning against the abbey gate, smoking a Gauloise that fumed an offensive odor. Hearing footsteps, he walked to the car, opened the rear door, then climbed behind the wheel.

Franchino stopped, looked up at the abbey, then back at Angelina. "I will see you in Rome."

"If God wills it."

Franchino slipped into the car and closed the door. *"Andiamo,"* he ordered.

The car started down the path. Franchino turned partway around in the seat and watched the figure of Sister Angelina recede into the blackness.

Thank the Lord, he thought to himself. And he closed his eyes.

Angelina reentered the abbey, praying to Christ for strength and guidance. She had thought she would never have to leave this place. Or think back to what had been. To New York. To Allison Parker! She remembered the first time she had met the girl. The day Allison Parker had walked into the rental office and confronted her with the newspaper listing. It had all been so painful. The charade as Miss Logan. The careful hours of surveillance, scheming to keep Allison Parker from succumbing to the will of Satan . . . Charles Chazen. And now it was to happen all over again. And she was once again part of it.

She gazed blankly at the sepulchral walls, abandoned for nearly a century, then climbed the staircase to the landing, stopping at the first open archway. Over the stone banister she could see the lights of Franchino's car just below. Once again she was alone, secure within the familiar walls.

She reentered her chamber and sat down by the window to meditate.

A high-pitched shriek sliced through the silence.

She turned. There was something in the room. Something moving.

Petrified, she grabbed the lamp, pointed it, illuminating the dank corners, then cried out, jumping backward toward the far wall. Next to the table was the biggest rat she had ever seen, leering sinisterly through a pair of glowing, marble-sized eyes.

She reached for a copper pot on the mantel as the

rat moved into the lamplight. She watched it slink toward her, stop in the middle of the room, and wait.

Another shriek. And a third. There was a second rat on the windowsill. And an even larger one on the corner of her bed. They began to move in on her, their front incisors flexing rapidly.

She threw the pot, missing the largest rat by inches. Terrified, she dropped the lamp and ran to the door. One of the rats bit at her leg, tearing flesh. She screamed, opened the chamber door, then stopped abruptly.

Three rats stood at the top of the staircase. Several more were on the landing. And more on the edge of the ceiling abutment.

Below and to the rear, she could hear the scratching sound of feet on concrete. She looked down. A wave of rats was heading toward the staircase from the cliffside trees. She clamped her palms over her ears, trying to close out the high-pitched skirling of the vermin.

"Oh . . . God!" she cried, the veins on her face popping through the flaccid skin.

Above her, rats began to pour over the roof.

She desperately backed along the corridor, holding the rail. As she turned, a rat jumped onto her face, digging its claws into her cheeks. She grabbed it by the throat, pulling it off. Crying, she fell to the ground. Another rat dug its teeth into her thigh.

Rats were everywhere. Below. Above. Screeching. Biting . . . clawing.

She struggled to her knees and crawled toward the chapel, leaving a trail of blood. She was nearly blind; yet she could see the chapel door, ten feet away, guarded by hundreds watching her with hideous eyes.

At the base of the chapel doors she reached up. The fury of the attack increased. Gasping for air, she fought the bolt, which gradually started to slip. Then a lurch. And her weight. The bolt skipped. The door creaked open. She dropped onto the chapel floor.

The deflected light of the moon fell onto the giant crucifix that hovered over her.

The rats convulsed.

Downstairs, Monsignor Franchino burst through the abbey gate. The main entrance was covered by thousands of convulsing rats. He picked up a stick and began to beat them. Frothing, they nipped and charged, bunching and groveling at his feet. He kept swinging, killing, moving upward into the inhuman cries of woe. He called out Angelina's name. No reply. Struggling, he reached the top of the staircase. The corridor floor was strewn with the vermin—many dead, others still writhing.

He stumbled to the entrance of the chapel and looked inside.

Lying on the floor in a pool of blood, and tattooed by the shadow of the cross, Angelina moaned and moved her head. He fell to her side. She was barely alive. She tried to move her lips; only a rivulet of saliva trickled out. He said the last rites and lifted her head.

"I'm sorry," he said. "I knew there was danger, and I had to return." He felt the creeping ooze of death slide over her skin. Then he lowered her head and pulled at her habit. She did not have her crucifix.

Looking at the dead furies from hell, he carried her back to her chamber and laid her gently on the cot. He did not have time to properly dispose of the remains. He would return to Rome and see to it from there. Forgive me, he thought to himself as he touched her face.

He left the chamber, descended the staircase, paused in the courtyard to lift his boot and bring it down on the throat of a struggling rat, one of the few still alive. He looked at the glazed eyes and tightened his already resolute expression.

"And so it begins," he said defiantly. "So it begins!"

SO IT BEGINS

1

"What do you think?" Ben Burdett asked as he turned from the mirror.

Faye Burdett rose from the stateroom couch. "Close the jacket," she replied.

He flipped the middle button into place and stood erect, dropping his arms to his side. He was tall, and the dark complexion of his pleasant face was unmarred by blemishes.

Faye patted down the tuxedo lapels, inspected the pleats in his shirtfront, and straightened the silk bow tie, which had been listing to the right. "You look great, honey," she said.

She kissed him and moved to the dressing table to make a minor adjustment in her own outfit, a gray-and-black pantsuit and black silk blouse. Behind her, Ben examined himself in the mirror, nodding approvingly. Then he turned and bent over the edge of his eight-month-old son's crib, proudly accentuating the frills of his dress shirt with his fingers. "What do you think, Joey?" he asked.

Joey looked up and spanked his hands against the mattress. Ben kissed him and then sat on the sofa, waiting for Faye to finish. He yawned, tired. Two weeks on the ship had dulled his senses. He was sporting a potbelly, a painful raw sunburn, and a droll expression that begged for city activity. But that was not to say that he hadn't enjoyed the cruise. He had—ad nauseam. Fortunately, though, they would dock in New

York City in the morning. He merely had to suffer through the final banquet—which Father McGuire had told them he was going to miss—and it would all be over.

Faye swiveled from the mirror and smiled, the dimples on each side of her mouth deepening against the tint of her skin. The pantsuit fit her perfectly. She was very thin, with long legs. Curly blond hair. Not much of a bustline to speak of. And a face that most admirers described as clean, pretty, and slightly off-beat.

"What time do you have?" she asked.

He pulled back the sleeve of his ruffled shirt and clicked the knob of his digital watch. "Ten to eight."

She glanced impatiently at the cabin door. "Miss Iverson should be here any minute."

"Don't hold your breath," he advised.

Twenty minutes later the baby-sitter—a woman of thirty-five, employed during the day in the ship's salon —arrived, half an hour late because of a mix-up on the duty roster, or so she said. Since dinner was scheduled for nine, they would certainly have missed the best of the hors d'oeuvres and a round or two of cocktails.

The ship was yawing gently as they emerged from the aft section, B corridor, and stepped onto the main deck, moving in the direction of the master ballroom. It was cooler than most other nights had been, but then again, they were no longer in the tropics. They could hear the rhythmic thump of the bow cutting through the waves. Above, the sky was clear and a brisk wind was blowing from portside. Except for two stewards and a lone gray gull that signaled the approach of land, the deck was empty.

They walked hurriedly by the empty chaises and entered the cocktail lounge. As Ben had expected, the buffet was nearly empty. Through the open ballroom door they could see the banquet tables filling rapidly. The room was wildly decorated, as if the toll of New

Year's Eve were just hours away. Streamers and colored balloons hung from the ceiling. A ten-piece orchestra played from the stage.

"Hey," Ben called, moving along the buffet.

Faye turned and stuffed some caviar into her mouth. "We can eat inside. Let's go."

"Okay. Okay." She licked off her fingers and quickly sipped from the glass of champagne in her hand.

He grabbed her by the arm. "And after dinner we'll get smashed. All right?"

She nodded, grinning prankishly. "That's the best suggestion I've heard in days!"

Laughing, they hugged each other, pressed through the ballroom door, and disappeared into the hail of balloons and streamers.

Dinner was over by eleven-thirty. While most of the passengers remained in the ballroom, Faye and Ben retired for aperitifs to the Captain's Lounge, a small salon nearer the bow.

Father James McGuire was waiting for them, standing at the bar, sipping from a glass of wine.

"Father!" Ben called as he walked into the room.

The priest placed his drink on the bar top and embraced them.

"We missed you at dinner," Faye said, flipping back a droop of hair from her forehead, while grinning enthusiastically. She liked the curve of Father McGuire's jaw, his blue eyes, his classic Irish features.

"I must apologize," Father McGuire said as he led them to a table. "I didn't want to miss the banquet, but I realized that if I was going to complete my treatise before disembarkation, I would have to isolate myself."

"There's no need to apologize," Ben said.

"That's right," Faye added as she touched Father McGuire's hand. "We're happy you were at least able to meet us for a drink."

The lounge began to fill with other passengers. Ben

walked to the bar and returned with two glasses of Amaretto.

"How was the dinner?" McGuire asked as he relaxed in his chair.

"Excellent!" Ben replied, describing the meal, but failing to tell the priest that his absence had made the banquet otherwise forgettable.

Having little in common with the passengers at table seventeen, most of whom were from small towns in the Midwest, Ben was fortunate that Father McGuire had been transferred over to them on the second day, replacing a couple from Billings, Montana. The priest, who taught at the Catholic Theological Seminary in New York City, proved to be one of the most enlightened conversationalists he and Faye had ever met. And certainly the relationship between him and the priest had not been hindered by the fact that both were professional writers, Father McGuire devoting himself to theological treatises, whereas Ben was mired in his first book, a novel about politics. And Faye's own job as an advertising copywriter had proven to be as equal a common ground, since Father McGuire had an intense interest in the communications media, especially where it embraced religion.

"I'm afraid room service was not so enticing," Father McGuire said as Ben finished his monologue. He lit a cigar and offered one. Ben accepted. "But perhaps that was fortunate. Rather than wasting precious time gorging myself, I remained devoted to the typewriter."

"I want you to know, Father," Ben said as he placed his arm around Faye's shoulder, "you're making me feel very guilty."

"How so?" Father McGuire asked.

"I haven't been able to get a word written, and you've completed an entire manuscript in two weeks."

The priest smiled. "Ben, you're writing fiction . . . creating ideas . . . and that's so very hard. I'm merely transcribing conclusions I've reached through years of study and introspection."

"Now, don't beg off, Father," Ben said, jabbing his finger at the air for emphasis. "You're writing something important, something that all your students will be able to appreciate. I'd be the last to minimize the difficulty, and I won't let you do it. And besides, I'm just creating . . . gristmill pulp."

Faye leaned over and kissed Ben on the cheek. "Everyone is going to love your book, honey."

Father McGuire agreed. "I've told you, Ben, that if every writer wrote what I do, the world of literature would be very dull. The desire to entertain is as valid as the effort to teach. Who is to say who performs a greater service for mankind?"

"You're both being very kind," Ben said, sheepishly sipping the Amaretto.

A pair of guitar players entered the lounge and began to play.

Ben leaned forward. "Faye and I want you to know how much we've enjoyed your friendship, Father. And we're not just saying this because the cruise is about over and it's appropriate."

The priest tugged uncomfortably at the white collar that encircled his neck. "Let me assure you that the feelings are mutual. We can all thank the couple from Montana who asked to transfer tables, since their departure allowed us to meet."

"They asked to be transferred?" Faye asked as she lit a cigarette.

"That's what I'm told," the priest replied. "One of the stewards said something about a disagreement and a request. I'm not quite sure."

Ben shrugged, "Perhaps they just wanted a change of scenery." Should he say anything? he asked himself, suddenly consumed with curiosity. The dining steward had told him that Father McGuire had requested the transfer and had asked the steward to find out if anyone at seventeen would be agreeable. Now, if that were so, why would Father McGuire have suggested the opposite?

Faye interrupted his thoughts, talking, laughing, finally walking to the bar to fetch another Amaretto. By one o'clock she had finished three more, and Ben could see that she was far more subdued than usual.

"Are you all right?" he asked, winking at Father McGuire.

Faye steadied herself. "Yes. Of course."

Ben looked at his watch. Before leaving for dinner they had decided they would not stay out too late, since the ship would be docking at seven A.M. and they would have to be ready to disembark by eight.

"Why don't we walk outside?" Ben suggested.

"Of course," Father McGuire said, easing to his feet.

McGuire and Ben helped Faye onto the deck.

"I like you very much, Father McGuire," she said. "As a non-practicing Catholic, I've never been one for priests, but you're different."

"I appreciate the sentiment, Faye . . . but remember, before I was a priest, I was a human being."

"Well-said!" Ben declared.

McGuire stood erect. "When I was at Dartmouth, I even played football. And I did my share of trouble-making."

Faye smiled. "Let me tell you, Father. From a woman's point of view, you're a very handsome and desirable man!"

McGuire laughed.

"You are!" she insisted, licking her lips.

McGuire blushed; so did Ben.

"What can I tell you?" Ben said, shaking his head.

McGuire flashed a very unpriestly grin.

"Come on, Faye," Ben scolded. "We're going back to the stateroom."

"Okay. Okay." She stumbled between them.

They walked along the railing, reached the B corridor, and paused prior to separating.

"I'll meet you in the morning," Father McGuire said, "in front of the pool deck."

"At eight?" Ben asked.

"Yes." McGuire leaned forward and embraced Faye. "Now, you get a good night's sleep. . . . And kiss Joey for me."

"I will," Faye said. "Good night, Father."

"Good night, Faye." He shook Ben's hand. "Till the morning."

Father McGuire turned and walked briskly down the deck. He had a strong, authoritative stride, a long gait, an erect upper body. He certainly had been an athlete in his younger days. And probably still was.

"And now, young lady," Ben said with a curious look on his face, "you're going to bed!"

She hiccuped, agreed, and walked unsteadily with him through the door to the stateroom corridors.

A dream that began where it ended, faded into oblivion as he opened his eyes and glanced at the clock—four-thirty A.M. He turned over, hoping to fall back to sleep. Next to him, Faye was buried deep in the pillows with most of the blanket wrapped around her legs. He pulled back his share, then grappled with the top sheet, aware that the ship was yawing more violently than it had been earlier that night. Frustrated, he tried to relax. But he couldn't. He could hear footsteps on the deck. Someone was walking slowly . . . almost trying not to be heard. It annoyed him. But what the hell, he thought. Forget it! Get to sleep. And he thought that that would no longer be difficult. He sensed a wave of drowsiness.

Then he heard the doorknob turn.

He sat up.

Someone was trying to get into the room.

Quickly he jerked out of bed, threw on his robe, opened the door, and stepped into the corridor.

No one was there.

He walked onto the deck, and following a hunch, walked toward the bow and cut along the swimming pool. Reaching the opposite rail, he glimpsed a man disappearing behind the main-salon cabin.

He bolted forward along the starboard bow, covering the area where the man might have gone. Then, exhausted, he stopped at the railing, gulping for air, and stood thinking, hands shaking. After several minutes he turned back toward the cabin.

On the deck above was a man staring out at the purple sky.

It was Father McGuire!

Startled, Ben climbed the staircase to the next deck. "Father McGuire!" he called.

The priest turned slowly. "Ben!" he said, surprised. "What are you doing out here at this hour of the night?"

"I might ask you the same question."

"I couldn't sleep," the priest said calmly. "The air is invigorating. I took a walk, and I've been meditating."

"I see."

McGuire touched Ben's arm. "You seem upset. And out of breath."

"Yes, I was running."

"Ben . . . is anything wrong?"

Ben nodded, his expression stiffening. "Someone was trying to get into my stateroom."

McGuire seemed perplexed.

"I woke up and heard the door latch turn. I opened the door, but no one was there. I walked out on the deck and caught sight of someone running away. I gave chase and found you!"

"And you think that I was the culprit? A nighttime prowler?"

Ben stared at the priest. Did he really believe that? No, of course not. Why in the world would Father McGuire have tried such a thing? They were friends. "No, Father," he said.

McGuire smiled. "I'm not even out of breath, Ben, so I'm hardly a candidate for a recent chase."

Ben hesitated, then said, "I'm sorry."

"Don't be. I'd be as upset. And as puzzled."

Ben leaned against the rail, focusing his eyes on the

twin smokestacks that rose into the sky like mighty
black obelisks. "Damn!" he mumbled. "Somebody
was fooling with my stateroom door."

McGuire nodded; he couldn't disagree.

"But whatever he wanted, he didn't get it." Ben
touched the priest's arm. "I'm sorry if I disturbed you,
Father."

"Not at all."

Ben returned to the main deck and reentered the B
corridor. Something was hanging from the knob on his
stateroom door. He walked closer. It was a crucifix!

He took it in his hands and rolled it between his fingers. It was large, about twelve inches long. And very
heavy. Made of a dark, glistening metal.

Why would someone have left such a thing?

Reentering the stateroom, he dropped his bathrobe
on the sofa, peeked at the baby, and climbed back in
bed. Faye was sleeping soundly.

He wound the chain of the crucifix about his palm
and held it up. A chill raced down his back. He had a
premonition. Nothing specific . . . but something.

He put it under his pillow, and rolling onto his side,
decided to forget about it until morning.

Father McGuire examined the crucifix carefully,
laughed through a cough, and returned it to Ben. "I
can't imagine why it was left, but more important, I
think it's a waste of time to speculate. Forget it. You're
now the owner of a lovely crucifix. And may God smile
on you for it." He patted Ben on the back. "Really."

Ben looked at the priest suspiciously, then jammed
the crucifix into his haversack as a porter approached
and informed them that Father McGuire's luggage
had been cleared and claimed.

"Did you mention it to your wife?" McGuire asked.

"Of course," Ben said as he waved to Faye, who
suddenly appeared out of the crowd at dockside.

She walked over holding Joey in her arms. "All
done. The porters are taking the baggage outside."

Ben nodded and grabbed the baby. "What do you think, Father?" he asked, holding the boy to his face. "Looks just like me, doesn't he?"

McGuire glanced at Ben . . . Faye . . . the baby. "The eyes," he said. "Otherwise—and I've told you before—he resembles Faye. Amazingly so!"

The baby gurgled and mumbled. Ben laughed and handed him back to Faye, who was dressed in a neat gray skirt and white silk blouse.

Two porters wheeled by a cartload of luggage. They followed, weaving along the enclosed dock.

"Can I give you a lift?" Father McGuire asked as they approached the exit. "The seminary has sent a car."

"Thank you, Father," Ben said, "but one of our neighbors is coming."

They walked onto the street and approached the curb.

McGuire laughed as Faye asked him about the crucifix, then laughed again as he dismissed its significance once more.

"It gives me the creeps," Faye said. "I want Ben to throw it away!"

McGuire nodded thoughtfully. "I can understand how you feel."

Faye looked at Ben, who smiled defensively. "All right, I'll throw it away, or better yet, donate it to a Catholic hospital."

McGuire's limousine pulled to the curb. The driver jumped out, loaded the priest's luggage, and opened the rear door. McGuire remained with Ben and Faye, planning a reunion, then embraced them and little Joey and smiled.

"I'll miss you all," he said, "and I'll anxiously wait for your call."

"You won't wait long," Ben assured him.

The priest eased into the limousine and waved out the back window.

Ben and Faye smiled and waved back, then retreated toward their luggage.

2

There was no way to mistake the approach of John Sorrenson's 1956 DeSoto. The relic came jerking around a corner, coughing noxious puffs of black exhaust, rattling like a box of spoons and forks, and trailing the remains of its right fender in the wind. It looked like an enormous tropical fish with long tail fins and a convertible top scaled from years of winter corrosion. Behind the wheel Faye and Ben could see Sorrenson's cylindrical head bobbing about, his hands gripped tightly around the steering wheel and his eyes so focused on the progress of the car that he seemed to be cemented to the windshield. They could not help but laugh—admiringly. In this day of unreasonable repair fees and inflation, the first-cello player for the New York Philharmonic had managed to maintain the grotesque anachronism and to do it on what even he admitted was a "trifling budget."

The car screeched to a halt; Sorrenson popped out. "Damn old bat!" he said. "Broke down on Forty-eighth Street!"

"It did?" Faye asked as she approached him with the baby in her arms.

That explained it, Ben thought to himself. They had been waiting over an hour. Several times he had considered taking a cab. But since Sorrenson never missed appointments, they had decided to wait.

Ben started to haul the luggage to the car. "What happened?" he asked, glancing at the old man.

Sorrenson buried his hands in the pockets of his gray cardigan. "I don't know," he said, sounding less urbane and self-controlled than usual. "I was driving down Ninth Avenue when she suddenly started to smoke and rumble. Well, if that wasn't the most terrifying thing! I pulled her to the side and sat there quite exasperated, since there wasn't a gas station in sight. Then I opened the hood and let her cool off. I jiggled this. And that. And gave her a stern lecture." He nodded omnisciently. "And then . . . well, I guess we reached an understanding, because very soon thereafter she started and ran like a top. Would you believe it?"

Faye kissed him on the cheek. "Yes, of course I would. You've always had a way with women and machines."

Sorrenson blushed, hugged her, and caressed the baby's chin. He offered to help with the luggage, but Ben refused to allow a man of seventy to haul heavy suitcases.

It didn't take long to pack up the car, and soon they were driving uptown on Twelfth.

"Now you have to tell me all about the trip," Sorrenson demanded.

Ben looked to Faye and took the baby.

"I only wish you could have been there, John," Faye said, pausing momentarily in the middle of the sentence to react to a sudden backfire. "It was fantastic."

"I told you, didn't I?" Sorrenson exclaimed with an eruption of parental pride.

"You were right," Ben said, remembering it was John Sorrenson who had suggested the cruise when they were trying to decide where to go and by what means. "In fact," he added, grinning curiously, "we've decided to take the same trip again next year."

Faye caught the final stages of Ben's enigmatic grin. "That's right," she said, catching the rhythm.

"That's wonderful!" Sorrenson cried.

"Everything was perfect," Faye added. "Including the sun."

"I can tell. You look absolutely magnificent. But you, Ben! You took too much!"

Smirking, Faye jabbed Ben with her elbow. Sorrenson cleared his throat and began a barrage of questions. Faye fielded most of them, then asked Sorrenson how he had spent the last two weeks.

"Doing the usual," he replied as he turned the car to Broadway, catching the curb on West Seventy-ninth. "We had several concerts devoted to Bach. I've spent time with my quartet practicing for the summer series. And we recorded an album, which you'll hear tonight, since I'm having everyone on the floor over for cocktails to welcome you back."

Ben cringed; he just wanted to go to sleep early. But then, Sorrenson had been responsible for the trip, so they probably couldn't say no.

"How is everyone?" Ben asked as 68 West Eighty-ninth Street appeared in the distance.

"Fine!" Sorrenson replied. "Max and Grace Woodbridge were over for dinner last night. He's started a new business. Plumbing supplies or something like that."

"Has Ralph Jenkins returned from Europe?"

Sorrenson nodded. "Just a few days ago. In fact, I ran into him in the hall and told him that since the two of you would be back today, I would have a get-together in honor of you all. And you know how Ralph Jenkins is!"

"No . . . how is he?" Ben asked. He really had no idea what Sorrenson meant. Ralph Jenkins had moved onto their floor three months before, and they had not had much time to get to know him, since as a board member of the International Society of Antique Critics he was often in Europe on business.

"You know," Sorrenson responded, "just mention a party, and he'll be there."

Sorrenson maneuvered the car down the street, pulling up in front of the awning to the twenty-story highrise where he had lived for the past twelve years. The car backfired angrily. He commented on her ill-temper and threatened to take her into the shop.

As Ben got out of the car, he agreed, "It's probably minor, but you're smart not taking a chance."

Ben and the doorman hauled the luggage into the elevator, followed by Sorrenson and Faye. The elevator rose and jerked to a halt on the twentieth floor, where they stepped out.

Sorrenson's apartment was immediately to the left, and theirs was in the other direction, two doors down the hall. In all, there were eight apartments in the south portion of the building: theirs, Sorrenson's, Lou Petrosevic's, Ralph Jenkins', Mr. and Mrs. Woodbridge's, Daniel Batille's, one belonging to two secretaries, and one belonging to an old nun who never left her apartment.

Sorrenson and the Burdetts entered the Burdetts' apartment and walked into the rectangular living room, which extended to an L-shaped dining area that opened onto the kitchen. Ben tipped the doorman, then hauled the luggage down the bedroom hallway as Faye turned on the lights.

"I don't believe all the dust!" she said, examining the furniture.

"What did you expect?" Ben asked as he returned and sat on the sofa. "We're lucky it's as clean as it is."

Sorrenson agreed, reminding them that if they had allowed him to come in and clean the place as he had volunteered to do, they would have found the place immaculate.

"I know, John," Faye said, "but if we let you do all

the things you volunteer to do, you'd never have time for yourself."

"I don't need time for myself," Sorrenson declared, sitting next to Ben.

Ben tapped his arm. "I won't tell the other members of the string quartet that you've said that."

"Tell them what you will. Tell them what you will."

As Ben and Sorrenson lighted cigars, Faye took the baby into the bedroom, then returned and prepared several cups of coffee, which she brought to the couch. Sorrenson was quick to inform her that he had to leave at one o'clock for a rehearsal.

"Then you have a half hour," Faye said. "Just enough time to look at pictures."

"You've developed pictures already?"

"Polaroids."

By the time they had pored over the stack of photos that Faye retrieved from the luggage, it was nearly one. Looking at his watch, Sorrenson jumped to his feet and quickly issued instructions for the evening. "Don't overdress," he warned. "It's just a casual affair. With some tidbits to eat. And some music. Nine o'clock. On the nose. Don't be late. It wouldn't do if the guests of honor showed up after all the food was gone."

Ben and Faye walked him to the door.

"Have we ever been late for one of your dinners?" Faye asked.

"No . . . but it's never good to start a precedent."

Faye kissed Sorrenson on his wrinkled cheeks and adjusted the cardigan so it sat properly on his shoulders.

"It's good to have you back," Sorrenson said.

"It's good to be back," Ben replied. "Especially when we have friends like you to return to."

Sorrenson blushed, then hurried out the door.

Faye tossed Ben out shortly after Sorrenson had left and told him not to return until six. Then she unpacked,

secure in the knowledge that she would get far more
done with him gone than if he were prowling the
apartment.

She gathered a pile of laundry to take to the laundry room later, then spent about an hour putting
everything away and another cleaning. That accomplished she took the baby and left the apartment,
returning forty-five minutes later with a shopping cart
crammed with groceries.

As she pushed into the building, Joe Biroc walked
out of the supply room.

"Mrs. Burdett!" he cried, the remnants of a Slavic
accent still detectable.

Faye smiled. "Joe!"

They embraced.

"And Joey . . . my little Joey."

Biroc grabbed the child and wrestled him in his
arms.

"Can you come up and have coffee?" Faye asked.

Biroc looked at his watch. "I go on at five. But if
you can throw on some instant, I have a few minutes."

"It's as good as done."

When they entered the apartment, Biroc sat down
in the armchair with the baby and waited while Faye
hurried about the kitchen. He was a huge man, almost
six-foot-five, with massive shoulders, giant hands, and
large sinuous muscles. Joey looked almost nonexistent
in his arms.

"Well, Joe . . . what's new?" Faye asked as she returned from the kitchen with two filled cups.

"There's not much to speak of," he began, "except
. . . my daughter had a baby."

"A grandchild? How wonderful!"

He nodded somewhat apologetically, reticent about
introducing his private life to the tenants of the building.

"Oh, Joe, I'm so happy for you. Is it the first?"

"Of course. Do I look so old that I'd have more
than one?"

They both laughed.

"His name is Todd. Todd Melincek. That's a nice name, isn't it?"

"That's a splendid name. In fact, Ben and I were considering it for Joey. Joey was almost a Todd."

"Is that so?"

Faye nodded. "Where does your daughter live?"

"Long Island."

"Does her husband work in town?"

"No . . . he has a plant near their house. He manufactures ladies' sweaters."

"Ladies' sweaters? That's a terrific business, Joe. If all the women in the country were like me, your son-in-law would be a millionaire—if he isn't already, that is."

"He has a way to go," Biroc admitted. "But even if he never gets rich, that wouldn't matter. He treats my daughter well. That's what's important."

"I couldn't agree with you more."

Biroc smiled and sipped the coffee.

"You know, I almost forgot," Faye announced suddenly as she jumped to her feet and raced to the bedroom. "We brought you something."

Biroc protested and warned that he had to go downstairs to start his shift. Faye was back in the room before he could leave.

"Ben and I couldn't resist . . . You've been so incredibly kind."

She held out a wrapped package. He took it and rattled it next to his ear.

"It doesn't tick."

"Open it!"

He pulled off the wrapping. Inside was a wooden box about ten inches long. He lifted the top.

"You shouldn't have," he said as he eased a hand-carved pipe out of its setting.

"We know how much you like pipes, and this was the prettiest one we had ever seen."

Biroc placed the stem in his mouth, then shook his head, put the pipe back in its case, and hugged her.

"I will put it at the head of my desk so it will always be in sight."

Moments later Biroc left the apartment. Smiling, Faye locked the door and returned to the kitchen to put away the groceries, pleased that Joe had enjoyed the present.

Ben came in at six o'clock. He stopped in the lobby to talk to Biroc, then rode up to the twentieth floor and knocked on Max Woodbridge's door.

Grace Woodbridge, a petite, gray-haired woman of fifty, incurably addicted to patterned blouses and long hemlines, answered. "Ben," she cried, holding a pan of steaming cornbread in her hands. "Max, it's Ben."

Max Woodbridge emerged from the den. "Ben, my boy," he said, approaching the door, "good to have you back."

Ben smiled. "I just want to say hello and thank you for watering the plants."

"Don't even mention it," Grace protested. "It was our pleasure. And besides, Faye has already thanked us. So enough. Here. Come in. Sit. Have some cornbread. You like cornbread, don't you?"

"Love it. But I just grabbed something at the deli."

"Just a little piece?"

"Bring it to Sorrenson's."

"I baked it for Sorrenson."

Max Woodbridge smiled, ran his hands through his rapidly thinning hair, then tightened the belt of his robe and shuffled his slippered feet on the rug. "You sure we can't get you anything?"

"Not a thing. Like I said, this is just a hello and a thank you."

"All right, but if you change your mind, you know where to find us."

"Of course. At Sorrenson's. Nine o'clock. On the nose."

"Good old Sorrenson," Max Woodbridge said, laughing.

"Yep . . . good old Sorrenson!"

Ben found Faye asleep on the living-room couch, her feet draped over the back. Next to her was a half-empty glass of wine.

He picked her up and carried her to the bedroom, laid her on the bed, then walked back into the hall, grabbed his haversack, and pulled out the crucifix. Deciding not to throw it away after all, he opened a desk drawer and shoved it under a stack of papers.

Returning to the bedroom, he took off his shirt, threw it over the dressing table, kissed the baby, who was asleep in his crib, then lay down next to Faye and fell asleep.

3

Ralph Jenkins was lecturing the guests on one matter of trivia or another when John Sorrenson opened his apartment door and ushered Ben and Faye into the room.

"You're half an hour late," Sorrenson scolded.

"I'm sorry," said Faye, "but Ben and I took a nap and we slept through the alarm."

Sorrenson shook his head.

"What did you expect?" Jenkins asked, glancing at Sorrenson while adjusting his thick bifocals. "They just return from a two-week cruise, and you want them to explode with energy?"

"Yeh, John," Max Woodbridge joined "they want to be late, they can be late."

"But you know—"

"Know nothing!" Grace Woodbridge declared, interrupting.

Sorrenson shook his head, fiddled with his tie, and laughed, admitting defeat. He was wearing an odd-colored suit, and if Ben's eyesight was correct, one brown and one black shoe. But that was John Sorrenson, the musician, the refugee from a rummage sale, whose appearance was made all the more striking whenever he was near the impeccably dressed Ralph Jenkins.

"Some wine?" Daniel Batille suggested, holding two bottles high in the air.

"White," Faye said. "For both of us?" Ben nodded. "Two whites."

Batille, who was working his way through graduate law school by tending bar, filled the glasses.

"Wine and music," Sorrenson declared, marching to the phonograph.

"Something mellow," one of the two secretaries suggested.

"I got just the thing." Sorrenson placed an old forty-five on the turntable and set the arm. "Vintage Sinatra!"

"Who's Sinatra?" the other secretary asked, deadpan.

Everyone laughed, offered toasts, moved around the living room—incredibly cluttered with knick-knacks, relics from garage sales, and mismatched wooden furniture—and laughed some more.

"You've just been in Europe, haven't you, Ralph?" Ben asked after Batille had doled out another round of drinks and the record had ground to conclusion.

"Yes. On a business trip." Jenkins, who was just past sixty, had a formal manner of speaking and a slight hint of an accent that Ben could never place and even though Jenkins claimed to have been born in the cantons of Bavaria, the accent had always seemed curiously non-Aryan. "My colleagues and I started out in England and ended up in Istanbul. We were looking for artifacts frōm the Bourbon period but weren't able to find anything of interest. However, we did uncover some leads, and next month, when I return to Europe, I'm going to pursue them."

"Then it wasn't a total disappointment?"

"Not at all, even if just for the opportunity to travel and develop new friendships."

Ben smiled. "Well . . . traveling must agree with you, Ralph. You look good. Rested."

"And so do you. But you know, it's good to be home. And besides, I'm going to be unusually busy this stay—writing an article for the *Ladies' Home Journal* and starting a book on antiques." He smiled. "How's your novel coming?"

"The dregs."

"Oh?"

"I didn't do a thing on the cruise."

Sorrenson returned from the kitchen with a handful of sandwiches and distributed them as Ben and Jenkins walked by the living-room windows.

Jenkins looked down at the street, staring thoughtfully. "What did you think of the construction?"

Ben looked out. Directly across from 68 West was an enormous excavation surrounded by a wood fence. He had noticed it earlier, assuming that a new high-rise was under construction. "What are they building?"

"You don't know?"

"No. How would I?"

"I thought I spoke to you about it before you left."

"Not a word."

Jenkins nodded. "The Archdiocese of New York is building a cathedral."

Daniel Batille and Sorrenson joined them.

"We're talking about St. Simon's," Jenkins said to bring the others up-to-date. "A lot of people in the neighborhood aren't happy about it."

"And I'm one of them," Sorrenson announced. "I don't want my view blocked by a goddamn spire."

"Is there anything we can do to stop the project?" Ben asked.

Jenkins shook his head. "I tried to find out before I left for Europe. I contacted the archdiocese, but that was a waste of time. Then I checked with the city, but the archdiocese had complied with the existing zoning regulations. I also checked the tax rolls and found that the land had been transferred to the archdiocese over fifty years ago. And not just the area where the cathedral is being built. But the entire block, both sides, including the land on which this building stands." He paused, studying the curious reactions. "I also discovered that the Equity Corporation to whom we pay our rent is owned outright by the archdiocese too."

"The archdiocese owns the building?" Sorrenson asked.

"Yes," Jenkins replied.

"I don't like this one bit," Sorrenson declared.

"What are you going to do?" Ben asked. "Move out?"

"I don't know. I just don't like the idea."

"John," said Max Woodbridge, "this may be the answer to our salvation. We stay here and take the elevator up when we go!"

"I don't find that funny," Sorrenson declared.

There was no doubt in Ben's mind that Sorrenson's displeasure was genuine. On the other hand, why should anyone get upset? What did it matter if the archdiocese owned the building?

"Maybe that explains our friendly nun," Batille said.

"You may be right," said Jenkins, picking up the

thread of the suggestion. "It makes sense that a nun would be supported by the church."

Grace Woodbridge, who had been listening, exploded with animation, drawing everyone in the room into the conversation. "I was told she'd been a captive of the Communists during the revolution in Hungary in 1956. She was attached to the archdiocese in Budapest, but was spending most of her time coordinating anti-Communist riots. After the outbreak of fighting, she was arrested by the KGB and tortured. The Vatican negotiated for her release and brought her here. Supposedly she's still remembered as a martyr in Hungary." Grace paused, shaking her head. "The KGB damaged her permanently. She's paralyzed, deaf, dumb, and blind, confined to that seat in the window."

"Is that true?" Ben asked.

Grace shrugged. "I don't know—that's what I was told."

"Who told you this?" Jenkins asked.

"A Hungarian refugee named Jan Nagy, who used to live on the fifth floor. He said he'd had contact with the nun while trying to escape."

"That's interesting," said Sorrenson, "but I wouldn't place too much credence in the story."

"Why not?"

"Jan Nagy was a mental patient. A nut. A schizo case. You can't believe anything he said."

Jenkins smiled curiously. "An old nun. Paralyzed. Blind. Deaf. Mute. Sitting at an apartment window. Never moving. Never leaving. With no visitors. No history. No visible way of life. I'm sure in a less-enlightened society such a person would have spawned some incredible stories." He laughed. "Another Count Dracula. Very intriguing."

Faye wrapped her arms about her chest and shivered. "Ralph . . . you're giving me the creeps."

"I'm just fantasizing, Faye. I'm sure she's just a nice old lady."

"A nice old lady?" Sorrenson shook his head. "I doubt it. In fact, we should try to find out exactly who or what she is."

Faye looked up. "John, I think we'd all be better off if we just forgot about her, left her alone."

"Why's that?" Ben asked.

"I don't know. I just have this feeling! Ever since we moved into the building, I've tried to forget that the woman is next to us—that our bedroom is right beyond the room where she sits. It's been very unnerving. . . . And, Ben, when we returned this morning, I sensed that she was looking down at me. I've never felt that before, and I don't know why I did then, but I did!"

Jenkins turned on an additional lamp. "I think we'd better change the subject."

"That's a good idea," Ben said, hoping they had not precipitated a witch hunt. The old nun had been there for a long time, and nothing had ever occurred to even suggest there was something sinister about her.

Sorrenson placed the new recording by the string quartet on the phonograph. The apartment, which had grown quiet, sputtered to life.

Ben joined Jenkins near the window. Jenkins had become strangely aloof.

"What's on your mind?" Ben asked. He could see Faye watching them curiously.

Jenkins sniffed and rubbed his hand along the base of his nose. "I was thinking."

"About what?"

"About the nun. And what Faye said, that we'd all be better off if we just forgot about her, left her alone."

"Oh, Faye's just frightened by the old broad."

Jenkins smiled. "Yes, frightened . . . but I think she's right."

Ben pressed his face against the cold window glass. Faye. Batille. Sorrenson. Grace Woodbridge. And now Jenkins. All of them spooked. Incredible.

"I think I'm going out of my mind," Faye declared as she bundled the laundry together on the dining-room table and stuffed it into the carrying cart.

"What do you mean?" Ben asked. He was curled on the couch with his shirt off, smoking a cigar.

"Well . . . not out of my mind, but don't you think that all of this is kind of weird?" Faye slid onto the couch. "Don't you think it's been something of a coincidence to suddenly have the Catholic Church breathing down our necks?"

"How do you mean?"

"First we meet Father McGuire on the ship. Then you're awakened in the middle of the night and find a crucifix on our door. I grant you, chance—possibly. But we come home and discover that the archdiocese not only owns all the land on both sides of the block, but this building as well. And of course there's the nun. Now, come on, Ben, those are a lot of coincidences."

He groaned and raised himself against the rear of the couch. "That's exactly what they are! Coincidences. I don't mind playing twenty questions with the neighbors, but let's not get wrapped up in this ourselves."

"Ben, please . . ."

"Faye, honey, I'm tired. We just got back to town. We should never have gone to Sorrenson's tonight. And frankly, all I want is some peace of mind and some sleep." He stared at her as she bit her lip; then, glancing at his watch, he said, "Hey, it's almost twelve. If you expect to get the laundry downstairs tonight, you'd better hurry."

"Okay. Okay."

"Do you want me to help?" he asked.

"No, I can manage," she replied. She grabbed the laundry cart, walked into the hall, and waited as the lights on the elevator panel slowly crawled upward. Damn that Ben, she thought. He was being a pain, especially since he was well aware of the disturbing coincidences himself.

The elevator arrived and the door slid open. She pulled the laundry cart inside. As the car descended, it was silent except for the whir of the mechanism's motor and the swish of wind in the elevator shaft. The indicator ticked downward; then the car slowed and stopped. The door opened and she wheeled the cart into the cinder-block-lined corridor.

The laundry room was at the end of the building, around a bend in the dark hall. Ahead, Faye could hear the bellow of the huge boiler. Behind, the sound of the rising elevator was barely audible.

She moved through the basement, telling herself to remain calm. She hated the place. But the laundry needed to be done, and if she waited for the morning, all the machines would have been taken by the early risers.

A sound. Movement. Somewhere ahead. Or was it her imagination? No. More sounds. Maybe another woman. Someone else trying to beat the rush to the machines. She stopped, listened, looked around.

There was no one there.

"Hello," she said as she moved slowly past the janitor's dressing room.

A slight echo. But no answer.

"Is anyone here?"

Breathing. Waiting. And no reply. Everything was okay.

She turned the bend. Ahead was the compactor room and the laundry room beyond, illuminated by a small red light.

Damn! The cart suddenly felt so heavy, as if she were pulling a load of bricks. And her legs seemed incapable of feeling, paralyzed.

She walked down the corridor and stopped. There was a dark blotch in front of the compactor room. Strangely, it seemed to be expanding.

Moving closer, she leaned over. It was blood—a trickle coming from under the door.

She wanted to run for the elevator. But could she? Someone was certainly hurt, possibly caught in the compactor.

She jiggled the knob and opened the door; it was black inside.

"Is anyone in here?"

No reply. She fumbled for the light switch and flicked it on.

She looked ahead.

Then she screamed, her lungs seared by a blast of hot air, her skin shriveled on her body.

"What the hell," Ben mumbled as he forced open his eyes and looked out at the blur of the room.

Someone continued to knock violently on the door, screaming his name.

"Coming . . . coming." Damn idiot's going to wake the baby. And Faye, too. She'd come back, hadn't she? "Hold your horses!"

He threw on his shirt and stumbled into the foyer.

"Okay," he said, snapping the latch and opening the door. "What! What's going on here, Joe!"

Biroc limped into the room, holding Faye in his arms. She was half-conscious and drained of color, except for her lips, which were cyanotic blue.

"Mr. Burdett. Oh, my God!"

Ben grabbed Faye and laid her on the couch. "Faye . . . honey? . . ."

No response.

"Faye!"

Gibberish.

Biroc opened the windows.

"What happened?" Ben cried as he ran to the kitchen, grabbed a damp cloth, returned and put it on Faye's forehead.

"Oh . . . Mr. Burdett!" Biroc said, shaking. "I'm not

sure. But there's a horrible . . ." He stopped, crying.

Ben grabbed him by the collar. "Get hold of yourself, dammit!" He shook him hard and pushed him onto the couch. "What happened?"

Biroc held his head to steady himself and jerked in two or three heavy breaths. "I was on the door, when the elevator opened and Mrs. Burdett ran out screaming. She didn't make much sense, but I could make out some words. She said there was a dead body in the basement. I left her at the door with Mr. Spezio from Three-H, took a flashlight and a club from the closet, and went downstairs."

"What was down there?" Ben asked, starting to come unglued himself.

"A body. And blood. In the compactor. Oh . . . my God . . . my God . . ."

"Did you call the police?"

"No."

Ben took Faye's hand and continued to press the cloth. "Or an ambulance?"

"No."

Ben ran to the phone. Goddamn hands were shaking so badly, he misdialed several times. Finally he asked the operator to get the police. When the connection was made, he repeated what Biroc had told him, then set the phone back on its cradle and returned to Faye.

She threw out her arms, trembling violently, foam bubbling from her mouth. He held her tight. Whatever Biroc had seen in the basement must have been horrifying to have made a man as stable and strong as Biroc go to pieces. There was much Ben wanted to ask, but he just sat there and quietly caressed Faye and waited.

There was no furniture, only a solitary chair in front of the center living-room window. The door was triple-locked. There was no light. In the chair sat a nun, Sister Therese. In her hands was a gold crucifix. Normally totally immobile, she was squirming, upset, her hideous face contorting terribly, her discomfort increasing.

Charles Chazen was in the building!

4

Chief Inspector Jake Burstein, Manhattan Homicide Division, felt his stomach ravel into a knot. He'd seen many corpses in his life, but this one was by far the most revolting. The entire body had been burned, then compacted like a package of garbage. Only the right arm, which extended out of the compacting chamber, remained completely intact, though it too had been burned almost beyond recognition. The skull was still in one piece, though most of it had been compressed. The torso was just a stump. The legs were crushed and black.

Burstein unbuttoned his raincoat—he had just arrived—and looked around the room. It wasn't very large, maybe ten feet square, made of gray cinder-block and unretouched-concrete floor. There was blood on the floor. And a trickle was still oozing out of the chamber. "Who found the body?" he asked, his voice heavily tinted by a Long Island inflection.

"A woman on the twentieth floor," said Detective Wausau, who was standing to Burstein's right.

"What's her name?"

"Faye Burdett." Wausau looked at the pad in his

hand. "Her husband called us. A doorman, named Biroc, saw the body too."

Burstein stepped around an NYPD forensic specialist who was dusting the floor, and several other unit men who were working on the compactor chamber beneath a temporary light attached to the water pipes on the ceiling.

"Who's in charge?" he asked.

The man nearest the compactor identified himself.

"Any prints?" Burstein asked.

"So far nothing."

Burstein poked a toothpick at the remains of the roast beef he had eaten for dinner. "How long's the victim been dead?"

"Not sure. But certainly not too long. The skin is still smoldering, and there are no signs of decay. No. I'd say he bought it this evening."

"He?" Wausau asked.

The forensic specialist pointed. "It's a man. Got a good set of genitals to prove it."

Burstein nodded and breathed deeply. The putrid smell of burned flesh was everywhere, intensified by the lack of ventilation in the room. He wiped his forehead with the sleeve of his raincoat and leaned against the wall. He was tall, thin, and bald; his face was soft and unblemished.

"How long until we can get some kind of identification?" he asked.

"I don't know if we ever will," replied the forensic chief.

"What do you mean? Peel some prints. Have his dental work checked."

The forensic chief held up the victim's hand; the ends of the fingers had been cut off. "No prints. And all the teeth have been removed."

Burstein glanced at the arm and the remains of the head, then pulled the forensic chief aside. "I want this entire basement checked for the missing fingers and teeth. And if there's any other way to identify the body, work on it. Scars. Marks. Something."

"Don't kid yourself. Whatever marks or scars may have been there aren't there anymore."

Frustrated, Burstein turned to Wausau. "Where's the doorman and woman?"

"Upstairs."

Accompanied by Wausau, Burstein left the room and entered the basement corridor, now clogged with uniformed police and detectives.

The building superintendent, a Puerto Rican named Vasquez, was seated by the janitor's dressing room. Burstein introduced himself and questioned him. Vasquez provided the names of the building employees and their responsibilities, then explained the normal procedures for the compacting of garbage. Most of the work was done in the morning. At that time, the garbage that had accumulated in the shaft overnight was compacted by the janitor, placed in disposal packages, added to the packages compacted the day before, and taken outside for collection. Although the janitor would have been in and out of the room all day, no one should have been inside after six.

"What do you think?" Burstein asked Wausau as they walked down the corridor to the elevator having finished their interrogation of the super.

Wausau shook his head. "Not much to go on."

Burstein smirked. "No, not much!"

"Chief Inspector Burstein," Burstein said officiously as he looked over the sallow faces in the room.

"Ben Burdett," Ben replied; then he introduced Joe Biroc, Ralph Jenkins, and John Sorrenson.

"You reported the murder?" Burstein asked.

"Yes," Ben said.

Burstein moved around the apartment and inspected the furniture; Wausau remained at the door. Sorrenson sat on the sofa and loosened the collar of his shirt; Jenkins moved down next to him.

"Where's your wife?" Burstein asked.

"In the bedroom. I gave her three Valiums, according to her doctor's instructions. She's in a state of shock, and he said he does not want her awakened or questioned."

The coy expression on Burstein's face matched the biting facetiousness in his voice. "Did the doctor say when she'll be in condition to speak?"

"No," Ben said.

"I see." He walked by Jenkins and Sorrenson. "Were either of you two here when Mr. Biroc brought up Mrs. Burdett?"

They shook their heads.

"We came in to help," Sorrenson offered.

Burstein sat down next to Biroc. "You okay?"

"Yes, sir," Biroc replied unsurely.

"Couldn't this wait until morning?" Ben asked as he hovered over them.

"I'm sorry. If the murderer had had some consideration for our welfare, he would have waited to kill his victim. But he didn't. So, unfortunately, I can't either. Now, Mr. Biroc . . . I want you to tell me what happened. Okay?"

Biroc nodded, then described the sequence of events.

Burstein listened. Wausau took notes. When Biroc had finished, Burstein adjusted the handkerchief that sat neatly in the pocket of his sport coat and began to pace aimlessly around the couch, switching his stare from Ben to Biroc to Jenkins to Sorrenson with irritating rapidity.

"Mr. Biroc, I'm told that the compactor is shut off at six. Is that correct?"

"Yes, sir."

"Who shuts it off?"

"I do, sir. Last night . . . I turned it off at exactly six-fifteen."

Burstein sat down on the arm of the sofa. "Did you see anyone in the basement?"

"No, sir."

"To your knowledge, did anyone go into the basement after you?"

"I wouldn't know. I'm sure there were women in the laundry room, and there's a rear entrance that people use to bring in bicycles. There are always people down there, Inspector."

Burstein turned to Ben, who was watching them like a hawk, eyes wide open, attention rapt. "Why was your wife in the basement?"

"She wanted to put the laundry in the washing machines so that it would be done overnight. She does that often. So do a lot of other women. There's absolutely nothing unusual about that."

Burstein raised his eyebrows. "Did I say there was? Mr. Burdett, I'm not insinuating that your wife had anything to do with the murder. That's the farthest thought from my mind."

Ben nodded.

Burstein smiled, returning his attention to the doorman. "Mr. Biroc, have there been any suspicious people in the building? Anyone who has done anything that might be considered off-balance? Anything at all that you'd know of?"

Biroc breathed deeply. "No. No one that I could point a finger at. Oh . . . you know, any building this size has its share of kooks. . . . Mr. Cram on the fourth floor talks to his English bulldog. Mrs. Schwartz on seven has a nasty temper."

Sorrenson interrupted. "I've lived in this building since the beginning, and I've known just about everyone who's ever lived here, and I can tell you that there's no one who would have done something like this. Don't you agree, Ben?"

Ben nodded. "Whoever did this must have come from outside."

"Why don't you let me reach the conclusions, Mr. Burdett? That way nobody gets into trouble."

"I don't like the tone you're taking, Inspector," Jenkins said suddenly. "I assume we're not under suspicion, so why should we be spoken to as if we were?"

"I beg to differ. Right now everyone is under suspicion! Is that clear?"

No one answered.

"There is one thing . . ." Ben said.

"What?"

"Well . . . I can't imagine how this would be of any help, but . . ."

"But what?" Burstein challenged.

Ben stepped forward. "Well . . . there's a nun who lives next door, who's as peculiar as anyone you'll ever find. Strangely enough, we were all in Mr. Sorrenson's apartment last night and she was the primary topic of conversation. But again, I can't imagine how she'd be involved—I'm told she's paralyzed, deaf, dumb, and blind."

Burstein's face was blank. Ben sensed that the policeman was responding to something, that he already knew of the nun or had heard something about her. Perhaps he had even seen her from across the street upon his arrival—sitting in her twentieth-floor window.

"What's the nun's name?" Burstein asked.

"I don't know," Ben replied. "No one does."

Burstein paced the room slowly, then walked to the living-room window and looked out. The city seemed a blur. Could it be a coincidence? he asked himself. He raked his memory, picking at pieces long relegated to a file somewhere in a police archive. It had been so long. The girl. The old blind priest. That complicated web of murders and unanswered questions that had nearly driven his predecessor, Tom Gatz, into a mental hospital. He seemed to remember. What was the address? Somewhere in the West Eighties? Somewhere close to where they were right now? He was curious. He would call for the file in the morning and check the addresses. Then he'd see. Just for the sake of knowing.

He turned back to the men in the room; they were staring.

"Who owns the building?" he asked.

"The Archdiocese of New York," Jenkins replied.

Burstein turned to Ben. "Is the nun in there?" he asked, pointing.

"Yes," said Ben. "She's always there. When you leave, look up at the window. It's night, so you may not be able to see very much, but you should be able to barely make her out. If not, you can try tomorrow."

"I want to speak to your wife's doctor in the morning," Burstein said after a long pause. "I want to know when I can talk to her. And I don't want anybody in this room to leave the city unless we're notified. Understood?"

The men nodded.

"Good," Burstein said.

Burstein and Wausau left the apartment. Outside, Burstein stopped in front of the nun's door. He listened. Nothing. He knocked. No answer.

"You're not serious about this, are you?" Wausau asked.

Burstein walked to the elevator and pressed the call button. "I want you to find a file for me . . . go back about fifteen years. It was a multiple homicide. A detective named Tom Gatz was the officer of record. Try Allison Parker, Michael Farmer, Joseph Brenner. It would be listed under one of those names. I want you to read it. Then I want to know what you think about an old blind and paralyzed nun."

The elevator arrived.

"Okay," Wausau said as he stepped inside.

"Then I want you to invent a good excuse for a warrant."

"What kind of warrant?"

Burstein looked back down the hall before stepping into the car. "I want to get into the nun's apartment."

The elevator door closed. And they were gone.

Faye was breathing slowly. Very slowly. At peace. With some of the anemic look replaced by a touch of facial color and life.

Ben leaned over and kissed her cheek.

The Valium was working. He hoped he would be able to sleep as well.

The baby was quiet too, having awakened only once during the confusion, then falling back to sleep quickly with a minimum of complaint.

Ben took off his pants and laid them neatly over the lounge chair. He didn't want Faye to wake up in the morning and see his clothes tossed in all directions. He would be neat for once. And cause her no more problems—no matter how trivial.

Into the bathroom. A quick tooth-brushing. A look at his heavy dark eyes. A click of the light switch. And into bed.

The soft bed. Under warm blankets. And the sound of Faye's gently moving chest next to him.

The ticking of the clock, too.

He stopped breathing, afraid to disturb the symmetry of the room—that strange, almost bucolic atmosphere of darkness and silence.

And he wanted to sleep.

He closed his eyes.

What had Faye said? "I think we'd all be better off if we just forgot about her, left her alone."

He turned on his side.

"Damn."

5

Inspector Burstein walked into the offices of Manhattan Homicide at eleven o'clock.

"Did you get any rest?" Detective Wausau asked as he stepped out of the detail room to Burstein's side.

Burstein shook his head and fought back a yawn, ignoring the last trace of the twisting migraine that had raced up the back of his neck shortly after he had crawled into bed at four-forty in the morning.

They entered the Inspector's office. Burstein placed his hat and coat on a peg, crossed the room, and sat at his desk, a cluttered monument to overwork and underpay. Pouring a cup of coffee from a thermos he had carried in his overcoat, he glanced over the duty roster, then looked up, stretching his features once more into a yawn. "What about Eighty-ninth Street?" he asked, unbuttoning the collar of his stay-pressed shirt and loosening his tie.

Wausau cleared his throat and adjusted his tortoise-shell glasses. "I spoke to Forensic," he said. "They checked for the body parts, but found nothing. . . . And there are no prints. They'll have a report here by noon."

Burstein nodded, while rearranging the papers on the desk. "Was the building covered?"

"Yes, but we're still running down three tenants, two of whom are women."

"Who's the man?"

Wausau opened his notebook. "His name is Louis Petrosevic. He's on the twentieth floor. Across the hall from the Burdetts."

Burstein stretched, then grabbed a pencil and began to scribble on the blotter. "When was he last seen?"

Wausau turned several pages, then answered, "Yesterday. At work. He sells copying supplies. We called his office and spoke to his secretary. She said he left at five o'clock to see a client, intending to go home afterward. As far as we can tell, he never made it back to the apartment."

The pencil broke; Burstein tossed it to the side and rubbed his hands over his face. "Okay," he said. He sipped the coffee. "That's a possibility."

"I went ahead and compiled a profile, just in case."

"Good."

The phone rang. Burstein answered it and referred the caller to one of the staff detectives. "What about the files?"

Wausau's face drew blank. "There are none!" he announced.

"What!" Burstein cried, shooting to his feet.

"I checked everywhere," Wausau said nervously. "Under every name you gave me. But there's nothing."

"Not even a catalog listing?"

"Sure. It's listed. They have it on the computer. But the files are gone. They've been misplaced or stolen. I checked for duplicates. Dead end there, too."

"God damn," Burstein cried bitterly. "God fucking damn. I want you to double-check." He paced nervously around the desk. "What about the warrant?"

Wausau popped a stick of gum into his mouth. "I spoke to the D.A. We need more than an intuition."

"That figures." Burstein looked through the bars on his window. There wasn't much of a view. Just a yard and the wall of the next building. He turned. "I need some time to think."

"You know where to find me," Wausau said. He walked out.

Burstein fished out a new pencil, scribbled a bit, closed his eyes, then grabbed the phone and slowly dialed. The line chattered noisily and began to ring.

"I was certainly surprised to hear from you," former Chief Inspector Thomas Gatz said in a familiar low-pitched twang that was forever irritating to the ear. The sound emanated from deep in his throat and took much of its form from the unnatural tucked-in position of his jaw, which caused the muscles to constrict and the vocal cords to compress. "How long's it been?" he asked, his attention focused on Burstein's inexpressive face.

"A year," Burstein answered, ignoring the din in the overcrowded luncheonette. "Maybe more."

Gatz looked down at the bowl of chicken broth that had been delivered moments before. A squat little man with an angular face, he had a pair of black eyes, a long nose with a lump on the bridge, and two unnaturally thin and colorless lips. On his head was an old fedora, which blended perfectly with his oversized suit. His shirt was soiled and spotted with coffee stains; it was also covered with ashes that had fallen from a chewed-up cigar that hung from his mouth and bobbed about as he ruminated.

"A year's too long," he complained, shaking his head. "So then why the call now? A problem?"

"You might say that."

"After all I taught you!"

Burstein lifted his brow. Had he really learned anything from the old cantankerous bastard? He smiled, then nibbled at the edge of a corned-beef sandwich. "You taught me a lot, but there were even cases that stumped you."

"Not many!" Gatz said with certainty.

Burstein smirked. "What have you been up to?"

"Not much. I was never made for retirement. Sure . . . there are things to do. But I'd rather be back on the force. There are times that I feel like busting inside."

"Why don't you take a part-time job?"

"I have one. Night watchman three nights a week at Con Edison. It's a snap, but boring as hell. You know, there ain't many good openings once you reach sixty-five."

Burstein mumbled sympathetically.

"Cut it! I don't need sympathy from a bald Jewish cop with a nagging wife and chronic hemorrhoids."

"And you're not going to get any, you old bastard!"

"Fuck you!"

They both laughed.

"You've been well?" Burstein asked.

Gatz nodded. "I've got arthritis. But other than that I'm alive. I keep myself busy enough to get by. Most nights, when I'm not at Con Ed, I watch old movies. There's a theater up here that plays the damn things. Three different ones a night. They start at eight and end near midnight. Yesterday they had *Wings, The Hunchback of Notre Dame,* and *Little Caesar.*"

"I don't think I've ever seen them."

"You're an uncultured bastard, Burstein. You know that?" He didn't wait for an answer. "Why I ever liked you, I'll never know."

Burstein laughed once more. The waitress came and deposited two cups of coffee. Then Burstein leaned toward his former superior and said, "Where in the hell am I going to find the time to watch old movies? I got two kids to put through school. And a wife to keep in groceries."

Gatz beamed. "The family okay?"

"Sure," Burstein replied. He dug out his wallet and lifted three pictures, placing them on the tabletop. "The two boys. And the wife." He pointed. "That's Michael. The oldest. You remember?" Gatz nodded. "He's in his third year at Boston College. When he graduates, he's going to law school. He's not gonna start out pounding the beat like you and I did."

"Worse could happen to him, but he becomes a lawyer . . . he becomes a rich man."

Burstein pointed once more. "That's Ricky. He's a freshman at Syracuse University. He's a good kid. He's studying to be a pharmacist."

Gatz picked up the picture of the younger son. "Good-looking boy, Jake. It's amazing how fast they've grown. I remember when you joined my squad. Ricky couldn't have been older than two or three."

"That's right."

"I look at this, it makes me think that I should have married and had kids." He laughed. "As it was, I did have kids . . . in a way. You and Rizzo. I loved you both. . . . When Rizzo died in the car accident, it took a piece out of me."

"I know," Burstein said.

The old man was baring himself, looking for a kind ear, a friend. But the mention of Rizzo must have disturbed him, because he suddenly changed the subject, returning to the topic of old films.

"Let me tell you about these movies," he said, removing the cigar from his mouth for the first time and tasting the broth. "In *The Hunchback of Notre Dame,* Charles Laughton plays the bell-ringer, Quasimodo. Remember that sergeant in Vice up on 188th Street? I think his name was Melvany."

"Yes."

"Looked a little like him. Christ, Melvany was the ugliest bastard I ever saw."

Burstein studied Gatz's face, the absence of emotion. It was time. "I want to talk to you about something—like you said, a problem."

"Quasimodo was found as a child by the Chief Justice of the French Courts, and lived in Notre Dame, where the Chief Justice's brother was bishop, and—"

"Listen to me."

"There was a gypsy girl named Esmeralda, who the Chief Justice loved—"

"Tom!"

"And the Justice killed the girl's lover—"

"Tom," Burstein cried again. "I want to talk to you about Allison Parker."

Silence.

"What about her?" Gatz said coldly, his voice betraying an underlying, deep-seated bitterness.

"There's been a homicide."

"So what?"

Burstein reviewed everything that had happened at 68 West Eighty-ninth Street. He'd never seen Gatz so attentive in his life. When he had finished, he added, "And the police files are missing."

Gatz stared in silence.

"What do you think?" Burstein finally asked.

"What do you think I think?"

"Well . . . I guess I know."

"I want to see the nun . . . speak to those people. And I want your permission."

"You have it, as long as you don't interfere with my investigation."

"I won't! And I appreciate you coming to me. You know how important this is. I'll let you know."

"You do that."

The luncheon ended abruptly as Gatz stood and dug into his pocket for change to pay his part of the bill. Burstein grabbed his hand and shook his head.

Gatz nodded. "You're a good boy, Jake," he said. Then he turned and left the restaurant.

Burstein rubbed his freshly shaved chin and stared at the rows of booths. He hoped he'd done the right thing. There was no way he could tolerate interference. But if he had not told his former boss, he could not have lived with himself. Gatz had waited an eternity. He could not deny him now. He only hoped that Gatz would stay out of trouble.

Several hours after leaving Inspector Burstein, Tom Gatz emerged from the kitchen of his rent-controlled Bronx apartment and sat down at his desk, holding a can of beer in his hand.

Two sets of open police files, removed from the police library years ago, lay on the desk blotter. Since Gatz had taken them, they'd been stored over the desk on the lower of two wall shelves. Unsurprisingly, he'd forgotten many of the incidentals, a fact that became painfully obvious by two o'clock that afternoon, after the first reading. Since then he had reviewed the material two more times, intent that he would have everything down to rote by midnight, convinced that if he were to appear at 68 West Eighty-ninth Street the next day properly prepared, he would have to discipline himself as best he could.

He had never thought he'd have the chance to vindicate himself. But if Burstein was right, the opportunity had presented itself. And he would try not to blow it. So he readjusted the light, put on his reading glasses, slurped from the beer can, and started through the material once more.

Joe Biroc bit into the stem of the pipe, enjoying the mellow taste of the Swedish tobacco. The night was cold; he was chilled. He tightened the collar of his overcoat and stamped his feet against the frost-coated ground, trying to spark the circulation in his legs. He looked at his watch. Ten P.M. He had been there for three hours, hidden in the corner of the dark alley beneath a tangle of encroaching clotheslines. Leaning down to pick up the capped jug of coffee at his feet, he yawned and repositioned himself against the wall of the body-parts garage. He looked up, staring at the lighted window three floors above. Former Detective Thomas Gatz was still seated at the living-room desk, still clearly visible. Gatz had not moved in more than an hour.

Biroc poured some coffee into a mug and tipped it to his lips. The coffee was still hot. It tasted good. He smiled, then returned the jug to the ground.

6

The high, shrill blast of the jet's engines cut through the cold night air as Alitalia Flight 7 turned off the taxiway and maneuvered toward a berth at the International Arrivals Terminal, John F. Kennedy International Airport.

Above, on the observation platform, Father James McGuire gripped the guardrail tightly. He had been waiting more than an hour, facing the bite of the Jamaica Bay winds while sensing that surge of adrenaline that often buffets expectation. The arrival of Franchino signaled the start of the final phase—whatever that phase was to be. Since their first meeting in July, he had followed Franchino's instructions to the letter, asking no questions, realizing that since he'd been involuntarily conscripted for an unknown purpose by a clandestine process originating within the Vatican, he'd had no alternative but to comply. But now maybe the suspense would end. Franchino's telegram had hinted at it.

Below, the passengers had begun to deplane. Franchino was the fourth person out. Father McGuire had not seen him in six months.

McGuire reentered the terminal building and took the escalator down to the arrival lounge to wait until

Franchino had claimed his luggage and cleared customs.

Franchino appeared twenty minutes later.

"Monsignor Franchino," McGuire called out as he saw Franchino walk through the doorway.

The two men embraced.

"Your plane was right on schedule," McGuire said.

"We should be thankful for that, Father," Franchino replied. "Few things in Italy are!"

Both men laughed.

McGuire pointed to the exit gate. "The car is just outside."

Franchino nodded and began to walk.

"Let me take this for you," McGuire said, pulling a leather suitcase from Franchino's hand.

"That's kind of you, Father. It was a long flight and I'm tired. Perhaps I'm getting to be as old as Cardinal Reggiani says." There was a twinkle in his eye; he didn't believe a word of it. "When a man enters his mid-fifties, many things start to happen—no matter how well he has taken care of himself. Do you take care of yourself, Father?"

"I think so, your Eminence. If I can, I jog in the morning and do calisthenics before I go to sleep."

Franchino smiled pleasantly as they left the terminal and climbed into the rear of a black limousine. McGuire tapped on the partition and motioned the driver to proceed. Franchino placed a black attaché case, which he had been carrying in his other hand, between them.

"I hope the flight was smooth and uneventful, Monsignor."

"It went by quickly. I'm thankful for that! I don't mind the flights from New York to Rome, since I take the overnight and usually sleep. But Rome to New York has been a problem for me. You've never been to Europe, have you?"

"No," McGuire said wistfully.

"We'll see that that oversight is corrected, once we have finished our duties in New York. I may take you to the Vatican to work for me. Or perhaps I shall place you on Reggiani's staff."

"Monsignor Franchino! You flatter me. I'm not sure I would be qualified for such an honor."

Franchino faced him squarely. "I respect your modesty, Father. But it is misplaced and unwarranted. You were chosen to assist me in this peculiar endeavor because of your abilities and talents. You are one of the most intelligent and practiced seminarians in the entire church hierarchy. Your future is very bright."

McGuire blushed; the farthest thought from his mind was secular achievement.

They rode in silence until the limousine had climbed the ramp onto the Long Island Expressway.

Then McGuire turned to Franchino. "There is a problem," he said cautiously.

"A problem?"

"Something unexpected."

Franchino did not like the unexpected; he had made himself very clear about that the first night they had met. "What?" he asked.

"There was a murder last night in the building."

Franchino stared, deep in thought. "Yes."

McGuire recited the details, then sat back, unsure of Franchino's reaction, not even sure whether the murder had any relevance.

"Of course," Franchino said, showing no trace of emotion. "My devoted, devious Charles Chazen. So this is how he makes his appearance."

"Who is Charles Chazen, Monsignor?" He thought he could hear Franchino praying under his breath.

Franchino smiled strangely. "Charles Chazen is Satan!"

McGuire felt a cutting chill race up his spine. "Satan?"

"Yes. Does that frighten you?"

"It might if I knew what you meant."

"It means exactly that. The man Charles Chazen is Satan. Satan personified!"

McGuire stuttered. "There is no one named Charles Chazen in that building."

"I'm afraid that there is now. I would be very surprised if a murder of that nature had taken place by chance."

"I don't understand," said McGuire, his eyes blankly staring ahead at the skyscrapers of Manhattan, now only a short distance away.

"You are not supposed to understand! You are to listen and do what you are told. And you are to say or repeat nothing. Not a thing you have done, learned, or seen."

"Monsignor . . . that has been our understanding —and my oath—since the very beginning. Do you question my fealty or my strength of character?"

"I do neither. I merely warn you that fealty and strength of character are like dust in the wind in the face of the power of Satan. This I tell you because I must. Until this moment, you have known nothing. Even now I can tell you little. But you now know the most crushing fact of all, the thing you must comprehend. It is Satan himself that we face. In all his fury!"

Father McGuire shuddered; he felt cold, dead, as if he had been trapped in a freezer. Could what he had just heard be true? Certainly Franchino was not the joking sort. But this? It defied the comprehension of the human mind. No matter the entire content of his education—it was impossible to grasp.

"Will I know more, Monsignor Franchino?"

"Eventually."

"Will I be able to comprehend it?"

"We have no doubt about your ability to do so. But only time will tell, my son. We must have faith in Christ, and he will guide us."

McGuire wiped his brow with a handkerchief.

"You will return to your duties at the seminary," Franchino continued. "I will be in touch with you constantly. And you must command the patience of a saint."

"I pray to God for it."

Franchino was silent as the limousine moved through the Midtown Tunnel. When it resurfaced, he said, "If Chazen killed the man, he did it for a reason. I would guess that he has taken the victim's place. That is why all means of identification were removed." He paused, thinking deeply. "There are many men in that building. But we must find him!"

"I will see to it," McGuire said.

"How is Faye Burdett?" Franchino asked.

"Not well."

The limousine turned uptown.

"Father McGuire," Franchino said casually, "my duties are dangerous. There is a chance that something may happen to me. In the event I die, you are to be my successor!"

McGuire turned in his seat. "But I don't know—"

Franchino interrupted. "If I die, you will assume my duties. You will be instructed. You will know everything I know. And will do everything I would have done. The only difference is that I have faced Chazen before. But no matter. You will have the strength. . . ."

"I choose to think that nothing will happen to you, Monsignor."

"If God wills it . . ."

The limousine cut crosstown and started up Broadway. Franchino changed the subject, though he could see McGuire teething at the bit. He remembered his own reactions, the initial confusion upon learning of the existence of the Sentinel. But that was years ago. It would do him no good to dwell on the weaknesses of the past.

The limousine turned onto Eighty-ninth Street and stopped in front of an old brownstone, about fifty feet from the excavation site of St. Simon's. Franchino felt a wave of dizziness as he climbed out of the car. It happened every time he returned to this spot, every time he stood within sight of Sister Therese.

McGuire walked to Franchino's side as the Monsignor looked up at the twentieth floor of 68 West Eighty-ninth. The angle was too oblique. He could see nothing. Yet, Sister Therese was there, alone, vigilant. He could feel her presence. The communication was evident, the telekinetics of her power pervasive.

He glanced at McGuire, who was also staring at the building. "You have noticed her?"

"Yes. Who is she?"

"Her name is Sister Therese."

"Is she part of this?"

"Perhaps." There was revelation in his voice.

They entered the basement of the brownstone. Inside, there was very little light. The corridor was strewn with garbage, and they could smell the mist in the stagnant air.

The door at the end of the corridor was closed. McGuire knocked. Footsteps approached from the other side. The door opened. The man in the darkness switched on the light. McGuire and Franchino entered and sat down on an old velvet sofa that had lost much of its stuffing. They said nothing. Neither did the man, until he knelt and kissed Franchino's right hand.

"Monsignor Franchino," Biroc said tremulously, "I am your servant."

7

"The name is Gatz. Detective Gatz. With a Z." Gatz smiled, revealing a mouth of beaverlike teeth that stretched across his face and left the impression that the lower part of his head was a huge dental bridge.

"Please come in," Ben said, noticing the piercing nature of the little ferret's ambivalent grin; it disarmed him.

Gatz stepped through the door with an uncompromising stride and an expression steeped in suspicion.

"I still don't understand," Ben said.

Gatz opened his coat and searched for a place to sit. Ben pointed toward the couch. Gatz nervously chewed on the end of his cigar and plopped down on the pillows.

"I don't make it a habit of being too specific on the telephone, Mr. Burdett. You know . . . wiretaps!"

"Isn't that a little paranoiac, Mr. Gatz?"

Gatz's stare sliced through the apartment. "I used to lay them. So it ain't my imagination, okay?"

Ben nodded. In his day, Detective Gatz must have been a tough cop.

"Let me repeat what I told you on the phone. I used to be chief of detectives, Manhattan Homicide Division. Inspector Burstein worked for me. So did a lot of other people. Because of the compactor murder, Inspector Burstein asked me to take a look. So I'm looking!"

"For what?"

"I don't know. Not exactly." He chewed off the end of his cigar, rolled it into a ball, and dropped it into the ashtray.

"I've told the police everything I know," Ben said.

"I'm sure you did, Mr. Burdett," Gatz replied coldly, crossing his legs. There were holes in the soles of both his shoes. And his collar was ripped. "The building you live in is about fourteen years old. Before it was put up, this entire stretch was occupied by several old brownstones . . . and one in particular. It didn't look very special. A plain brown building. But shortly before it was torn down, there were several murders committed there. I was the detective in charge. Officially, the murders were never solved."

"That's an interesting bit of history, Mr. Gatz, but this is fifteen years later! You're not seriously suggesting that the murder in the basement had anything to do with those homicides, are you?"

"I'm not suggesting anything."

"And why the hell are Faye and I the center of attention? Because she found the body?"

"In part, Mr. Burdett. In part!"

Ben's voice flushed angry. "Well, then . . . give me the other part."

Gatz stood, walked to the wall, and listened. "The other part? . . . The nun!"

"Now, listen," Ben said as he exploded across the room and jammed his face next to the detective's. "I've had enough of this. That old woman has lived here for a long time and hasn't bothered anyone. If the police or the building management don't like her, they can have her evicted. I don't give a shit. Okay? She leaves us alone. We leave her alone. We have nothing to do with her. She has nothing to do with us!"

"I wouldn't bet on that, Mr. Burdett."

"Well, I would!" Ben shouted.

"Mr. Burdett," Gatz said, mellowing his expression, "I didn't come here to argue with you. I came to help. Someone in this building may be in terrible danger. I don't know who it is for sure . . . but it may be your wife."

Ben's face tightened.

"Look. That brownstone was a plain old building— physically plain—but there was something very distinctive about it."

"What?"

"In the middle of the fifth floor, in the window, there was a man—a priest. An old blind and paralyzed priest who sat without moving, never leaving his place. Does that ring a bell?"

"A coincidence," Ben said defiantly.

"Oh? . . . Is that so, Mr. Burdett?"

Ben stared.

"Where's your son?" Gatz asked.

"Downstairs. In the park with a neighbor."

"And your wife?"

"In the bedroom."

"I'd like to talk to her."

"She's still not well."

"After two days? Mr. Burdett! She wasn't the one who was attacked. She only found the body. I can understand that she'd be shaken, but . . ."

Ben frowned. He too had found it strange that Faye had remained in such intense shock for so long a period.

"If she's asleep," Gatz said, "I'd like to take a look at her. I won't disturb her. It's very important."

They entered the bedroom. The curtains were drawn. Only a wisp of dull light crept through the window.

They could hear Faye breathing softly. They approached her. Ben took her hand. She opened her eyes. They were red and glazed.

"How do you feel?" he asked.

Faye licked her lips and moved her fingers in his hand. "Tired. So tired. And dizzy."

Ben sat down and stroked her hair, which was knotted and unkempt. She mumbled. He moved down closer and listened. "Mr. Gatz is a friend," he said.

Gatz stared at her face and hands.

"A friend of mine. He wanted to see you and wish you well."

Gatz nodded. "I heard what happened, Mrs. Burdett. I'm sorry."

Faye barely moved. Her eyelids fell. She was too full of tranquilizers and sleeping pills to respond.

After a long pause Ben stood. "Have you seen enough?"

"Yes."

They walked back to the living room.

"You think she's in shock?" Gatz asked as he

placed his foot on the coffee table and relit the stump of the cigar.

"Yes."

"Look, Burdett, I'd like to have a talk with you. But somewhere else. Away from your wife."

Ben looked toward the bedroom. "All right. But only for a short while."

"That'll be long enough."

They left the apartment, took the elevator to the lobby, and walked onto the street, crossing to the other side. There they stopped. Gatz pointed up at the nun's window. They could see very little—just the outline of a body.

Ben watched the facial muscles in the former inspector's face twitch and roll. Gatz's concentration was intense, almost crazed.

"She's been there—without fail—since I moved into the building," Ben said.

Ben waited for a comment. There was none. Gatz just stared upward.

O'Reilly's Pub, on the corner of Columbus Avenue, was a perfect place for an intimate discussion.

They took the first booth in the rear, ordered two Heinekens, and waited until the beer had been placed on the table.

Then Gatz cleared his throat and leaned forward. "I know you're skeptical. I also know damn well I may go through this and you might tell me to get lost. It's happened before. But I don't think you will, because I'm positive I'm going to convince you, and it may be easier than you probably think right now."

Ben crossed his arms and eased himself back in the seat. "I'm not thinking anything, Mr. Gatz. Not a damn thing. I'm all ears."

Gatz slugged a mouthful of beer and flicked a fly off the tip of his nose. "It started fifteen years ago. An assistant district attorney named Michael Farmer was getting rich taking bribes in plea-bargaining sessions. There were a lot of guys on the force who knew about it, but there was little anyone could do without proof. Farmer and I were at each other's throats. I never liked him. From the moment I met him, I knew he was a sleazy, ambitious grade-A son of a bitch." He paused, smiled, then continued. "He was married to a socialite whose maiden name was Karen Birmingham. She wasn't too good-looking. Or even rich. Farmer married her for position and power, since her father, a partner in a Wall Street law firm, was big in the Republican party. Unfortunately, Farmer couldn't keep his cock in his pants. He got the hots for a young fashion model named Allison Parker, who fell in love with him but didn't know about the wife. Once Miss Parker found out about her, she exploded and gave Farmer an ultimatum: either the wife goes or she does. Farmer asked for a divorce. Karen Farmer freaked out. A week later they found Karen Farmer in the alley of their New York apartment building—an apparent suicide. I was put on the case. I knew he'd had her murdered. She had probably threatened to tell the district attorney about the bribes, and he realized that he had to get rid of her. Unfortunately, I couldn't prove it. The medical examiner ruled the death a suicide. No charges were brought. I was pulled off the case, even though I'd been able to find threads of supportive evidence. Anyway, all you need to know is that Farmer's wife died, that I knew he'd had her murdered, and that a couple of months later the guilt-ridden girlfriend, Allison Parker, tried to slit her wrists. Once again I became involved, and once again I got nowhere."

Gatz stopped and ordered another beer. Ben could see rage and frustration moving across Gatz's features like a kaleidoscope.

Gatz pulled a half-smoked cigar from his pocket, lit it, and jammed it into his mouth. "Nothing happened for two years. Then one night hell broke loose. A girl was found roaming the streets in her nightgown at four in the morning hysterical, claiming she had murdered her father. I went to the hospital, and who did I find? . . . Allison Parker. From what she told us, we were able to construct the following scenario: After Miss Parker recovered from the suicide attempt, she moved in with Farmer and began to play house. Everything was fine for two years, until she received a call from her mother, who told her that her father was dying of cancer. She went home to Indiana to be with the family, refusing to let Michael Farmer visit. The old man lingered on for a couple of months. It was a terrible strain on Miss Parker, because she hated the bastard. But he eventually died and she returned to New York, convinced that she had to get away from Farmer, find her own apartment. She saw a rental ad, met the agent, a woman named Joan Logan, and saw the apartment on the third floor of a brownstone at 68 West Eighty-ninth Street." He stopped as Ben flinched, then continued. "While she was inspecting the premises, she noticed a priest in the Five-A apartment window. The agent dismissed the priest, whose name was Matthew Halliran, as an old harmless, blind, and paralyzed neighbor. Miss Parker took the apartment. But soon she began to have fainting spells. Then, during the next few weeks she met her neighbors. First a man named Charles Chazen, his cat, Jezebel, and parakeet, Mortimer, who lived in Five-B, down the hall from the priest. Then two lesbians in Two-A who came on a little too strong. Finally, she attended a birthday party for Chazen's cat and met Emma and Lillian Klotkin, Anna Clark, and the Stinnets, the Klotkins' cousins from across town. That night she heard footsteps and clanging in the apartment above. But Four-A was supposed to be empty. Miss Parker went and complained to Miss Logan, who told her that except for the priest, there were *no* other neighbors, and hadn't been for years. Miss Logan returned with her to the building and escorted her through each of the apartments—all empty and decrepit except for the priest's, which they could not enter. Miss Logan left. Miss Parker tried to call Michael Farmer, but couldn't reach him or her best friend, a model named Jennifer Learson. So she stayed in the brownstone. That night she woke at four o'clock again. Overhead, she heard footsteps and clanging. She grabbed a knife and flashlight and climbed the steps to the fourth floor. Halfway up, she stepped on the cat, which had the parakeet, dead, in its mouth. Then the cat ran away. She entered Four-A and in the dark bedroom walked smack into her dead 'father.' Terrified, she stabbed him and ran out of the building—hysterical. And that's where I became involved. We checked the brownstone. There was no sign of violence. No blood. And no neighbors. We tried to find Miss Logan but couldn't. We checked on Allison Parker's father and had his body disinterred. He was rotting in the box. We typed the blood on her arms; it matched her own and could have come from any number of wounds. So there were only two conclusions we could reach: first, the girl had had a nightmare or a series of hallucinations—which certainly was not inconsistent with her psychiatric history—or she had actually met the missing neighbors and killed someone. If the second possibility was true, I knew that Michael Farmer had to be involved. Unfortunately, there was nothing I could do without a body. But within a week we had one—a detective named William Brenner, an underground, small-time trickster. He was found in the trunk of a car not far from Eighty-ninth Street, dead of multiple stab wounds. We typed his blood—it matched the blood found on the girl. I was convinced that for some reason Farmer had sent Brenner into the brownstone disguised as the father and Miss Parker had killed him by mistake. I was also convinced that Brenner had been involved in the Karen Farmer murder. But for a long time I had no way to connect Farmer and Brenner. Then came a fatal night when everything jelled. My detectives discovered information in Brenner's apartment that linked Michael Far-

mer to Brenner, both at the time of Karen Farmer's
death and on the night that Allison Parker supposedly
'killed' her 'father.' I ordered an arrest warrant, then
went to pick up Michael Farmer. At the same time, Jennifer Learson called, reporting that Allison Parker had
gone to the brownstone. And so had Michael Farmer.
There was supposedly a bizarre religious plot involving
the Catholic Church. We went to the brownstone and
found Michael Farmer dead, his skull crushed. Father
Halliran was dead too. Heart attack. And Allison Parker was missing. We issued an all-points and obtained a
warrant for her arrest."

Gatz stopped and caught his breath.

"Is that all?" Ben asked.

"No," Gatz replied. "We questioned Jennifer Learson for days, and she filled in many of the gaps. According to her, after Allison Parker was released from
the hospital, she and Farmer had continued to argue
about what had actually happened. Frustrated, Miss
Parker went to the rental office. Miss Logan was gone,
the office abandoned. The calendar indicated that
Miss Logan had disappeared the night Miss Parker had
'killed' her 'father,' and that jibed with our own information and our inability to locate the agent. That
night Farmer and Miss Parker went to dinner and afterward went into the Ripley's wax museum off Broadway, where Miss Parker saw a statue of a dead woman,
one who had been executed at Sing Sing Prison
many years before. It was Anna Clark—a participant
at the cat's birthday party. Panicked, Miss Parker ran
away. Left alone, Farmer went to the *New York Times*
to find out who placed the newspaper ad for Miss Parker's apartment. The *Times* editor told him that the
ad was never ordered and never appeared. Farmer went
home. Miss Parker showed up later that night and said
she had been in a church. Farmer, who admitted to
Jennifer Learson that he had sent Detective Brenner
into the house to see if there were any neighbors or
if any strange things were happening, suddenly de-

clared that something peculiar might really be going on. They searched the brownstone. They were not able to get into the old priest's apartment, nor did they find any evidence of neighbors or a murder, but they did find a book. When Farmer looked at it, it was printed in English. When Miss Parker looked at it, it was in Latin. Farmer had Miss Parker write down what she saw, then took the scribbling to Columbia University to have it translated by a Professor Ruzinsky. He translated:

"To thee they course by lot hath given
Charge and strict watch that to this happy place
No evil thing approach or enter in.

"We tried unsuccessfully to track Ruzinsky. A year later his body was discovered in the woods near Bear Mountain. But to go back. Farmer took the translation to the archdiocese and confronted a priest—a Monsignor Franchino—who was responsible for paying Father Halliran's rent. Franchino denied recognizing the translation and denied any irregularities concerning Father Halliran.

"Farmer wasn't convinced. He broke into the archdiocese, opened Franchino's safe, and stole a series of files, which he showed to Jennifer Learson. The files dated back hundreds of years and covered hundreds of individuals. All of these people had the same M.O.: all had attempted suicide; all had disappeared off the face of the earth one day and then reappeared with manufactured identities—as priests or nuns, blind and paralyzed. Why? Neither Farmer nor Learson could say. But Farmer found one last file—a file for Allison Parker and a Sister Therese who she was to become. He concluded that Allison Parker was being programmed, hypnotized—that's why she suddenly wanted a new apartment alone, that's how she saw the rental ad that wasn't and the Latin inscription in the book. He also concluded that she was to be Father Halliran's successor as some sort of Guardian or Sentinel.

And that this was to happen the next night. So he went to the brownstone to stop it. The rest you know: Farmer was found dead . . . so was the priest . . . Allison Parker was gone. Jennifer Learson said that Farmer had taken the files with him to the brownstone, but we were never able to find them.

"We checked everywhere. The Archdiocese of New York, the landlord—a man named Caruso, who later disappeared also—and more. No one had ever heard of a Monsignor Franchino or the inscription. And we had no idea what had happened the last night in that brownstone. Six months later the case was closed."

"And should remain closed," Ben said, banging his fist against the table. "This is the most incredible crock of shit I've ever heard."

"Look, my cocksure, ignorant friend, whether you like it or not, the nun next door is Sister Therese— who is Allison Parker—the successor to Father Halliran. She's to be replaced. And I'll bet that your wife is going to be next. She's going to become the next Sentinel."

"Why? And for what?"

A sardonic grin crept over the detective's lips. "To guard against the approach of Satan."

"What?"

"You heard me. The Sentinel is God's angel on earth, the successor to the angel Gabriel, who was commanded by God to watch for and prevent the approach of Satan."

Ben shot to his feet. "Gatz, you're crazy. Do you think that anyone would believe a word of this?"

Gatz stood too. "Yes . . . I think you will. I located the source of the inscription. As well as additional information that I stole from the archdiocese. Tomorrow, if you come to my apartment, I'll show you proof."

"And if I say no?"

"Then you're a fool . . . but you'll be there." He scratched his address on the back of a napkin.

Ben grabbed the napkin, scowled, and tucked it into his pocket. There was a long silence. Then Ben said, "Okay."

Gatz nodded smugly.

In silence Ben paid the bill.

"Ben . . . what a time we had in the park!" John Sorrenson announced. He was holding Joey in his hands as Ben and Gatz approached. "I'm winded. Fortunately, I don't have any rehearsals today."

Ben grabbed the baby, who had reached out to him. "That's good, John . . . and I appreciate your helping."

"Don't be ridiculous. Anytime. He makes me feel young again."

Ben turned to Gatz. "This is my son, Joey. And my neighbor John Sorrenson."

Gatz shook Sorrenson's hand.

"Mr. Gatz is a private detective who is helping the police with the murder."

Sorrenson seemed to pale. "I'd rather not talk about that right now. I haven't slept the last two nights."

Ben nodded and looked at the doorman.

"Biroc's been sick," Sorrenson said, noticing the questioning look on Ben's face. "That's Mr. Suarez, a temporary."

"I hope it's not serious," Ben said.

"No. Mr. Biroc has the flu. He'll be back Monday."

Gatz stepped between them. "Mr. Burdett . . . if I could have another minute of your time . . ."

"Okay." Ben turned to Sorrenson. "John, could you take Joey upstairs?"

"Sure," said Sorrenson in his affable manner. "I want to look in on Faye anyhow."

"The door's open."

Sorrenson took the baby and disappeared. Gatz led Ben to the curb. He reached inside his pocket, took out a picture, and handed it to Ben. "Allison Parker."

Ben turned away from the sun to see the glossy

clearly. Allison Parker was certainly attractive. Angular and tall. With skin like silk, long brown hair that fell over her shoulders halfway down her back, two enormous blue eyes, and a delicately sculptured nose.

"Keep the picture," Gatz said.

"Why?" Ben asked.

"Just keep it. I have plenty others."

Ben leaned against the fender of a car. "Is that all, Mr. Gatz?"

Gatz nodded. "Just be at my apartment tomorrow at one. And do me a favor. What I told you? Not a word to anyone."

"Okay."

Gatz turned away unceremoniously and walked to the corner.

Ben watched him as if he were looking through a fog. Suddenly everything had become unreal. Then he looked at the picture of Allison Parker, and shaking his head, entered the building.

8

The next day Ben taxied to the Bronx, climbed out of the cab at the address Gatz had scrawled on the napkin, stood to the side as the cab spun away, then glanced up and down the tenement block. It didn't look like the best of places to live. There was a grocery store on one corner and a shuttered luncheonette directly across. All the buildings were eroded, decorated with broken doors, crooked fire escapes, and scribbled graffiti. The sidewalks were cracked and littered with garbage; the street was dotted with potholes filled with stagnant water and mud; the air smelled of poverty and decay. A peculiar place, he thought, for an ex-homicide detective to live, though Gatz's meager pension would probably not have allowed him to move to a better location.

Gatz's tenement building, a five-story, red-brick dinosaur fronted by a rusted fire escape, was located mid-block. Ben entered and climbed to the third floor. There were four apartments. Gatz's was in the rear.

He knocked several times; there was no answer. He looked at his watch. It was five to one. Goddammit. Gatz should be there. Especially after having made the one-o'clock meeting sound so crucial. Could he have forgotten? Not likely. Perhaps Gatz had gone out for a few minutes and would soon be back.

Ben returned to the first floor and knocked on the superintendent's door. A short, balding man answered. A double for Winston Churchill, the man was dressed in a pair of baggy pin-striped pants and an undershirt. He had a bottle of beer in his hand.

"There are no apartments available," he said as he belched. "And there's a wait list once one comes free."

"I'm not looking for an apartment," Ben said.

"Oh . . . then you're peddling?"

The super tried to close the door; Ben stopped it.

"Look . . . I'm not peddling. And I don't want an apartment." He paused, thinking rapidly. "I'm from the police department. I'm an auditor." He thought that that would have the most impact. "I had a one-o'clock appointment with Mr. Gatz about his pension. But he doesn't seem to be in."

"He doesn't?" asked the super rhetorically as he scratched his right underarm. He was one of the grossest human beings Ben had ever seen. "Then he isn't!"

"Do you know when he left?"

"No. I don't ask for a report from the tenants. If they want to leave, they leave. If they want to shit, they do it. I don't care if they throw themselves off a cliff as long as the rent is paid on time. Okay?"

The super tried to close the door again; once more Ben stopped it.

"Look . . . do you mind if I make a call?"

"Nope . . . but you can't. The phone is out of order. And do me a favor. Don't hang around in the hall while you wait. The tenants don't like it. It gives them the jitters."

"I'll wait on the stoop," Ben said, not too pleased with the prospect of waiting in the street. "Can I ask you some questions?"

"Look, mister—"

"Just a few? Police business?"

The super paused, then nodded reluctantly. The name on the door was Hardman. It seemed appropriate.

"What do you know about Mr. Gatz?"

"Not much."

"Has he lived here long?"

The super rubbed his bald head and sucked in the excess stomach that extended over his belt. "Ten, twelve years," he said. "But he keeps to himself. Doesn't go out much and doesn't say much. No. Gatz don't like to talk. He was a cop. He's retired. He don't bother nobody. And he pays his rent on time. Okay? That's all I know."

"Did he ever mention a girl named Allison Parker?"

"Who?"

"Just a girl." Obviously the detective had never mentioned her.

"I ain't interested in Gatz's sex life either. He gets his nooky, he gets his nooky. Who from? That's his business. As long as he don't corrupt the morals around here, he can get fucked all day long. Though I tell you, I don't go for no slobs. He better not bring any slob hookers in here. Or any kind of dirty broad!"

Ben focused on the urine stain on the man's pants. Slob hookers? Dirty broads? The man should have a long look in the mirror. "Would it be possible for you to let me into Gatz's apartment? I could wait for him there."

"Are you crazy, mister? Let you into a tenant's apartment?"

"Gatz mentioned that you would, if he were late."

"Bullshit. He knows better than that. Look, if you're from the police department, I'd like to see your badge."

"Badge?" Ben stammered. "Uh . . . I'm not a cop. Just an auditor. Wage earner. Just like you."

"Then if you're not a cop, take your goddamn questions elsewhere or come back with someone who has a nice shiny badge. I don't like snoops. And I don't like wasting my time."

Once again he started to close the door, but stopped. Someone called him from behind. He turned. A petite woman, dressed in a yellow housedress, hair pulled back, a dish in her hand, walked out of the kitchen.

"I overheard you talking, honey," she said.

The woman was attractive, almost appealing, poles apart from the man who seemed to be her husband.

"Gatz is in his apartment," she said. "I took out the garbage a half hour ago and saw him coming into the building. He said it was a very important day for him. Someone was coming at one o'clock and he felt his entire life was about to change. He asked if I could pick up some groceries for him because he had to stay and wait. He was very adamant about waiting. He's up there."

"That's impossible," Ben said suddenly. "Unless he's in the shower."

"There are no showers," the super explained.

"Then he must have heard me. I pounded on the door for two or three minutes." Ben was puzzled. "I'm going to try again."

The super turned to his wife and stared.

"He's up there," she said once more.

The super turned back to Ben. "I'll go with you."

The woman quickly receded into the background.

The super closed the apartment door and led the way.

"My name's Hardman," the super said as he started to climb the staircase.

"Ben Burdett," Ben replied.

They reached Gatz's door and knocked. There was no response. As the super shrugged, Ben faced him squarely. The super looked down the hall, then grudgingly opened the door with his passkey.

They entered.

The apartment had been ransacked. The dresser drawers had been pulled out and overturned. Clothes from the closets lay all over the floor. The draperies on the windows were ripped. The mattress in the bedroom had been slit and torn apart.

What the hell had gone on here? And where was Gatz? Since Mrs. Hardman had seen him a half hour ago, whoever had attacked the place must have done so within the last few minutes. Certainly Gatz had not stood around enjoying the sight. He would have tried to stop it, called for help. But obviously he hadn't. Maybe it had happened during the night? No. That made no sense. Gatz would have said something to Mrs. Hardman in the street.

Ben looked around. "I think you'd better call the police, Mr. Hardman."

"Yes," the super said unsurely. He reached for the phone that lay on the floor, off its cradle, and dialed. "Police, please," he said, once the connection had been made.

Ben started to sift through the debris. What could burglars have been searching for in a tenement apartment? Could it have had anything to do with Allison Parker?

He searched the bedroom and bathroom, finding nothing. Then he examined Gatz's desk.

"What are you looking for?" the super asked.

"I don't know," Ben replied.

"You'd better wait until the police get here."

Ben turned and smiled; the super had lost a great deal of his bravado. "Once they get here, I won't be able to look."

The super entered the kitchen. Ben could hear the faucet open as he looked over the desk shelves. They were empty. Most of the books had been thrown to the floor. He picked up several and looked them over. Nothing of interest. He examined the dust prints. The upper shelf had wide marks that surely had been caused by the books. But the lower one had thin lines that seemed to have been formed by narrow files or magazines. He looked at the floor once more. There was nothing in sight that might have fit.

He snapped his head around as the super called his name, then jumped over the toppled desk chair and raced into the kitchen.

The super was standing beside the refrigerator. The door was open, and inside was Detective Gatz—staring out at them . . . dead.

"Christ!" Ben cried.

"What do we do?" the super asked in an uncharacteristic mousy voice.

"Nothing. The police will be here in a couple of minutes."

"Right in my building," the super mumbled. "Right under my nose. Half an hour ago he was talking to my wife. I can't believe it." He shut the refrigerator door. He looked as if he were ready to throw up. "God."

"God isn't going to be of help. Why don't you sit down? Or throw some water on your face?"

The super walked into the bathroom. Ben returned to the living room and looked through the debris once more. Finding nothing, he turned the desk chair upright and sat down. He had to get hold of himself. The police would be there within minutes. Then the questions would start all over again. Surely they would ask why Ben had come to meet the detective. And he would have to say something to satisfy them. Of course, as soon as he mentioned the compactor murder, the police would start to draw parallels. But there was nothing he could do about it. There was no way he could disappear. The super knew he'd been there. And he had given the super his name.

The super returned and sat down on the edge of the overturned sofa. He was pale. A hint of saliva lay on his chin. He had thrown up.

"I guess Gatz's pension won't mean too much to him now," the super said softly.

"No," Ben said. "Not a thing."

The super covered his face with his hands. Ben sat back and crossed his legs. Suddenly the room was very silent.

And they waited.

As Ben had anticipated, the police grilled him for over an hour. He told them that Gatz had contacted him on the advice and with the approval of Inspector Burstein from Manhattan Homicide, specifically to discuss the compactor murder. He told them that Gatz had explained nothing at their first meeting, so they would have to call Burstein to find out the particulars.

That's exactly what they tried to do, but were unable to locate him. They did tell Ben that a Detective Wausau had corraborated Ben's story, at least in principle, since Wausau had no idea exactly what had occurred between his superior and Gatz either.

Shortly before four o'clock the police released him. He left the tenement and took a taxi to Manhattan Homicide.

Throughout the trip downtown, he lay against the back seat staring through the windshield, reexamining everything Gatz had told him and reliving the horrible events of the last few hours. Gatz's murder still seemed incredible. Gatz was no weakling. It would have taken a very strong man to strangle him. But whatever had happened, Gatz was gone. That was the bottom line. If Ben was to pursue Gatz's story further, he would have to do it with Inspector Burstein, who, Gatz had indicated, had had contact with Allison Parker and had witnessed, in part, the strange sequence of events.

The cab dropped him off in front of division headquarters. He went inside and asked the duty clerk for Inspector Burstein. The duty clerk placed a call upstairs. Minutes later Detective Wausau came down, accompanied by a second detective.

"Mr. Burdett," Wausau said, extending his hand.

Ben shook it and waited while Wausau introduced the other detective, a man named Jacobelli.

"Let's go into that conference room," Wausau said, pointing toward a doorway at the end of the main corridor.

"I'd like to see Burstein," Ben said as he started to walk.

"First I want to ask you some questions . . . about Gatz."

"Look, Detective Wausau, I've been under interrogation for the last two hours, and I told the Bronx Homicide people everything I know. You spoke to them. If you want to speak to them again, go ahead. But I want to talk with Burstein, and then I want to go home to my wife. Okay?"

"Tell me about Gatz!" Wausau insisted. "From the beginning."

Reluctantly Ben repeated everything, avoiding the specifics of the conversation he'd had with Gatz in O'Reilly's Pub. That he would reserve for Burstein, especially since Gatz had warned him, during the walk from O'Reilly's to the apartment, to say nothing to the police.

Wausau pumped him for over an hour, drawing random conclusions about the relationship between Gatz's death and the murder in the Eighty-ninth Street compactor.

When Wausau had finally finished, Ben turned on him angrily. "Now, goddammit," he said, "I sat in this stinking interrogation room when I didn't have to, and I gave you all the information you wanted. Now I just want to talk to Burstein. I don't think that's an unfair request, do you?"

"No," Wausau said. "But that's going to be difficult."

"Why?"

"Because he's dead."

Ben felt a sharp jolt; he staggered.

"He and his wife died in their sleep last night. We found out an hour ago. His house burned. The preliminary report from the NYFD investigation squad states that the fire was set. Arson."

Ben was numb. Wausau told him to go home; they would contact him. Ben walked out of the building and stopped at the curb. There he turned and looked up at the sky.

"God!" he cried, not knowing why. But loud enough that if God were listening, he could hear.

9

The body in the compactor. Gatz. Inspector Burstein.

Were their deaths related? Maybe. Certainly any connection among the three could just as easily have been explained away as happenstance. The old nun probably had nothing to do with the corpse in the basement. Gatz had most likely been murdered by a burglar. Burstein had been the victim of a lunatic pyromaniac. But deep inside, Ben knew that all three murders were connected, that Burstein and Gatz had been eliminated because they had known too much. With Michael Farmer dead, and the old priest—Father Halliran?—and now Burstein and Gatz, there was no one among the innocents who had any insight, except Jennifer Learson, of course, who had disappeared a long time ago. If someone was trying to cover all traces of the truth, it seemed likely that they had disposed of Miss Learson too, or if they hadn't accomplished that as yet, could reasonably be expected to make her their next objective. But whose objective? If he believed Gatz, he could not help but conclude that the plotters were connected to the nun, and following that trail would inevitably lead right to the Archdiocese of New York. It seemed beyond comprehension, the implausibility made all the more pressing by the austere surroundings of St. Luke's Cathedral, where he had been sitting for the last half hour, trying to make some order out of the chaos. If only there was someone he could ask, someplace he could go to search for the truth. But there wasn't. He was helpless. And so was Faye who was still lying in bed mesmerized by shock, and according to Gatz, even more subject to the sway of events than he or perhaps anyone else who had ever lived, except for Allison Parker and her predecessors, of course. He opened his eyes; the afternoon light that poured through the stained-glass windows intensified the unreal world he had been contemplating. Suddenly the church seemed threatening. True, the place was a sanctuary, but in the context of events, what kind? And for whom? And for what purpose?

The place was silent. There were only four people inside. It was warm, but certainly not hot enough to cause him to sweat as profusely as he had, nor to make the air as stale as it seemed. He felt as if he were going to suffocate. He opened his collar, stepped out of the pew, and turned toward the rear. A priest walked into view.

"Father!" Ben called. He approached the man. "I wonder if you could help me."

The priest smiled. "Of course, my son."

"I've been told a story, and I'd like to check it with you."

The expression on the priest's pleasant rosy face encouraged him.

"I've been told that every several years, the church selects a lay person, manufactures a secular identity, disguises and sets up the person as a sentinel or guardian." He paused, waiting for a reaction.

The priest looked puzzled. "For what purpose, my son?"

"I'm not sure."

"My son, if you can't be more specific, there's no way I can help."

"I can't be specific, Father. But I know many people have died because of this. There is even the possibility that the church has been behind several murders, committed to protect the identity of this person."

The priest was horrified. "My son. This story seems highly unlikely. But to suggest that the holy church would be involved in a violation of the commandments of God, let alone murder, is offensive and out of the question. Who told you this story?"

"A policeman."

"Where is he?"

"Right now? Probably in the Bronx County Morgue. He was murdered this morning."

The priest shook his head. "In my opinion, the entire story is a fabrication. Why it was fabricated, I do not know. But I can assure you the church would have no part of it."

"Perhaps you're right," Ben said after a long, strained pause. "Perhaps this is all a dream. Perhaps I'm going out of my mind." Why was he talking to this man? If by some incredible quirk of fate this priest was familiar with the matter, he certainly would not admit to it. And of course it was more logical to assume that a low-level churchman would have no idea as to intrigues undertaken by the hierarchy. No, he was wasting his time, even possibly placing himself in danger. He had to get out of there. "You're probably right, Father!" He started to inch toward the exit. "The policeman must have been wrong. He was probably a little paranoid. And who knows why he was murdered? Someone might have had a grudge against him. That's it. A grudge." He stepped onto the concrete steps that led down to the street. He could still see the priest watching him curiously; he was sure that the priest was convinced that he was a little mad himself. "Thank you, Father. I appreciate the attention and concern. Thank you."

He reached the sidewalk and started to walk, picking up speed. He had to get home, see Faye, try to relax, escape from it all. But deep inside, he knew it was only beginning, if only because he could not just wait and let fate dictate their future. He had to find out more.

He would start in the morning!

"What are we doing? Having a party?" There was a smile on Ben's face as he stood in the doorway.

"I feel so much better, honey," Faye said. She jumped off the couch and embraced him.

"You see," cried Sorrenson from across the room. "I told you she just needed a couple of days. And some tender, loving care."

Grace Woodbridge emerged from the kitchen with a tray filled with cups and saucers. "Coffee and tea."

"Put it on the table," Faye suggested. She led Ben into the room and pushed him down on the couch next to Ralph Jenkins.

"You sure you're all right, honey?" Ben asked.

"I woke up about an hour ago feeling like a million dollars." She took the baby from Jenkins and rocked him in her arms. "And seeing John and Ralph and then Grace made me even better. You know?"

"Yes . . . I know."

"Where were you?"

"Just out. Were there any calls?"

"Not while I was here," Sorrenson said. "And I've been here since you left."

"Then you missed your rehearsal," Ben assumed.

"Oh . . . what's a rehearsal when you're needed by friends? And I'm not the only one who made a sacrifice, if you want to call it that. Ralph passed up a meeting of the Antique Guild."

"A nothing meeting," Jenkins said. "Did you meet with the policeman?"

"Yes," Ben replied. He had not told Jenkins the purpose of the meeting, only that such a meeting was taking place. He hoped the sound of his voice did not betray the seriousness of it all. "Everything's fine," he added.

"Well, that's good," said Grace Woodbridge as she set up the servings. "It's about time someone said something is fine around here. Max left the apartment this morning, moaning and groaning. When I got here, Faye was still asleep and John and Ralph were talking as if the ultimate cataclysm was about to happen. Everyone has started to imagine things. And I'm sick of it. I won't let Faye become a party to it. It's all over."

"You bet your life," Faye said.

She stood and spun around with the baby in her arms. He giggled at the sensation. The others laughed as they had not laughed in days.

Grace Woodbridge passed around the dishes. Ben pulled Faye down to the couch and kissed her. "You don't know how happy I am to see you like this. John. Ralph. Grace. I appreciate your staying with

Faye today. Maybe it is over." Did he really believe it? "What do you think, Joey? Is Mama going to be all right?"

The baby waved his hands and stretched a toothless smile. Everyone laughed again.

Ben stood and walked to the window. Next to it was a typewriter set on a table. In a manila envelope were several hundred pages of neglected text and notes.

"I want you to get back to your book, honey," Faye said as she sipped from a cup of tea.

"Yeah," Ben said halfheartedly, thumbing the pages.

Jenkins walked to his side. "I expect a masterpiece from you, Ben."

"You do? That's good, Ralph. But the way things have been going around here, I'll settle just to finish it."

"I know you better than that. You'll get back to it, lick it, get it published, and have a hit on your hands."

"From your lips to God's ears."

Jenkins nodded as Sorrenson approached; behind them Faye and Grace Woodbridge had started to examine the latest issue of *Vogue*.

"You might be interested to know that I checked into the identity of the nun," Sorrenson said softly.

Ben looked him straight in the eye. "You did?"

"Of course. I told you I would. Now, don't ask me how I did it, but I found out that the nun's rent checks are paid by an M. Leffler."

"Who's he?" Jenkins asked.

"Ah . . . I found that out, too. I have a friend who works at the archdiocese. I asked him if he had ever heard of such a person. He said that M. Leffler is the archdiocese's comptroller."

"So what does that tell us," Ben asked.

"Simply that in addition to owning the building, the archdiocese also pays the nun's rent. We suspected it, but now we know!"

Faye's voice interrupted them. "Hey, what are you whispering about?"

Ben turned. "Nothing, honey."

"You're talking about the nun, aren't you?"

Ben cleared his throat. "Well, kind of."

"Really. I told you we should forget her. If Sister Therese wants to sit there, let her."

"What did you say?" Ben asked, startled.

"Sister Therese. That's the nun's name."

"How do you know that?"

She shrugged.

"Did someone tell you?"

"No. I just know."

Ben looked at Jenkins and Sorrenson, who shook their heads. Then he sat down next to Faye and took her hand.

"What else do you know?"

"What do you mean, Ben?"

"You know what I mean."

She said nothing; he grabbed her by the shoulders, and she flinched.

"What was her name before she became Sister Therese?" He was almost screaming.

Sorrenson, Jenkins, and Grace Woodbridge were astonished.

"What was her name?"

Faye shuddered. "Allison . . . Allison Parker."

Ben sat back. Everyone in the room looked on tensely. No one dared say a word.

"Allison Parker," Ben repeated, nearly in tears. "Yes. That's her name. Allison Parker."

Sorrenson, Jenkins, and Grace Woodbridge had been long gone when Ben walked out of the bedroom in response to the bell, answered the door, and ushered Biroc into the foyer.

"I hope I didn't wake you, Mr. Burdett," Biroc said apologetically.

Ben looked at his watch. "No, Joe. We were just

going to sleep. I didn't see you on duty yesterday or today."

"I wasn't in yesterday, and today I started late and only worked half a shift. The building management suggested that I take it easy. You know . . . after what happened."

"Sure," said Ben. "How can I help you?"

"Oh, no, Mr. Burdett. I didn't come for a favor. I came to see if Mrs. Burdett was all right. I didn't want to come up so late, but it was eating at me."

"You're welcome here anytime. And Mrs. Burdett is much better. She'll be very happy you called."

Biroc smiled. "That's good to hear. I was very concerned." He opened the door and stepped into the hall. "Mr. Burdett, if there's anything you need tomorrow while I'm on, please call down. No matter what. I'll see to it."

"You're a good friend, Joe."

Biroc nodded. "Good night."

"Good night, Joe."

Ben closed the door.

Lying in bed, he felt as if someone had poured ice water over his body. He was cold—not superficially, as one would be in the dead of winter, but deep inside, almost as deep, he thought, as the substance of his soul.

Next to him Faye was reading a book. He stared at her and listened to the baby move restlessly about his crib, which was secreted across the room in the darkness. Ben had been silent for the last ten minutes, ever since he'd said good-bye to Biroc, tiptoed into the bedroom, and climbed into bed. He was ready.

"Faye," he said.

"Yes, honey," she replied without removing her eyes from the book.

He leaned forward. "Could you stop reading for a minute? I'd like to ask you something."

She laid the book on the quilt. "Sure."

"Don't you think it's peculiar that you knew the nun's name?"

She looked at him and nodded. "Someone must have told me. What other explanation is there?"

"But you don't remember anyone telling you, right?"

She pouted impatiently. "I told you that already."

"Okay. One other thing."

She nodded.

"Did you ever try to commit suicide?"

The expression that crossed her face was the strangest he had ever seen.

"Did you?"

"Why do you want to know?"

"Let's just say I do. It concerns me."

"Ben. We've been married for seven years. We've known each other for twelve. Of all things to ask. And of all times."

He shuffled uncomfortably on the bed. "I'm just curious."

She looked at him squarely, her eyelids blinking in rapid confusion.

He raised himself up on the pillows. "Faye . . . it's simple. If you've never tried, just say so."

She tossed the book angrily aside, pulled up the blanket to the nape of her throat, and looked off into space. "And what if I did try to kill myself?" she said, her voice so distant that she sounded as if she were somewhere else. "Would it make a difference?"

"No. I just want to know."

"All right." Her eyes pierced him. "I did try. When I was much younger."

He said nothing for a long time. Then he asked, "Why?"

"Let's just say I did. I swore that I would never talk about it. In fact, for many years I repressed the entire incident."

"Faye . . . I—"

"I said I don't want to talk about it. Please. I never want it mentioned again. I want you to promise."

He waited, then said, "All right. I promise." He had the answer—that final bit of information he needed to reinforce his resolve to take action. What action? He didn't know. But something. "Why don't we go to sleep?"

She didn't answer.

He reached up, turned off the reading lamp, and rolled on his side, facing away from Faye. He knew she was staring at his back. He could feel it. But he would not turn back to say anything else. He'd said enough. Now he wanted to think, sleep, then get up early and get to work.

10

When Ben left the apartment at eight o'clock, it was already raining heavily, and there wasn't a free cab in sight. He took the bus downtown on Central Park West, transferred at Fifty-seventh Street, rode to Third, and got off in the face of a driving wind. Crossing the street, he ducked into a corner delicatessen, sat down at the counter, ordered a cup of coffee, then pulled the *Madison Avenue Handbook* from his raincoat pocket and studied the list of New York's model agencies. Some were nearby, a few farther downtown; if traffic permitted, he could conceivably cover all of them in one day. He hoped, though, that wouldn't be necessary, that he would hit a lead to

Jennifer Learson early. But he doubted it would be easy; it had been fifteen years. In a transient business like modeling, built on beauty and youth, there were probably no models and few employees of any kind who had remained in the business that long a period of time.

After a second cup he left the delicatessen and covered the midtown agencies on foot. No one had ever heard of Jennifer Learson, and though there were two or three bookers who could remember a model named Allison Parker, no one could recall what had happened to her.

By the time he reached the lower-midtown agencies, he was almost convinced he was wasting his time. However, one booker at a small firm remembered something about a model who had been involved in a series of murders and who had disappeared. She recalled that a woman named Rusty had worked for the girl's agency. The company was long since defunct, but Rusty was still in the business, booking at Blanchard Models.

He thanked the woman, checked the directory for the address of Blanchard, then grabbed one of the few available cabs he had seen all day and taxied several blocks to a converted-brownstone office building.

Blanchard Models was on the second floor. The owner was an attractive, pleasant woman in her early forties. There were eight employees. Rusty was one of them. Miss Blanchard was kind enough to take her off the booking board.

"My name is Ben Burdett," Ben said, shaking Rusty's thin, freckled hand.

Rusty was tall, slim, about forty, with an encouraging smile, a reddish complexion, and a mild, enthusiastic voice.

"And I'm Rusty."

Ben nodded. "Rusty . . . you may be able to be of great help to me."

"I'll try, if I can." She could see the urgency in his expression.

He sat down on the lounge next to her.

"I'm looking for a girl named Jennifer Learson."

Rusty was surprised. "Jennifer Learson? God, I haven't heard her name in ages. Sure, I knew her. She was one beautiful woman."

"So I'm told," Ben said. He looked at her, coaxing with his eyes.

"She was the best friend of a model named Allison Parker. I booked for them both. What happened to those girls is a tragedy."

Ben moved in closer, so close that he could feel the drift of her breath as she spoke.

"What happened?"

"Well . . . I really don't know the specifics. You'd have to ask the police. They were good models. In fact, when the roof fell in, they were both doing very well. Especially Allison. Oh . . . they weren't stars yet, but there is no doubt in my mind that they would have made it. No doubt at all. They were like sisters, always together, laughing. If I remember correctly, Allison was from Indiana, and Jennifer was from Macon, Georgia. They'd been in town for a couple of years. In fact, when they first got here, they roomed together in the Village—at least, until Allison moved in with her boyfriend, a lawyer named Michael Farmer."

Ben lit a cigar and watched her closely; once she started talking, he could see that she had a lot to say and no hesitation about saying it.

"It was terrible. Poor Allison disappeared off the face of the earth after her boyfriend was murdered. Oh . . . it was in the papers—all over them. There was an investigation, but I don't think the police solved anything."

Ben drew his tongue across his lips, coating them with a thin film of saliva; then he nodded again, somewhat more resolutely, to urge her to continue.

Rusty sighed and clasped her hands in her lap. "The one I really feel sorry for is Jennifer."

"Why?"

"Well . . . she went through some bad times. Of course, so might have Allison. But no one ever saw Allison again, so no one could possibly relate to her experiences. Do you know what I mean?"

"Of course."

"Jennifer didn't come in for a long time after the murder. When she finally did, she looked like a different human being. She had completely changed. As I said before, Mr. Burdett, she was a beautiful woman. She had dark hair, a dark complexion, a magnificent figure, and a smile that could melt granite. But what a sight she'd become. She was as pale as a ghost, and she had lost twenty pounds—she couldn't have weighed more than ninety-five. You'd have thought she had just gotten out of a concentration camp. There were terrible wrinkles under her eyes, and she was racked with the shakes. We had lunch the day she returned. She told me she had been questioned by the police. Then she rattled off a lot of gibberish about Allison and Michael. I was sure she wasn't all there. Her thoughts were all jumbled, and nothing she said made any sense. You know what I mean? It was like listening to a lunatic. And was she paranoid! She kept telling me about a plot by religious fanatics; she said they were after her. She was even carrying a gun to protect herself. I tried to calm her down, but she wouldn't listen. Or couldn't. She said she hadn't had a date in months. Hadn't even left her apartment. She was afraid they would grab her. Now, what was I supposed to say or do? I was in shock. Well, she tried to get back to modeling, but got nowhere. Who was going to book a girl who looked like she had just risen from the grave? I told her to get away. Take a year off. She said she had to work. She was seeing a psychiatrist four times a week, and the bills were running very high. Then she disappeared, reappearing again months later. She seemed to be getting worse. Worse-looking. More paranoid. Kind of manic-depressive. In fact, one of the girls thought she was schizo. And I wouldn't have bet against it. About a year after she first came back, I tried to call her. She had a bunch of residual checks that had built up. No one answered her phone. I went to her apartment and buzzed. She let me in. She said she wasn't answering the phone because 'they' were after her and she didn't want 'them' to know that she was home. You should have seen her place. It hadn't been cleaned in months. There were TV dinners all over. Garbage on the floors. Tons of dirty dishes in the sink. There was a terrible odor of human feces and urine. God, it was awful. I tried to convince her to leave the apartment, but couldn't. I gave her the money. She told me she was through with modeling; she had found a better way to make a living. And I was quick to see that she needed a lot of cash. She had scars on her arms. She was shooting something. Cocaine. Heroin . . . who knows?"

Ben was fascinated. "And this all happened within the space of a year?"

"Yes . . . over fourteen years ago." Rusty paused, then continued. "A couple of months later, I found out how Jennifer was earning a living from a model named Victoria, who had known both Jennifer and Allison. Victoria and her boyfriend were walking near Broadway, after coming out of a theater, and saw a drugged-up girl standing on a corner soliciting. It was Jennifer. Victoria tried to talk to her, but Jennifer didn't respond. Just then a pimp came out of a building and introduced Jennifer to a Puerto Rican john, who led her into his car and drove off. Victoria was shocked. She tried to speak to the pimp. The pimp refused to answer and disappeared into an alley."

Rusty stopped talking; she was tense, perspiring heavily. Ben offered a handkerchief; she took it and wiped her face.

"That was the last I heard of her for at least two years. Until one night . . . I remember it distinctly. It was Christmas Eve. I was home. The phone rang, and it was Jennifer on the other end. I could barely hear her. She said she had taken an overdose. I called the police. They went to Jennifer's apartment and rushed her to Bellevue. I found her parents' phone number and called her father. He said he didn't care what happened to her. If she died, she died. He hung up. It was incredible. Anyway, I spoke to Jennifer a month or two later; she was being treated as an outpatient at the Bellevue psychiatric clinic. She was more paranoid than ever. Then she disappeared again. When she next called, about a year and a half later, she said she had been confined to an institution, but was completely normal and cured. She said she wanted to return to modeling. I told her to come in, but I knew that no matter how much progress she had made, too much time had passed. She showed up just prior to closing, thank God. She was still under thirty. But she looked ninety. And she had wild eyes, like a rabid animal's. I was scared. I made one of the other bookers stay. I told Jennifer there was no way she could return to modeling. I was afraid she would get violent. But she didn't. She just stood, as if she had expected to hear what I had said, and calmly left the building. And that's the last time I saw her."

Ben bit into the end of his cigar; he felt a tremor run up his spine. My God, he thought. My God. He could hardly moisten his mouth. It had dried like the caked floor of a desert lake.

"You're sure that you never saw her again?"

Rusty looked off into space, searching her memory. "Yes . . . I'm sure."

"And you have no idea where she is?"

"I didn't say that."

Ben's body stiffened. "Where is she?"

"She was confined to a mental institution."

"Which one?"

"Providence State Hospital. In Riverhead, Long Island. But whether she's there now, I don't know. All I can tell you is that I want nothing to do with it."

"Of course."

Rusty stood; she was shaken.

They shook hands.

"I don't know how to thank you," Ben said.

"Forget it. I hope I was of some help."

"Yes. You certainly were."

He thanked Miss Blanchard for her consideration and walked to the door with Rusty at his side.

"Mr. Burdett," Rusty said as Ben was about to leave, "I forgot to ask you why you wanted to know about Jennifer. Why you seem to be so interested in her whereabouts."

Ben smiled and stared at her feline eyes. "Why?" he asked rhetorically. "Because I think I've found Allison Parker."

"Over the last six or seven years," Dr. Taguichi said softly, "she's been admitted several times. From the very beginning there was not the slightest doubt about the diagnosis. But what truly amazed us—beyond the depth of her psychosis—was the extent of the symptoms and the crossover into other syndromic subtypes."

"What do you mean?" Ben asked.

They began to cross the neatly pruned exercise yard of Providence State Hospital.

"Well . . . there are certain symptoms, general ones, that are common to most schizophrenics and which allow us to make a diagnosis. In Jennifer Learson's case—as I said before, she displayed firm paranoid tendencies. She was tense, suspicious, guarded, even hostile at times. And she had a fixed sequence of delusions of a persecutory nature."

"What kind of delusions?"

Taguichi told him; it sounded like a repetition of Gatz's epic. Ben told Taguichi that he had reason to believe that Jennifer Learson's story had some basis in fact. Taguichi admitted that that might be so, then continued to evolve a picture of a very disturbed girl.

"Even granted that the persecutory delusions—a religious plot carried out by the Catholic Church—had some foundation in fact, I can assure you that the further manifestations did not. She was convinced that clerics were following her, trying to kill her. Alternately, she was convinced that she was to be the next living victim, the next guardian, the successor to her friend Allison Parker, whose personality and fate were clearly developed in her mind. These of course suggest coexisting delusions of grandeur. She experienced delusions in which she claimed to be the Virgin Mary. She heard voices. She saw visions. One time she thought she was on fire, burning at the stake like Joan of Arc. Another time she perceived that her heart was growing. Mr. Burdett, this is classic paranoid schizophrenia. But as I said before, she also elicited a gamut of general schizophrenic manifestations. She had severe disorders of verbal behavior. At times she was totally incoherent. At other times she spoke in wholly indecipherable symbolic terms. She was subject to mutism, echolalia, and verbigeration—all forms of verbal and expressive dementia. With each successive visit she showed an ever-increasing and serious deterioration of appearance and manner. One day we found her eating her own stool."

Ben grimaced; a surge of stomach acid sickened him.

"In addition, she was particularly subject to affective disorders, reduced emotional responses, and emotional blunting."

"Doctor . . . this sounds like a very sick girl. Why was she ever let out?"

Taguichi nodded thoughtfully as they reached the end of the exercise yard and entered the building to their right.

"In the beginning, Miss Learson was a voluntary internee. We were able to keep her schizophrenia under control and release her periodically. She responded well to daily doses of chlorpromazine, which she took as an outpatient. When that drug proved ineffective, we alternated several other phenothiazines, with mixed results. We also utilized several forms of psychotherapy, but with negative results there, too."

"Did she return voluntarily?"

"No. She was committed by her family after a sequence of self-mutilatory acts, one homicidal episode involving a man who was supposedly paying her for sexual services, and an alarming increase in the frequency and the nature of her delusions and hallucinations."

They climbed a staircase to the second floor and started to walk down a white corridor.

Ben shook his head. "Perhaps I'll be able to make some headway with her. Perhaps something I say will get through."

"I'm afraid not, Mr. Burdett. She is one of the few truly hopeless cases in the institution. Of course, that's an opinion. But a good one. Even if she were still in the paranoid state, she would be difficult to reach. But during the last four years, since her involuntary confinement, her clinical course has taken an alarming turn —a possibly terminal psychiatric turn."

Ben looked at the doctor with weary eyes.

"She has become a catatonic."

"A what?"

"She has lost contact with the outside world, Mr. Burdett. Her trauma is very rare today, although many years ago it was common. Modern treatment has all but eliminated such conditions. However, these treatments have failed with Miss Learson. She has not responded to drugs. She has not responded to insulin coma. She has not responded to electroconvulsive shock. Nothing has helped. For the last two years she has lain immobile on her cot, salivating, at times eliciting a cataleptic response, frozen body positions . . . what-have-you." Dr. Taguichi could see the horror in Ben's eyes, the look of frustration. "I'm sorry."

They arrived in front of a door, which Dr. Taguichi opened; they stepped inside.

Ben could hardly keep from screaming; he felt even

sicker than he had felt outside. The girl who lay on the cot could conceivably have been a beautiful woman at one time. But now she was a dirty old crone. A shriveled, frozen body without any expression, even a hint of life.

As they stood in the room, Dr. Taguichi explained Jennifer Learson's condition in greater detail. For one brief instant Ben thought he saw some movement. Then it was gone. He spoke to her, listed names that he thought she might recognize: Allison Parker, Detective Thomas Gatz, Michael Farmer, Monsignor Franchino. She remained mute, imprisoned in a self-created hell. He felt his own emotions start to get away. He looked at Taguichi. Certainly he could not let himself crack in front of the hospital's chief of psychiatry.

He smiled faintly.

"It's unfortunate," Taguichi said. "We've done just about everything that can be done for her, though of course we'll keep trying."

Ben looked at the wooden cot, the simple pine table and chair, the empty gray walls; the cell could have been cropped out of a mid-nineteenth-century work of social fiction.

"I'd like to go," he said, sensing his own break with reality, his giving way to revulsion at the thing that Jennifer Learson had become.

Taguichi nodded and escorted him out of the building. At the entrance to the hospital they stopped.

Ben had been visibly affected; Taguichi assured him that there was no way he could have avoided it. No one ever entered the world of the mentally ill without a marked emotional withdrawal.

"If there is anything else, any new development, I'd like you to call me, doctor."

"Of course," Taguichi said.

Ben drew deeply at the fresh Long Island air. He wanted to tell Taguichi why he had come, why he had lied about his familial relationship to Jennifer Learson.

But for reasons of his own safety and Faye's, he could not.

He looked straight at the doctor, lowered his eyes, and sighed.

Within seconds Dr. Taguichi was gone and Ben was on his way to the train station in Riverhead.

Ben had been standing on the platform for about fifteen minutes when the grinding sound of wheels on rail chattered through the air.

He picked up an old magazine and approached the edge of the platform, being sure not to get too close to the rail pit.

The train appeared around a bend and pulled into the station, opening its doors.

He entered, took off his jacket, and sat in the car's last seat. The train started to move. He sat back, relaxed, and opened the magazine. He had nearly finished when his eye caught the headline of a small article. He held the magazine up to the light. The headline read: SYRACUSE GIRL SURVIVES ORDEAL ON ADIRONDACK MOUNTAINTOP. TELLS STORY OF MURDER AND THE SUPERNATURAL.

He began to read.

11

Shortly after three in the morning Ben emerged through the roof door and moved toward the front face of the building.

"Over here," a voice called.

He strained his eyes but could see nothing; it was like looking into a black hole.

"Mr. Burdett."

He turned. Two men dressed in sneakers and black sweatsuits stepped toward him.

"Sorry I'm late," Ben said.

"Forget it," replied Frykowski. "This is Turner."

Ben nodded to the second man, who smiled and adjusted the wool ski cap on his head.

"Is the platform down?"

Frykowski nodded. "We dropped it this afternoon."

"Have any trouble getting into the building?"

"No. We told the superintendent the job had been ordered by management."

Ben walked to the edge of the roof and looked over the wall. The platform was hanging three feet below. He checked the grapnels. They were secure.

"You sure these'll hold?"

Frykowski laughed. "We do this every day, Burdett, and we take no chances. Once a week we check out the entire apparatus. Pulleys. Ropes. Everything."

Frykowski smiled and climbed over the roof railing onto the platform. Turner checked the winches and followed.

"Ease over the wall and step down as if you were getting into a hot bathtub. Don't make any quick moves."

"Okay," Ben said, throwing one leg over the rail.

Frykowski and Turner grabbed Ben's arms and lifted him into place. The platform shook under his weight.

"Just relax," Frykowski said. "We'll do all the work. We only have several feet to descend. It'll be over in a minute."

Frykowski and Turner moved to the opposite sides of the platform and grabbed the pulley ropes; the platform gradually began to slide.

"You know, Burdett, I don't like to ask no questions or cause no problems. But this is the craziest thing I've ever done. I saw the old nun in the window, and I gotta believe she ain't gonna be too happy about this."

"She's deaf, dumb, blind, and paralyzed."

"But still—"

"Keep your voice down," Ben cautioned.

The platform reached the top of the nun's window.

"Now slow," Frykowski said.

"We're all right," Turner replied, tightening his glove-covered hands on the ropes.

Ben fell to his knees and placed his palms against the glass. Slowly more of it appeared, fronting a dark lace curtain and the face and body of the old nun. Even at that close range it was so dark that the contours of her features remained obscured.

"Tie it off!" Frykowski commanded.

Turner secured his rope, nodded, and remained to the side. Frykowski tied off his end, moved toward Ben, and looked in the window.

"It beats me," he said, shaking his head. "An old broad holding a crucifix, sitting in a window. If I were you, I wouldn't go near this pussy."

"I appreciate your concern, Frykowski, but I paid you to get me down here, not to lecture. Okay?"

"Sure. Sure."

A gust of wind ripped past the platform. Ben grabbed frantically for the railing. Frykowski laughed.

"Nothing's gonna happen, Burdett."

Ben reached for the base of the window frame.

"Help me get it up."

They fought the window. It wouldn't move. Ben stood, looked over the top of the lower frame, then returned to his knees.

"The lock's open; it must be jammed."

Frykowski took two chisels from his pocket. He handed one to Ben. They inserted the tools along the edge of the frame, sliding them through the frozen mortar. Ben tried to lift the window once more. It seemed to give. They poked with the chisels several more times. Ben tried again. This time the window slid quickly to its apex.

Ben pulled the curtain aside. "I don't believe it," he mumbled, fighting back the impulse to scream.

The woman was the most repulsive thing he had ever seen. The shriveled skin. The knotted veins in her hands, the swollen, distended blood vessels that crept perilously close to the surface of her face. The matted web of hair. And the eyes, encased in cataracts.

She was dressed in the black robes of the sisterhood. Her hands were callused and old, topped by long, pointed nails. And if she were breathing, there was no way to tell.

"This is bad news, man," Frykowski said, gritting his teeth.

"What is it?" Turner called from the side.

"Nothing. You stay there." He turned to Ben. "I want to pull us up. Right now!"

"It'll only take me a minute. Please."

Ben took a wineglass, wrapped in a handkerchief, from his pocket, and tried to pull the nun's hands off the cross. Her grip was incredibly strong. He asked Frykowski to help. Reluctantly Frykowski tugged until the nun's left hand slipped off the metal. Ben spread her fingers and wrapped them around the glass, carefully pressing the tips. Then he rewrapped the glass in the handkerchief and placed it back in his pocket.

A violent gust of wind, then another, tossed the carriage from side to side.

"We're going up," Frykowski said.

"One second," Ben pleaded as he pulled out a Nikon.

"Up!"

Turner started to untie the pulley ropes.

Ben set the exposure and started to snap at the nun.

"Up," screamed Frykowski once more as he raced to his side of the carriage and grabbed hold of his rope.

Turner freed the system and started to pull.

"You'd better hold on, Burdett," Frykowski warned.

Ben continued to snap.

Another gust swiped them. The platform lurched, nearly throwing everyone off. Ben quickly pushed the camera into his pocket.

"All right, let's go. But close her window."

"Fuck the window, man!" Frykowski screamed.

Turner pointed upward. "Look!"

Ben and Frykowski followed the line of Turner's hand.

"The rope!"

Both lines of the right support were withering.

"Christ!"

The platform started to sag toward the building; Ben grabbed for the rail.

"That won't help," Turner cried. He stumbled to the center of the carriage. "Into the window."

Frykowski grabbed for the window frame. So did Turner. Ben fell back. The camera popped out of his pocket and onto the platform. He dived, caught it just as it was going off the end, and stuffed it inside his shirt.

Turner was already inside the window. "Come on, man!"

Streaming sweat, Frykowski pulled himself into the apartment. One of the lines broke. Ben grabbed the outer edge of the platform and started to inch back toward the window.

Frykowski and Turner leaned out, groping for Ben's legs.

Everything was turning; Ben looked down at the street. It seemed to be reaching up to him. Above, he could hear the strands breaking.

The final support broke, the platform careened violently into the side of the building. Only the left support lines prevented it from crashing to the street. There was shouting, but Ben could hear nothing. He was dangling by his hands, twenty stories above the ground.

"Shimmy up and swing over," Frykowski cried.

Ben pulled up, trying to climb. The heavy burlap ate into his hands; his body was getting heavier, hanging like a slug of lead.

A blast of wind whipped across his face. He looked down, then up. The other line was beginning to wither.

"Help me," he begged.

But Frykowski and Turner could do nothing.

"Pull harder!" Frykowski called. "Harder!"

Ben squeezed the rope. His hands were soaked. So was his body. Down the wall, he could see the lights in the Woodbridges' apartment snap on.

He started to pull, trying to climb, reaching just beyond the break point as the line ripped through. Shuddering, the platform broke away and crashed to the street.

More lights came on.

He started to swing toward the window. The men leaned out, trying to grab him. They were short. He pushed off the ledge next to the nun's window and jackknifed toward Frykowski, who grabbed his leg and secured his arms. Seconds later Ben was inside the apartment, on the floor behind the nun, heaving phlegm and racked by tremors.

The apartment was dark; other than the chair in which the old nun was sitting, there was no furniture.

Frykowski and Turner fell to the floor. They could hear voices in the hall. Ben recognized John Sorrenson's. Then Daniel Batille's and one of the secretaries'.

Ben caught his breath, aware of what could have been. Another inch. Another few seconds. And he was dead. "I thought you said you'd checked the ropes."

Frykowski coughed. "We did. And they're new—purchased less than a month ago. And we've used them at least ten times. I could understand one breaking. But all four?"

"Maybe someone cut them."

"No way. They're kept locked up. And I told you,

we checked them. There was nothing wrong with those ropes."

Ben looked around the room. All he could see was the nun's back. She loomed over him like a horrible vision in a nightmare.

"Something made those ropes break!" he said.

"Why don't you ask the nun?" Frykowski snapped. "I told you she wasn't going to like what we were doing. Just look at that thing. You think that's human? Do you? Well, if you do, you're nuts! That ain't human! I don't know what she is or where she came from, but I want nothing to do with her." He stood, helped Turner to his feet, and struggled to the door. Outside, the commotion had ceased. "She's all yours. But let me give you a word of advice. This adventure tonight cost me a platform—"

"I'll reimburse you."

"—and almost cost us our lives. If that doesn't ring any bells in your head, you're fucking crazy!"

Frykowski flipped the locks and opened the door. He peered out, pushed Turner ahead of him, followed, and shut the door.

Suddenly Ben was alone with Sister Therese. He stood and checked for the camera. It was still there. So was the wineglass. Both had survived the ordeal undamaged.

He moved toward the nun, then stopped, staring. The crucifix in her hands was identical to the one that lay under the papers in his drawer.

He felt the darkness moving in on him, and a crawling sense of claustrophobia. It was as if something was forbidding him to move forward.

"What do you want from us?" he asked.

She did not answer. He retreated to the door and closed his eyes, wishing that she would go away. Then, breathing deeply, he opened the door and walked out.

Ben wiped the sweat from his forehead. "When I returned to the apartment, Faye was still sleeping.

The noise hadn't awakened her, but it had woken everyone else. When I left this morning, I ran into one of my neighbors, Daniel Batille, who couldn't understand why I hadn't heard the crash. I dropped Faye and the baby off in the park and came right here. How're you doing?"

"Fine," said Nicky Macario as he manipulated the glass under the desk lamp. "I'll have something in a minute."

Ben watched him dust.

Macario, whom Ben had met at the Knickerbocker Athletic Club, had been one of the NYPD's most talented print experts, and even though he had been off the force for several years, operating a restaurant in Greenwich Village, he had forgotten very little.

"So you don't know why the ropes broke!"

"No," Ben said, leaning against the wall of the closet-sized room. "They must have been defective."

Nicky nodded. "I still can't figure out why you went through all the trouble."

Ben raised his brow. "I can't tell you that, Nicky. Just take my word that it's very important to me. Okay?"

"Sure. No skin off my back."

Macario worked for several minutes more, then turned and handed Ben the glass. "Congratulations," he said. "You went through hell for nothing. There are no prints."

"No prints? I made firm impressions."

"The outlines of the fingertips are there, but there are no patterns inside."

"I don't understand."

"Neither do I." Macario shrugged. "But that's what we have."

"Damn," Ben cursed.

"What are you going to do?" Macario asked.

"Buy you dinner for your time."

"I'd rather you bring the wife into the restaurant when she feels better. But I didn't mean for me.

I meant about the man. What are you going to do?"

Ben shook his head and emitted a hollow laugh. "I don't know," he said.

After leaving Macario's, Ben had a cup of coffee at a luncheonette, then taxied to the theater district and got out on Forty-seventh Street in front of the Technicolor labs.

The developing manager, whom Ben had spoken to earlier that day, was waiting for him. He took the negatives and told Ben to take a seat. It would be a while.

Ben sat in the waiting room and read the paper, pausing once to call Faye to tell her that he'd be home within the hour. Then he returned to his seat and started to skim a copy of *Sports Illustrated*. He was interrupted moments later.

"All done," the developer said as he popped through the lab door.

He handed Ben several prints.

"Strange-looking old woman."

Ben nodded as he examined the proofs. "These are perfect," he said, patting the man on the shoulder. "Just what I need."

"Where did you find the old thing?"

"Just sitting around," he said sarcastically. "Look, I wonder if you could do me a favor?"

"If I can."

"Keep the negatives for safekeeping. In case I lose these pictures, I want you to have the negatives to strike some more prints. There's no way I'd be able to get the nun to sit for a portrait again. She was not a good subject the first time."

"I see. Well . . . I don't see why not. Sure. I'll keep them. Just let me know when you want them."

"Absolutely."

Ben thanked him and left the building, stopping on the corner of Broadway to study the pictures in the revealing light of the afternoon sun. The nun was reality—a horrible, decrepit, revolting reality, but a living fact nonetheless. He shivered involuntarily, then put the pictures in his pocket, walked to Forty-second Street, and entered the subway.

12

At ten A.M. Ben disembarked from American Airlines' Flight 42 in Syracuse, New York, and walked out of the main terminal, holding a folder containing the newspaper article, the glossy of Allison Parker, and the pictures of the old nun. He hailed a taxi and directed it to 625 Iroquois Street in a busy suburb in the northern section of the city. There he pressed the bell on a three-story, white colonial home and waited.

After the fifth ring, a tall Lincolnesque man opened the door.

"Mr. Burdett?" he asked with a degree of certainty in his voice.

Ben nodded. "Mr. Thompson?"

"Yes. Please come in."

Ben entered and followed Thompson into the living room, a quaintly decorated rectangle with a distinct air of country charm.

"Please sit down, Mr. Burdett," Thompson suggested.

Ben chose the rocking chair.

"I can't tell you how much I appreciate your kindness," Ben began uncomfortably. How to begin? Where? "I know this is very hard for you, but I had to see your daughter."

Mr. Thompson's eyes reflected the agony of ceaseless pain. "Please, Mr. Burdett. You are as important to me as you say I may be to you. If there is any hope, I'll use any means I can find to help Annie. . . ."

Ben nodded. "She's upstairs?"

"Yes. With the nurse. After we've talked, we'll look in on her."

Ben examined the man carefully. He had fine features, a dark stubble of beard, strong blue eyes, and a look of intelligence. Yet, he seemed to be wound into knots. Both his hands were clasped tightly into fists; there was an annoying quiver in his jaw and a claylike color to his skin.

"For the last two years, Mr. Burdett, it's been hell for me. Can you understand that?"

"Of course."

"I love my daughter more than life. She's all I have left. My wife died when Annie was only a baby, and I've raised her by myself. Believe me, Mr. Burdett, Annie was the most lovely girl. So pretty. So gentle and loving. I don't think she had an enemy in the world. Do you have any idea what this has done to me? No one could. It's as if someone had torn out my insides. Better she should have died. Then I could have killed myself and it would have been all over."

"You shouldn't talk like that, Mr. Thompson."

"I know. I should pretend it didn't happen. Relegate it to a remote region of the brain. Forget that I haven't slept one night in God knows how long. Forget that my daughter has become a zombie." He shook his head. "But please don't feel scolded, Mr. Burdett. I'm used to such advice. The psychologists. Psychiatrists. Doctors. Police. All of them have said the same thing, though of course in much more eloquent terms."

Ben lowered his eyes; he felt like shrinking through the floor. He bled for the man; he bled for himself.

"Mr. Thompson. It's very difficult for me to speak to you. I want you to know that. If anyone appreciates your situation, it's me. But instead of condemning ourselves and the people we love, we must try to work together. I know what your daughter went through. You know my situation. And if there's anything I was unclear about on the phone, please ask."

Thompson stiffened. "No, you were very precise."

"I live with a terrible reality," Ben said. "I'm convinced your daughter saw the nun, Sister Therese . . . the nun whose successor may just be my wife."

Thompson nodded ever so slightly.

"If we can establish that both nuns are one and the same, we might be able to give credence to the facts as told to me by Detective Gatz. Then . . . anything might be possible."

"What?"

"I don't know. But something. We might be able to locate the priests involved in the plot. We could go to the top of the church hierarchy. We could go to the police. The newspapers. The district attorney in Manhattan."

Thompson's eyebrows shot swiftly upward. "Do you know what you're saying, Mr. Burdett? Go to those people for help? Let me tell you something. From the day my daughter was discovered in that clearing, the police, the press, the district attorney—all of them have been pointing their grimy little fingers at her, at a girl incapable of defending herself. If you'd like, I'll show you a stack of letters and articles that will turn your stomach. The district attorney even considered empaneling a grand jury to charge my daughter with murder!"

"You're joking."

"No. They found no footprints, no fingerprints, no sign of anyone other than Annie and Bobby Joe. That was certainly enough circumstantial evidence against her, wasn't it?"

Ben shook his head. "Was she lucid when they brought her off the mountain?"

"At times. At other times she wasn't. Unfortunately, her condition worsened rapidly—helped along by the attitude of the authorities."

"What do the doctors make of it?"

Thompson shrugged. "They don't know their asses from their elbows. First they said it was a psychosis. Then a physical ailment. Then a little of both. None of the tests have proven anything. Frankly, I haven't let any of them in this house in months."

"I understand," Ben said, moistening his lips. He looked toward the kitchen. "Would you have some water?"

"Of course," Thompson replied.

Thompson walked slowly to the kitchen and returned with a glass. Ben noted just how ponderously he moved, even though he was tall and slim, built like a distance runner. The mental strain had taken a physical toll.

Ben sipped from the glass, placed it on the coffee table, and took out the pictures. He handed over Allison's glossy first.

"That was Allison Parker. The picture was given to me by Gatz."

Thompson nodded without saying a word.

Ben handed him the pictures of the nun.

"I shot these two nights ago."

Thompson slowly sifted through the stack; he began to sweat.

"Gatz insisted that both women are the same. I compared the pictures of Allison and the nun, and I can't be sure. What do you think?"

"I don't know," Thompson said thoughtfully; he reexamined each again, fighting back a growing look of astonishment.

Ben saw tears in the man's eyes.

"This is her," Thompson suddenly said, indicating

the pictures. "This is the woman Annie saw . . . my poor baby."

"How do you know?"

"I know. She fits the description. You read the description in the paper. You know damn well it fits. You knew it the moment you took those shots."

"But I wanted to hear it from you."

"Well, now you've heard it!" He started to sob uncontrollably. "My God. Oh . . . my God."

Ben leaned over and touched his shoulder. "Please . . . I know how you feel, but you've got to control yourself. We need all the self-control we can muster."

Thompson screeched; Ben recoiled, horrified by the sound. It was as if Thompson's soul had escaped and cried out against the hopelessness he had known for the last two years.

It took several minutes to quiet Thompson down.

"I'd like to see your daughter," Ben said when the man had stopped whimpering.

Thompson nodded and drew a pair of hairy, strong hands across his face. "I'm sorry. I get like this. There's no way I can control it."

"I know," Ben said, his voice filled with empathy. "Come." He helped Thompson to his feet.

Thompson returned the glass to the kitchen, then led Ben up the staircase to the second floor, where they entered the last room at the end of the corridor.

The room was a mausoleum, a tomb for Annie Thompson. It was silent, devoid of sunlight, overwhelmed by a shroud of lifelessness. The lace curtains on the windows were unruffled, permanently closed. The antique dresser was bare. The air was still and uninviting.

Annie Thompson was in bed, buried under a patchwork quilt. Next to the bed were two chairs. An old woman occupied one. Thompson introduced her as Annie's nurse. He explained that he did not have much money, but that the little he did have, he spent on his daughter's welfare.

Ben stood in the doorway, staring. The girl in the bed was nearly a carbon copy of Jennifer Learson—from the color of her skin to the dead expression on her face, to the morbid odor that seemed to emanate from her pores.

He walked inside and looked at Annie's face; her eyes were open. He was convinced that she could see him, even though there was no reaction.

Thompson spoke softly to her, reassuring her that they were there.

"Can she hear?" Ben asked.

Thompson shrugged. "No one knows."

Ben touched her skin. Cold. Dry. He pinched his fingers together to relieve the unpleasant sensation.

"Hello, Annie. I'm here to help you. I know you can't talk, but maybe you can understand me. I'm a friend of your father's. I came to show you something."

Thompson tilted his head. What was Burdett up to?

"I'm going to show you a picture. If you recognize the person, see if there is someway you can let me know. Blink your eye. Move a finger. Anything. I'll see it."

"Do you think you should?" Thompson asked.

"We have nothing to lose."

Ben leaned close to the girl, his shadow crossing her face; he could feel the uneven flow of her rancid breath on his nostrils. He took out the pictures of the nun and chose the one he thought was best. He turned it faceup, and placed it in front of her eyes.

They waited.

"She doesn't understand," the nurse said meekly.

"Shh," Ben warned, raising his finger.

Slowly Annie's eyelids began to twitch. Something was happening. She started to move about in the bed.

Thompson sat down and grabbed her hand.

"She recognizes the nun!" Ben said.

The terror of the realization stalked across the room.

"She recognizes it!" Ben repeated.

Annie's face was animated.

"She does. Yes. She does!"

Thompson called to her and draped his body over her chest; he was crying.

"This is the nun you saw, isn't it?" Ben asked.

The girl's reaction was intensifying.

"Isn't it?"

The girl retched. Ben jumped back. Thompson hurled himself on her as she exploded, foaming at the mouth.

"Christ!" Thompson shouted. "Help me grab her."

Chaos broke. Annie kicked and screamed. The nurse moved in. So did Ben. Annie kicked Ben in the balls and he doubled over, holding his groin, writhing in pain.

Thompson grabbing at Annie. The nurse shouting. Annie—remote, catatonic for years, dead—suddenly flaying, screaming, all the pictures of the nun now clutched in her hand.

"Oh . . . God."

Still hunched over in agony, Ben tried to grab her legs.

"See if we can tie her down."

She kicked Thompson's face. Blood spurted.

"Dammit," Ben cried as Annie bit into his hand, jumped up from the bed, and beat at them, her face a picture of supernatural rage.

There was more blood, grappling, cursing. Then suddenly Annie ran toward the door, knocking the nurse onto her face. Ben grabbed for her nightgown; it ripped off in his hand. Annie was naked.

She collided with the door frame, still holding the pictures.

"Stop her!"

Thompson hurled himself into the corridor, dived

for her feet, smacked off the banister, and fell down the steps to the first floor; he lay still, bent obtusely like a coiled spring.

Ben looked down the steps; the nurse was next to him, shaken, useless.

"Annie!"

She opened the door and raced into the street.

He skirted down the steps, stopped briefly to look at Thompson—out cold, maybe even dead—then followed the naked girl outside.

She was already halfway down the block, heading toward a crowded intersection, attracting the amazed stares of at least a dozen people.

"Stop her!" Ben shouted.

No one moved; they stood frozen, orchestrated by the sound of the noon whistle that suddenly ripped through the air.

Ben charged down the street, running as fast as he could, fighting the pain of struggling lungs. Two people grabbed at Annie, slowed her down. Ben moved faster, gaining, feet pounding into the gray concrete slabs of the sidewalk.

"Annie!" he said as he smacked away the pouring sweat that was eating into his eyes.

She stumbled, almost fell, stumbled again, turned about aimlessly, cried out, held up the pictures. She was at the intersection; she turned directly toward Ben and focused on him, almost as if she wanted him to clutch her, hold her, save her from the torment that was her life.

He stopped, no more than ten feet away. They looked at each other. Behind her, traffic flowed in spasms, cars stopped everywhere, people watching. The streets were clogged with pedestrians, their attention glued to the incredible scene—a naked girl, holding pictures, crying, a man chasing her, the two of them fixated on each other like wild animals.

"Annie . . . I want you to come with me. I can help you." He stopped, inching air into his lungs, trying to get his breath back. "Please, Annie. I know you can understand me."

She said nothing; she continued to foam at the mouth. And she was shaking, vibrating as if her body temperature had been raised beyond human limits.

What was going on? Ben considered. A girl locked in a catatonic trance for years, suddenly alive, wild. Should he wait or run at her?

"Everybody . . . please stand back." He could see the crowd moving in; he could hear whispers, interspersed with laughter. "This is a very sick girl. Please."

He started to talk to her again. Behind him he heard someone say that they were going for the police. But he couldn't stop now. He had to deal with Annie. He tried to reassure her. Did she understand what he was saying? He couldn't tell.

Her agitation increased; she started to waver. A tear dropped down her cheek. Her lips moved. Then she cried the most unearthly sound he had ever heard, far worse than her father's screech of woe.

He moved toward her; she raced into the street. Cars skidded to the side; she wove about them. One car swiped his hip. He cursed and continued to follow.

A bus turned the corner. Annie threw herself in front. The driver tried to stop, but skidded. The bus hit her flush and jammed into a stalled car, crushing her. Blood poured from her mouth and nose. As Ben raced up, he could hear her body-shuddering death. He tried to pull her out, but she was already gone.

"Oh . . . no," he said, once more feeling a sickening surge of bile. "Oh . . . my . . ."

The crowd was all over him; police sirens rang in the distance. Someone hit him on the head. He fell to the macadam, dizzy, fighting unconsciousness. An eternity seemed to pass. Then his vision cleared. He raised himself to his knees and tried to find the pictures. There was no sign of them. He crawled under the bus and under the nearest cars. The pictures were gone.

He stood and began to back away. He had to get back to the house and try to revive Annie's father. And he had to get away from there before the police arrived. He did not want to go through another interrogation.

He left the scene of the accident and returned to the Thompson house. Mr. Thompson was still on the foyer floor. The nurse was in the living room, crying.

"Mr. Thompson . . . ?" Ben asked as he walked into the room.

"Dead. I called the police and an ambulance."

Ben nodded. "I see."

"They asked me for your name, but I didn't know it. They told me to tell you to stay."

"I see," Ben repeated. He had to get out of here.

"They should be here soon."

"Fine," Ben said. He looked about wildly. "I have to go out to my car. I'll be back in a minute."

The woman nodded, numb.

He reentered the hall, stopped momentarily to look at Mr. Thompson's body, then walked out into the street.

Annie had found peace; so had Mr. Thompson. Maybe they were better off, Ben thought as he walked very quickly to the corner.

Maybe.

Ben closed the phone-booth door and looked at his watch. He had ten minutes to board the New York-bound jet. Plenty of time.

He took out a scrap of paper and dialed the number written on it—the number of Technicolor in New York. A receptionist answered the phone. He asked for the developing manager and waited. Several minutes later the manager took the phone.

"Mr. Burdett . . ." the man began in a strained voice.

"Look," Ben said, "I have to catch a plane, so I'll make this quick. I lost all the pictures. I want you to strike some duplicates off the negatives."

Silence.

"Hello?"

"Yes, Mr. Burdett. I hear you. But I can't."

"Why not?" Ben felt himself start to choke.

"Someone broke into the lab last night and took the negatives."

After a long pause Ben asked, "Just those?"

"Believe it or not, just those."

Ben pulled the receiver away from his ear and looked at it.

"Mr. Burdett?" the man's voice called out of the phone. "Mr. Burdett?"

Ben said nothing. He dropped the phone, stepped out, and walked to the glass window that looked out over the runways.

A thought kept repeating itself in his mind, repeating like the headline on a wire-service ticker tape: HE WAS IN FOR THE FIGHT OF HIS LIFE.

13

"Ben!" Father James McGuire called as he walked along the balcony.

Ben smiled and stepped off the staircase. "I hope I didn't interrupt anything."

"Of course not," McGuire said, shaking his hand. "What a surprise."

"I was in the neighborhood and I couldn't resist stopping in."

Father McGuire was genuinely pleased. "Well . . . I'm glad you did. I was wondering when I might hear from you. In fact, I was thinking of calling you myself. I'll show you. I have it on the calendar for Thursday."

Ben nodded. "It's good to see you, Father."

"Come. Let's go into my office and share a glass of wine. And tell me about Faye and the baby."

McGuire pointed down the corridor to the last door on the right, then led Ben into a small, cluttered room devoid of all but the rudiments of religious trappings.

McGuire poured two glasses of wine from a glass decanter, handed one to Ben, and sat down behind his desk. Ben could barely see McGuire's head over the pile of books, reports, and artifacts.

"What brings you to the neighborhood, Ben?"

"My book. Several chapters are set on nearby streets. For authenticity, I'm walking around, taking note of street names, and getting an accurate picture of the neighborhood and architecture." He sipped the wine. "This is superb."

McGuire was pleased. "I'm glad you like it, Ben. Wine is one of my avocations. You're drinking Ducru-Beaucaillou, vintage sixty-four. It was one of the better years."

Ben smacked his lips together and let the aroma drift into his nostrils. "Is this where you do most of your writing?" he asked.

"All of it," McGuire replied. "I shut the door and shut out the world."

"I wish I had the discipline."

"It's mind over matter, that's all."

Ben smiled, sat back in the leather chair, cleared his throat, and bounced the base of the wineglass nervously on his knee.

McGuire watched him carefully. "Well, Ben, tell me about Faye. Is she well?"

Ben hesitated. "Yes . . . but she was sick briefly. We had a disturbing occurrence in our building. There was a murder, and Faye found the body. It had a very strong impact on her. She was in shock for several days."

McGuire's expression ebbed and rose with precision. "What a terrible thing! Is she all right now?"

"She's still tense. And she hasn't been able to go back to work. Perhaps next week she'll feel well enough to return to the grind."

"Send her my best wishes for the quickest recovery. If there's anything I can do, Ben, such as visit, I'd be happy to do it."

Ben gestured, leaned forward, and angled his head. "No. She's fine. We have some very caring neighbors. But of course, you're always welcome to stop by."

McGuire's fingers raced rapidly over the silver letter opener on the blotter; Ben noticed something withdrawn about his manner, and no matter how pleasant and inviting his words, that impression was unavoidable.

"Is anything wrong, Father?" Ben said.

"Wrong? Of course not. Why do you ask?"

"I don't know. You look very distant."

McGuire nodded. "I get like that when I'm working. An occupational hazard. Please forgive me. Now, tell me about the baby."

"The baby is fine. Fortunately, he's too young to notice the strain on his mother."

"Yes, that's most fortunate."

"Well, how have you been, Father?"

"Fine, but the demands on my time have been immense. You can imagine what energies I must devote to my teaching and seminary duties, in addition to my writing. I wish I had the solitude of a cruise once more."

Ben looked at the clutter on the priest's desk. Whatever McGuire was doing, he was doing it with intensity. "I hope you'll be able to take a break and join us for dinner as soon as Faye is able."

"That will be my pleasure, Ben. You know that."

The two men sat in silence. The conversation had been as inane and bland as any Ben could remember.

"Father . . . there's something on my mind."

McGuire stared, eyes wide open.

"There's a young lady I know named Jennifer Learson who's been confined to a mental institution. The doctors are desperately trying to find a clue to her breakdown. There's a priest named Monsignor Franchino who might have some insight, having had contact with the girl some years ago. Have you ever heard of him?"

McGuire rubbed his chin and arched his brow. "No. The name isn't familiar. Is he connected to the Archdiocese of New York?"

"I don't know. I believe he was a New York resident, but I haven't the slightest idea about his affiliation."

"How long ago did this happen?"

"Fifteen years."

McGuire shook his head. "Fifteen years? Even if he was affiliated with the Archdiocese of New York, who knows what might have happened in the interim? He could be dead. He could have been transferred . . ."

"Or he could still be here. Or within reach."

McGuire nodded. "Can you describe the man?"

"No. . . . And I don't want to become a burden, but I need help. I called the archdiocese and asked if there was any record of such a person, and they told me there wasn't. Of course, there might have been a reason to withhold the information. Or perhaps the records were incomplete. On the other hand, they might reveal that information to a member of the clergy."

"They might."

"And if Monsignor Franchino belongs to another archdiocese, a priest would have a better chance of locating him than I would."

"Perhaps."

Ben smiled.

McGuire laughed. "I'd be happy to help. I'll make

some inquiries and call you as soon as I know something."

"You're sure it won't be an inconvenience?"

"Of course not, Ben."

Ben stood and grabbed McGuire's hand. "I don't know how to thank you."

McGuire stood too. "Don't thank me yet, Ben. I may not be able to locate the man."

"I thank you for the effort."

They walked to the door.

"Father, I've got to confess," Ben said, "I didn't just drop in. I came by specifically to ask you to help me."

"I know."

Ben seemed surprised. "How do you know that?"

"You're a bad liar, Benjamin Burdett."

They laughed once more.

"I'll call you as soon as I can," McGuire said.

Ben turned and started to walk down the corridor. He stopped when he heard McGuire call his name.

"Ben . . . I was curious. Do you still have the crucifix?"

"Yes . . . it's in a desk drawer."

McGuire nodded. "Till we speak again."

Ben waved and descended the staircase.

Father McGuire called that evening at eight-thirty.

"Ben," he said, "I think I've found your man."

Ben almost dropped the phone.

"He's attached to the Archdiocese of New York, although he wasn't listed in the directory."

"What does he do?"

"I don't know. I tried to determine his duties and position but wasn't able to do so."

"And Monsignor Franchino did not volunteer any information?"

"No, he did not."

Ben tightened his grip on the phone. He could hear the baby crying in the other room. Faye was with him. They had just finished a simple dinner, and Grace Woodbridge had left after a brief visit.

"Can I see him?"

"Yes. I arranged a meeting."

"When?"

"He suggested lunch tomorrow at the Cornell Club. I told him that I would check with you and if he did not hear from me to the contrary, it would be confirmed."

"Of course it's all right." Ben could not hide his jubilation.

"Twelve o'clock."

"I'll be there on the nose. What did he say when you mentioned Jennifer Learson?"

"That's the problem, Ben."

"Problem?"

"He insisted he has never known or met Jennifer Learson. When I told him the connection was fifteen years ago and suggested his memory might be rusty, he persisted but accepted the possibility. So he agreed to the meeting. But I must tell you, he is very skeptical."

"We'll see, Father. . . . Franchino is not a common name."

"Well, I hope I've been of some help."

"I don't know how to thank you."

"Just let me know what happens."

"Absolutely."

"Good night, Ben."

"Good night."

Ben had already returned to the living room and had dropped in front of the television when Faye walked out of the bedroom.

"Who was on the phone, honey?"

"Oh . . . just a friend." He flicked channels with the remote control.

"Which one?"

"What is this—twenty questions?"

Faye eased herself onto the couch and wrapped

her arms around his neck. "You sounded very excited. You're not seeing a woman on the side, are you?"

Ben laughed and rubbed her shoulders. "That's the most ridiculous thing I've ever heard. What woman? Where? I don't even have the strength!"

"You've always been very strong with me."

"You're special."

"Come on, Ben," she pleaded.

"The baby sleeping?"

"Yes."

"Why was he crying?"

"Who knows? Ben. You're trying to avoid my question."

Ben crunched his lips together and waited as she pushed against him to prod. "All right . . . it was Father McGuire."

"Father McGuire?" Her voice peaked with surprise. "Why didn't you let me speak to him?" She pulled away. "How could you have done that? You know I would have loved to speak to Father McGuire."

"Don't get excited, honey . . . you'll see Father McGuire soon enough. I went to visit him this afternoon at the seminary and asked him to join us for dinner . . . when you feel well enough to go out."

"I feel fine now."

"He called to tell me how much he enjoyed the visit. I said nothing to you because I wanted it to be a surprise."

"What?"

"You know—dinner with Father McGuire. We'll do it sometime next week. But now there's no surprise."

"Okay, so there's no surprise."

He turned his attention to the television. She sat quietly, still holding him, her eyes closed. Then she got up and flicked off the set.

"Hey," he yelled.

She looked down, hurt and uneasy. "I want to talk to you. Please."

"Okay." He realigned himself on the couch.

She sat on the floor. "You know . . . we really haven't talked to each other since I found the body. First, I was a vegetable. Then, you've been busy—at what, I don't know, but busy. I almost feel I don't have a husband."

"I'm sorry, honey. I've been preoccupied. The book—"

"You haven't touched the book!"

"All right. Until several days ago, you weren't doing very well, and I've been upset about your condition. That's why I haven't been very talkative. This has been very difficult for both of us. And now I just want the entire incident forgotten."

She rubbed his hand; her face was tense with emotion. "It's been so hard," she murmured, almost in tears. "I don't know why this all had to happen. Everything was so good. And now . . ."

"It's all over," he said sternly. "I don't want to dwell on it. I don't want you to eat at yourself. Honey, you didn't do anything wrong. You just found a dead body. So what? You're fine again. You can go back to work whenever you want. So there's no reason it shouldn't be all smiles around here. Just a few days ago when Sorrenson, Jenkins, and Grace Woodbridge were here, you were perfectly happy. What happened?"

"I don't know. Maybe I've been thinking too much. Ben . . . what would you think about moving?"

He'd given it a lot of thought, but Gatz had said that moving would not help. "Why?"

"I don't know. To get away from the building. The memories."

"Oh, Faye, you'll get over it!"

She shivered. "Ben! I don't want to live next to the nun anymore. I can't stand it. Just knowing she's there drives me crazy."

"But, Faye, she's been there since we moved in. . . . Why should you want to leave now?"

"Because I do! This whole place is strange. How do you explain the platform that fell? Max Woodbridge told me the building management hadn't ordered it. What was it doing here, and why did it fall?"

"Faye, how in the world am I supposed to know the answer to that?"

"Do you know that the nun's window is open?"

"You're kidding." Had they forgotten to close it?

"No . . . look from the street. Just look."

"Okay. It's open."

"And they haven't discovered the identity of the murderer. He could still be around. And no one has found Lou Petrosevic. And so on."

He looked straight through her. "What do you want me to say?"

"Nothing. I just want you to understand what's going on inside me."

"Okay. I understand. I'll even think about moving. Okay?"

She nodded.

"Is that all?"

"No," she said bluntly.

"Then what, honey?"

"You've been acting very strangely, Ben. I'd like to know why."

He strained to keep his composure. "How so?"

"Granted, my state of mind has prevented you from working on the manuscript, but still I expected you to remain around. Whether you realize it or not, you've been gone most of the time. The night the platform fell, I woke up—even though I told you I hadn't—and you weren't here. In the middle of the night! And then I got a call from American Airlines to check on your credit-card number. You went to Syracuse on Thursday, when you said you were going to the library to do research. Now, you know I've never questioned you or watched when and where you came and went, but wouldn't you be curious if you were me and suddenly your husband was disappearing and covering it up with stories that didn't hold water? Wouldn't you be?"

"Yes, I would," he agreed.

"Well?" she said.

"The night the platform fell, I was outside the building. I couldn't sleep, so I took a walk."

Faye didn't move. "And Syracuse?"

"I was there on business. The *Village Voice* asked me to investigate a story. I flew up and met the people and reported back to the paper. If you'd like, I'll give you the phone number of the assignment editor and you can call her and check."

Fortunately, she said that that would not be necessary.

"I mean, if all this has been bothering you, you should have said something. The explanations are very simple. And besides, you know that I've never withheld anything from you. Or lied to you. Right?"

Faye was embarrassed. "Right."

"Then let's forget this whole thing. If you want to talk about moving, we can do that in the morning. Or better yet, think about it. Decide if moving is what you want. If it is, we'll see. Okay, honey?"

"Well . . . I guess . . . okay."

"We've made a big thing out of nothing."

A very hesitant "I guess so."

"But now it's forgotten."

She laughed to herself and nodded. "Do you want me to put the TV back on?" She started to get up.

"No . . . I just want you to lie next to me and relax. That's all I want. Now, come on."

She slid close to him and enveloped his arms and legs, caressing his back with her supple lips.

"I love you," she whispered.

"And I love you, too. Don't you ever doubt that for a minute. Promise me!"

"I promise," she said in a whisper.

He closed his eyes and felt his body melt into hers; it was good . . . oh, so good. They had not had each other since coming home from the cruise. He yearned for her, sensed the pain of wanting swirl

through his groin. At times like this he could almost
convince himself that the drama he was living was no
more than a transient nightmare—almost. But no matter how relaxed or how absorbed with sensation, there
remained the unforgettable experiences of the last
weeks, the prophetic words of Gatz, the face of Jennifer
Learson, Inspector Burstein, Annie Thompson and her
father, the body in the compactor, a man named Franchino, and so many illogical coincidences and ab-
surdities—the crucifix, the platform incident, Gatz's
death, the nun. And on and on—a cauterizing onslaught pursuing him like a Harpy. Where would it
end? And how? All that was left was Monsignor Franchino—hopefully the right Franchino, unearthed after fifteen years of anonymity. Tomorrow would tell.
He looked at Faye in the darkness and wanted to say
something, but couldn't. He tightened his grip and
kissed her on the face, fighting to untether his mind
and keep it away from the haunting mystery.

Monsignor Franchino.

Tomorrow.

"That's a very interesting story, Mr. Burdett," Monsignor Franchino said as he poked at the appetizer
on his plate. "Very interesting."

Ben smiled and placed both hands on the table.

The dining room was filled; most of the patrons
were dressed in conservative business suits. The overhead lighting was flat, the noise subdued and unintim-
idating. They had been there more than a half hour.
Monsignor Franchino had been several minutes late.

"But apart from its total preposterousness, I'm not
the Franchino who was involved, if in fact there was a
Franchino involved and there was something to be involved in."

"I see," said Ben, his mouth full of food.

"But let me ask you an obvious question." Franchino carefully plucked a crumb of bread from the
white hair on his right hand. "Assuming such a sce-

nario occurred and I was the man, why would you confront me?"

"What better way to get at the heart of the matter?"

Franchino nodded and popped a forkful of food into his mouth. "I checked the records of the archdiocese, and there have been several Franchinos who have been assigned to its auspices."

"Monsignors?"

Franchino smiled. "No."

Ben resumed an expression of neutrality. He was determined to make Franchino defend himself, even though he sensed that the priest was toying with him, playing with him as an expert litigator juggles a jury.

"Were you in New York during the period I mentioned?"

"I already told you I was not involved."

"I understand that, but—"

"Mr. Burdett, if it will make you happy . . . no, I wasn't. I was in Rome. At the Vatican."

Ben sipped from a glass of wine. "You know, Monsignor, we've been talking for almost an hour. I've listened carefully to you, and there should be no reason for me to doubt you. But unfortunately, I do."

Franchino's entire body seemed to rise, though he stayed seated. "You're accusing me of lying?"

"Let's just say I don't believe you. You may call Gatz's story preposterous drivel, but I've seen and heard too much to reject it outright. And of course there's the nun."

"A very unfortunate woman."

"Perhaps."

"You're very uncharitable, Mr. Burdett. I checked her background. She's supported by the archdiocese. She spent most of her years teaching at a parochial school in the Bronx. At various times she supplied her services to the critically ill as a staff member at St. Vincent's Hospital. At age fifty-six she was stricken by multiple sclerosis and has since become a charge of the church."

Ben narrowed his eyes. "Why did you agree to this meeting if you're an innocent? Why didn't you tell McGuire that you were not the man—period!"

"Father McGuire was very insistent."

"Oh, come now, Monsignor Franchino, how insistent could he have been? I told him nothing. And I'm sure the good father didn't twist your arm. No, Monsignor Franchino, I suspect you consented to this meeting to find out who I know and what I know."

Franchino's eyes blazed. "I don't wish to be abrupt, Mr. Burdett, but you're a suspicious, highly inventive man who is either playing some obscure game or subject to a psychotic disorder."

"Is that so?"

Franchino straightened the sleeves of his frock. "And I am not used to being accused of mortal sins. Of murder, subterfuge, of coordinating sinister plots against 'unfortunates.' "

"I haven't accused you of anything."

"But you've implied."

"My wife's life may be at stake. And so might my own. If you read inferences into an honest attempt to uncover facts, then so be it. And of course, if I'm right, you have every reason to feel accused."

The busboy removed the appetizer dishes as the two men sat in silence, staring at each other, sipping their wine. Moments later their main courses arrived, and Ben resumed the conversation.

"Did you ever meet Father McGuire before?"

"No."

"A wonderful man. Very bright. He's a credit to the church."

"I'm sure."

"We spent some time together on a cruise. The last night, a man tried to break into my stateroom. He failed, but left a crucifix on the handle of the door."

"You seem to be the object of an inquisition." Franchino laughed. "Perhaps you should consult the police. Or hire a private investigator."

"Or perhaps I should try to get an audience with the Cardinal."

"It's a free country, Mr. Burdett." He bit into his entrée, roast beef, well-done. "The food is very good. I hope you enjoy it."

"I'll try, Monsignor. Of course, it would be far more digestible if I were in a good state of mind, and I surely would be in a better frame of mind if you told me the truth."

"But I have, Mr. Burdett!"

"Pardon my language. I'm not used to speaking to a priest this way, but you're full of shit!" He kept his voice low, his tone pleasant. "Gatz told me that Michael Farmer had met with Franchino and had communicated the results of the meeting to Jennifer Learson."

"We've been through this already."

"Not quite. Farmer was very exact about his description of the man. So was Miss Learson. And Gatz. It seems our Franchino had a pair of very large, muscular hands. On the back of the palms were long curly tufts of white hair." He grabbed Franchino's right hand; Franchino made no attempt to pull it away. "Like these hands, Monsignor."

The obdurate expression on Franchino's face made Ben shake.

"You were the man Michael Farmer met fifteen years ago. You were the man who possessed the files. You were the man who was intimately involved with Allison Parker, who is the nun in the window. And you're the man who's after my wife!"

Franchino shot to his feet, towering ominously over the table, trying to control his temper.

"Good day, Mr. Burdett," he said, throwing his napkin onto his plate. "The meal is paid for. Please enjoy it. I wish you and your wife well. I trust you will not inconvenience me again."

Ben said nothing; Franchino stormed out of the room. Ben waited, then walked to the window facing

Third Avenue, looked out, and watched the priest enter a cab.

He smiled.

He had the right Franchino.

14

It was raining when Monsignor Franchino reached the roof of 81 West Eighty-ninth Street, next to the excavation site of St. Simon's, and trained his binoculars on Sister Therese's window. It was open, but that did not disturb him. Biroc had reported the platform incident within hours of its occurrence. It was Biroc too who had followed Burdett to Syracuse, seizing the pictures from the dying girl, and Biroc who had stolen the prints from Technicolor. Joe Biroc was a very useful man.

Franchino focused the binoculars on Sister Therese's eyes. The thick cataracts shone like beacons. But as hideous as she seemed, she was a vision of beauty, God's angel on earth, who in her devotion had preserved her soul and achieved salvation. Soon she would be granted rest eternal and join her God, as had Father Halliran before her.

Father Matthew Halliran, William O'Rourke by birth. Fifteen years a memory. Were it not for the vivid beat of droplets against his face and the numbing cold that bit his skin, he might have questioned the rapid drift of time. Looking through the binoculars, he could see the vision of what had been, a recreation of that night many years ago when he had stood on this exact spot and had focused a similar set of binoculars on the third-floor apartment occupied by Allison Parker. It too had been a rainy night. Realizing Chazen was prepared to move against the girl, he had hurried there just as a figure had walked across the street and entered the brownstone, a figure later identified as a Detective Joseph Brenner. A short time thereafter, Allison Parker had appeared on the street, covered with blood, hysterical, running through the rain. He had watched her disappear before entering the brownstone to survey the damage. What had happened? What had Chazen done? And who had entered the building? Unexpectedly, he found Detective Brenner's body, skewered with knife wounds. He quickly removed it from the building, deposited it in the trunk of an abandoned car, then returned to apartment Four-A to remove whatever traces of blood he could find, even though he was certain Chazen would alter the rooms to prevent the police from discovering evidence of struggle. The job done, he left the apartment, only to confront Chazen, standing at the base of the third-floor staircase. Never had he known such terror. As sweat poured from his body and his very soul ached, he had stood and faced the thing, praying to Christ for strength, guidance, the power to survive. And from somewhere it had come. Before his eyes, Chazen passed through the dimension and was gone.

Franchino remembered driving to the archdiocese that night and spending it facedown on his cot, crying. And then the images bled away and he confronted the present—Sister Therese, Ben and Faye Burdett, the rain, the cold, the tiny twinges of angina that had started earlier in the day as he accepted the fact that Chazen was about to commit himself once more.

"Faye," Ben called as he squinted across the bedroom.

There was no light in the room, no movement.

"Faye!" She must be in the kitchen, he thought.

What time was it? Three? Christ.

The baby rolled over and coughed in his sleep.

Ben turned on the light and jumped out of bed, his head aching. Damn thoughts of the previous day's lunch with Franchino had eaten a hole in his brain.

"Faye!" he called as he entered the living room.

No one on the couch; no one in the kitchen. The bathroom? No.

He listened. It was raining outside. Where had she gone?

He dressed quickly and left the apartment, eavesdropping at the doors on the floor, hoping to hear voices, her voice. Perhaps unable to sleep, she had gone to Sorrenson's or Jenkins'. But there was nothing.

He rang for the elevator, and when it arrived, rode down to the first floor.

The night doorman was asleep on the couch, a dripping umbrella tilted against his legs.

Ben woke him.

"Yes . . .?" the doorman said, startled.

"Did you see my wife?"

The man looked up. "I must have fallen asleep . . . Who did you say, Mr. Burdett?"

"My wife!"

"No . . . not that I recall. I shouldn't have fallen asleep."

Ben nodded, thinking quickly. The street? Maybe. But why? She'd have been crazy to go out in the rain in the middle of the night. But then where?

"If you see her, buzz me."

"Of course, sir," the doorman said as he struggled to his feet and adjusted his coat.

Ben returned to the elevator and started up to the twentieth floor.

Where? Why? More questions. His mind was a jumble.

The elevator stopped and the door slid open, screeching into the silence.

He stood on the lip of the car, body against the door frame. Suddenly he knew. The basement! She was down there!

He moved back inside and pressed the basement button. Once again the car started to descend. This time, though, it seemed to be crawling; he could almost taste the seconds moving by, taunting him. Suddenly he felt claustrophobic.

The basement appeared beyond the sliding door. He stepped out. Somewhere down the corridor, he could hear the drip of a faucet—perhaps in the janitor's room. The pipes were knocking, too.

Call out? No.

She had not been in the basement since the night the body had been discovered. Why had she come down here now? It made no sense.

As he turned the corner, he heard something behind him. There was someone there, and it wasn't Faye.

Some more steps, and now he was convinced that there was life nearby. He could sense the pressure of a heaving chest trying to still its breathing so as not to betray itself!

Could it be Faye? He was sure it wasn't. Faye was ahead of him somewhere.

The corridor was spinning around him as he stumbled toward the compactor room, stopping ten feet away. This was the spot. . . . Blood. A body. Death. . . . What was she doing here?

"Faye . . ." he called. If she was in the compactor room, she would hear him.

No answer, but an intensified sense of presences assaulted his senses. There was someone ahead, and someone behind.

Gripping the cinder-block walls, he inched toward the room and looked inside.

The red light was on. Faye was standing in front of the compactor, erect, petrified.

"Faye!"

She didn't move.

He entered and grabbed her; she was stiff. He called her name again and shook her. She was in a trance. Although she could see him, she registered nothing.

"Come on, honey . . . I'm going to take you upstairs."

He turned her around; her feet were locked. He would have to drag her to the elevator.

He grabbed her by the waist, then stood still. There were voices in the corridor, low, sibilant whispers and catlike rustles on the concrete.

"Faye . . . do you hear me?"

Laughter in the hall.

Maybe it was nothing—neighbors, kids off the street, the janitor—but at this hour in the morning?

"Is anyone there?" he called, simpering like an idiot.

Silence replied.

He stuck his head out into the hall. As he began to call out again, he felt a stab of pain. He grabbed for his face. Blood poured over his hands. Another stab of pain. The sensation of crashing fists.

Three men were around him, punching and kicking at his head. Through the rain of blood he could just make out their faces. They were teenagers, all black. One was holding a knife. The tallest had a scar across his forehead.

Ben held up his hands to protect himself. The boy with the knife slashed it across his wrist. The others continued to punch.

More blood.

They dragged him into the compactor room, then bound him and poked at his genitals with their feet.

"You scared, man?"

God . . . someone had to come down to stop this. Please!

"Scared?"

"Lookit the snatch!"

"Leave her alone!"

"Shut up, you motherfucker."

Ben groaned as a kick landed in his groin.

The tallest boy ripped off Faye's blouse and bit her breasts. Another screamed something in Spanish.

Ben cried as he saw the knife slash across Faye's chest and blood rush down her skin.

They pulled her to the floor, kicking her in the chest. She broke from the trance.

"Ben," she cried, seeing him doubled over.

She reached for him; one of the boys stepped on her arm and ground his heel into her flesh, lacerating the skin.

They fell on her, slobbering their tongues on her face. Each time she resisted, they punched until huge crimson welts covered her cheeks. Within minutes she had been beaten into a stupor.

Ben tried to protect her; they grabbed his head and beat it against the wall. Then they pulled off their clothes and dragged Faye across the room and up against the compactor chamber.

"Please leave me alone. Don't hurt me!"

"Shut up, you sleazy cunt!"

"Beg, cunt! You're gonna beg for all the cock you can get!"

"No!" Ben screamed.

The tallest boy grabbed Faye's lips and forced them open. He inserted his penis as the others jabbed at her groin.

She babbled hysterically as they slapped and beat her.

Ben rolled on his stomach and lifted his head, watching the shuffling bodies. Then he crawled toward

Faye, sliding over his own blood, reached up, and grabbed one of the black, hairless legs.

"I'll kill you all!"

One of them stood and cocked his foot. Ben saw it coming toward him, the black boot filling his field of vision. He felt a thud against his forehead.

And then there was nothing.

Wiping water and perspiration from his face, Monsignor Franchino raced across the street, passed under Sister Therese's window, and ran through the alley to the rear entrance of the building. Grimly he navigated the trenches of water, entered the basement, and walked quickly toward the compactor room.

Whatever had happened, had happened there.

How long had he been on the rain-pelted roof? It no longer mattered.

The room was ahead.

No sounds . . . except maybe whimpering.

He felt the angina again. The pills? He'd left them on the railing of the roof.

What was Chazen doing? And why?

God give him strength!

It was stifling hot. Hard to breathe. Or could it have just been his terror manifesting itself?

He held onto his crucifix as he approached the compactor-room door and stepped inside.

Ben Burdett was seated, his back against the wall, his face covered with bruises. On his lap was Faye's head. She was staring up at the ceiling, fixated on nothing. Her breathing was slight.

Ben froze his attention on Franchino.

Franchino advanced and knelt. He said nothing.

Ben wet the laceration on his lip, sniffed to clear his nose, and tightened his grip on Faye's body. She mumbled in pain.

"Monsignor Franchino . . ." Ben said. "Monsignor Franchino."

The sun had risen, painting the city with a spectac-
ular coat of uncontaminated light. In the street below
the Burdetts' apartment the first noises of day had begun to echo. Faye was in bed, sleeping uncomfortably,
her head covered with bandages. Ben and Monsignor
Franchino were seated at the dining table, exhausted,
sipping coffee. Ben had frantically tended to Faye
alone for the last half hour, and now, as he faced
Franchino, he was still in a near-fury.

"It's time you and I discussed the truth, Monsignor!"

Franchino lowered the angle of his stare and drank
from his cup.

"Or are you still going to play dumb?"

"No. I'm not going to play anything."

Franchino's manner was somber, but far more open
than Ben could remember it being at lunch.

"What were you doing in the basement, Monsignor?"

Franchino breathed deeply. "I came down to find
you." He was still perspiring, the sweat welling in the
grooves and pockmarks of his face.

"How did you know we were there?"

"I knew."

"But how?"

"Does it matter, Mr. Burdett? I knew you were
there. I knew something was going to happen."

"Why didn't you stop it?"

"I couldn't."

Ben spilled some coffee on the tablecloth. "Why
couldn't you?"

"I did not have the power."

"Look, Franchino, I went through these riddles at
lunch. I'm in no mood for them now. Three black
teenagers trap us in the compactor room and proceed to beat us. Five minutes after they leave, you arrive—the cavalry to the rescue. Then you say you
knew it was going to happen but did not have the power to stop it. Franchino, I've got to admit that if this

were happening to someone else, I'd have a good laugh. But it's not, and I'm not laughing."

Franchino leaned across the table. "Sister Therese next door was once Allison Parker. Sister Therese is the Sentinel. Everything you were told by Detective Gatz occurred and is true. The quotation Gatz showed you is accurate. The role of the Sentinel is as you understand it. There is more that you don't know, but what you do know is sufficient."

Finally, the truth. After all the digging, it had been dropped into his lap. "Why are you telling me this now?" he asked.

"Because I need your help."

"How?"

"I will explain."

"Does Father McGuire know anything about this?"

Franchino paused, then said, "No. I had never met Father McGuire before he contacted me."

"I see," said Ben before he paused to wipe the perspiration from his face. "So Sister Therese has been sitting in that window watching for the approach of Satan." Should he laugh?

"Precisely."

"And what if Satan should choose to appear in Ethiopia or some other godforsaken place?"

"It wouldn't matter. Although the Sentinel sits in the window of an apartment in New York City, her purview is the world. The apartment is a physical value that humans perceive. The Sentinel's abilities are ethereal, omnipotent, and omniscient. She can be anywhere at any time. She is God's angel on earth, the instrument of his powers. In reality, she can sit anywhere. The physical perch of the Sentinel has been changed many times over the years, more at the whim of the Sentinel's priestly guardians than for any other reason. Father Halliran sat in a brownstone on this very ground. Sister Therese sits as you see her. And Sister Thomasina—or Faye Burdett, if you will—her successor, will sit as well, maybe here, maybe in some other location."

Controlling his anger, Ben said, "So Faye is to be the next . . . Sentinel."

"Yes."

"Do you really think that I'm going to let you get away with this?"

"You have no choice. It is God's will. And, my son, do not think of this as a horrible fate. The Sentinel is blessed. God has extended his hand, his forgiveness. For when Satan perverted Eden through mankind's sin and God declared that no longer would his heavenly angels sit and watch for the approach of Satan, he decreed that one of mankind would be his angel on earth, would sit in penance for sin, the attempt of suicide. Yes . . . to be chosen as the Sentinel is a blessing, my son."

"Blessing, my ass! You're going to rob her of her life. Shrivel her like a prune. Blind her. Deafen her. Paralyze her. And you can sit there and tell me that this is a blessing?"

"My son. Do not think of the world solely in terms of mortal flesh. Beauty dies, people age, people die. Mortal bodies pass to dust. Flesh is but aimless matter. It is the soul that carries the essence of life, the spark of God and Christ. To that you must look. Faye Burdett's soul is in mortal danger; she has sinned. She must atone, serve penance, or she will be damned to eternal hell. Faye Burdett has been chosen to stop Satan. She can move into the light of God's grace, have her praises sung throughout God's kingdom. . . . If I were you, I would pray that she attains this noble station."

Ben's voice rang with sarcasm. "Why must I pray, when you've said it is God's unstoppable will?"

"Because there is an opposing will that is nearly as strong—the will of Satan. By eternal edict, if God's angel on earth should be perverted, be suffered to sin against itself, then the chain shall be broken, the Sentinel shall be no more, and mankind shall have wrought

Satan upon itself once more. Satan will try to subvert your wife. He will try to make her take her life before her transition to the role of Sentinel. We cannot let that happen, or mankind is doomed. Beyond all else, we cannot let that happen!"

Ben was shaking his head. "How do you propose to prevent it?"

"I don't know. But first we must identify the fiend."

"Have the Sentinel do it for you."

"I only wish that were possible. Satan's powers are immense. He can change his form, his place, anything. He is most difficult to root out, but that is precisely what must be done. I can deal with him only if I can locate him. The Sentinel senses Satan's presence. Satan is in the building. But he is cleverly disguised. He is waiting. Most likely in the form of the poor soul whose body was found in the basement compactor. I am sure that Satan destroyed the body and took its place. Yes . . . he is here. Even I can sense his presence. I have confronted him before. There is a vibration in the air that makes me tremble."

"You, Monsignor, afraid?"

"We must all be afraid! Do you not understand that, Mr. Burdett?"

Ben nodded slowly, acutely aware that the ravages of terror had already permeated his body.

"And what is your role?"

"I am merely God's servant. I am here to protect Sister Therese and see that Sister Thomasina properly assumes her destiny." He pointed at the window. "Sister Thomasina shall sit like no other Sentinel before her. A cathedral shall rise to shield her, to stand as a monument to her martyrdom. It shall succor her, enhance her glory, honor her in the eyes of her children. There you shall soon see the rising foundations of her domain and her ultimate resolution, a blessed chamber overlooking the city . . . the transition . . . then immortality!"

"And if you fail?"

"God help us all."

Ben stood and walked slowly around the table; Franchino remained entranced.

"You want me to help you?"

"Yes."

"How can I do that? You, the old nun, and all the crazy priests and sorcerers around here haven't been able to do it. How the hell am I going to?"

"I promise you that you can. You must listen to me, do as you're told. Seek the answers to questions that I will propose. And then——"

Ben slammed his hand violently against the table, his body hunched over the priest, shaking. "You want me to help you destroy my wife!"

"Mr. Burdett!"

Ben grabbed the monsignor's collar and pulled his head over the table; Franchino made no move to protect himself.

"You want me to destroy her! You bastard!"

Franchino slowly straightened himself and removed Ben's hands.

"I suggest you control yourself, Mr. Burdett. Explosions of temper will not help you or me. I did not want to tell you, to give you too much hope, but there is an alternative."

"What do you mean?"

"I can't be specific. But there is a way to alter your wife's fate without endangering mortal man. It can be done with your cooperation, and *only* with your cooperation. It will be difficult. But if you do not defy me, I offer you relief from your agony."

"You know damn well I'll do anything."

"I'm sure."

"That's assuming, for one brief moment of lunacy, that I believe all of this."

"Mr. Burdett, after what you've been through and seen and heard, if you have any questions about the reality of the Sentinel and the danger that exists, you are a fool, a sick, simpleminded fool."

Ben just nodded.

Franchino stood. "I will contact you with instructions. You must arrange for me to meet everyone on this floor."

"Why just this floor?"

"Because Satan is here!"

"Okay. . . . But before you go . . . what really happened in the basement?"

"You and your wife were beaten."

"By whom? Three black teenagers from the streets?"

Franchino approached the door. "No. There were no teenagers down there. There were no people other than you and your wife. It was a staged event, created and choreographed by Charles Chazen, Satan."

"Why?"

Franchino opened the door and moved halfway out. He looked puzzled. "I don't know why," he said, and closed the door.

Ben sat down at the table again. He placed his head in his hands, sat quietly for several minutes, then began to cry.

15

"I was worried," John Sorrenson announced as he nibbled the end of a scraped carrot. "It was not like you and Ben to close yourselves up in the apartment and disappear. And for ten days, mind you!"

"We thought it best to have as much solitude as possible," Faye replied, avoiding the truth. Ben had warned her that no one could be told what had happened in the basement or in any way suspect that they had been nursing themselves back to health. "Ben and I needed to be alone. It was just something we had to do."

"But to shut yourselves off . . . to avoid your friends . . . not even to speak to us!"

"John, if I could only make you understand . . ."

Sorrenson scratched his head. He wasn't wearing his hat today, but had on a vivid plaid suit, a pink shirt, and a red bowtie. And his cheeks were especially rosy, giving him the appearance of a clown. "Fortunately, Biroc told me he had spoken to you and that you were both all right. If not, I might have called the police."

Faye smiled. "John, I can always count on you to look out for our welfare."

"Indeed you can. Indeed."

She hugged him, careful to keep the glass of wine in her hand from spilling.

As Max Woodbridge had observed shortly after arriving for the dinner party, Faye looked better than ever. The ebullient smile had returned to her face, as had her healthy color. Of course, the progression did not seem that unusual; prior to the second basement incident, she had seemed well on the mend, and since no one had any inkling that something else had happened in the interim, they had no reason to suspect an interruption in her continuous improvement.

Across the room, Ben was standing alone, watching. Except for Sister Therese and Lou Petrosevic, everyone on the floor was there. Including Charles Chazen! Franchino had assured him of that. But who?

"I was just speaking to your friend," Jenkins said as he approached. "A very interesting man. I'm surprised that you've never invited him over before."

Ben broke from his thoughts. "I have. But he's been busy. This time we got lucky."

"How so?"

"He teaches history and religion at the State University of New York. When I told him about the nun, he became curious and wanted to take a look."

Jenkins nodded. "What does he think?"

"He thinks she's a very unfortunate woman."

"But without religious significance?"

"Believe it or not, Ralph, those were his exact words."

"What's his name again?" Jenkins asked, tapping his lips with his index finger.

"Franchino."

"William?"

"Yes."

Ben looked across the room; Monsignor Franchino was seated on the couch, dressed in lay clothing.

"Well, let me tell you, Ben, he may not know much about the nun, but he knows a great deal about antiques."

"Is that so? He's never mentioned antiques to me."

"He said his former wife was an aficionado."

"That could be," Ben agreed.

"But of course," Jenkins said, smiling at Faye as she hurried by, "I'm sure Mr. Franchino has encountered antiquities himself. Anyone who fluently speaks as many languages as he does has to have lived throughout Europe, and that's the surest way to develop an appreciation for different styles of furnishings."

"I thought Bill spoke only Italian and English."

"That's not the half of it, Ben. Try German, Spanish, French, Russian, and Polish, too."

"I'm impressed," Ben said, noticing Franchino rise and move toward them—acutely aware of every move, sound, and word in the room. And why not? Charles Chazen knew Franchino's identity; Franchino did not know Chazen's.

"Ben," Franchino said, "I can't tell you how much I'm enjoying this."

"I'm so glad you were able to come."

"And your wife couldn't be lovelier."

"Thank you," Ben glanced at Faye. "By the way, I didn't know you were a linguist, Bill."

"A barely passable one," Franchino replied.

"You're being modest," Jenkins insisted.

"Modesty is a very difficult assignment for an egomaniac," Franchino said. He looked at his watch as they laughed. "I can't stay much longer, Ben. I have work to do at home, and as usual, an insufficient amount of time."

"I never thought time was a problem for teachers," Jenkins observed, straightening the lapel of his nattily tailored suit. "You know, off hours, sabbaticals, summer vacations, and that sort of thing."

"I wish that was true," Franchino replied. "But when you're a tenured professor, the faculty expects you to publish, and that takes long hours of work."

"What are you working on now?" Ben asked, having prepared the question long before.

Franchino paused as Batille joined the group. "I'm investigating Renaissance religious beliefs in Slavic Europe."

"Eastern Orthodoxy?" Batille asked.

"In part," Franchino replied, "but I'm more concerned with ethnic variations and non-Catholic influences."

"For example?"

"Well . . . there was a sect in the provinces of what is now Bulgaria that conducted a ritual that combined concepts of black magic and the established tenets of Eastern Orthodoxy. They believed in the indelible power of the cross. Once a year they gathered, looking for the sign of Satan."

"And what was that?" Sorrenson asked, having walked up behind them unnoticed.

"It was their belief that a crucifix, forged of white

iron ore from eastern Bulgaria, possessed properties that would leave a mark on the legions of Satan— and Satan himself—a narrow burn under the border of the metal shaft. They conducted intricate ceremonies with these artifacts and vowed to condemn the marked ones to death."

"Was anyone ever marked?" Sorrenson asked.

"We can't be sure. We do know from authenticated extracts that many were sent to the stake."

"Are any of those crucifixes still in existence?" Ben asked. He knew the answer already. That afternoon Franchino had identified the crucifix from the ship as one of the relics. A coincidence? Hardly.

"Yes. There are several. I've identified at least three of the hundred forged—all of them housed in a private collection in Bucharest."

"So you're saying," said Batille, "that the mere touch of the crucifix will leave a mark."

"If touched during the ritual."

"What baloney!" Sorrenson said.

As Sorrenson questioned the accuracy of history, Ben pulled the crucifix from the top desk drawer. "Is this one?" he asked, turning it in his hand.

Surprised, Faye walked over. "I thought you threw that away!"

Ben looked at her, shrugged apologetically, and gave the crucifix to Franchino.

Franchino inspected it. "Unfortunately, no. If it was, it would be quite valuable."

"Do you know the ritual?" Ben asked.

"Yes," replied Franchino.

"Then do it. Who knows? Maybe . . ."

Sorrenson waved his arms. "Ben, this is a dinner party, not a séance."

"Come on, John, it'll be fun." He looked at Faye. "I leave it to you."

Faye said nothing.

Max Woodbridge walked to Ben's side. "This isn't the right time, Ben."

"It isn't?"

Ignoring Woodbridge, Ben announced that Franchino would demonstrate the ritual.

But Franchino said, "Maybe I shouldn't."

The room was silent.

"Do it!" Ben repeated.

Franchino hesitantly arranged the reluctant guests in a circle, drew a line across the floor, bisecting it, stationed himself midway, and had the lights turned down. Then he began to mutter in Latin. Garbled sounds, guttural-toned. Again and again. Slowly his voice became louder.

The echo of breathing intensified, the strain of pumping lungs—the Woodbridges together, Ben and Faye facing each other, the secretaries and Batille across from Sorrenson and Jenkins.

Franchino raised the crucifix over his head, increased the speed of his incantations, and started to move.

Was the ritual anything other than a deception? Ben asked himself, feeling dizzy, disoriented.

Suddenly Franchino screamed, the sound emerging from deep in his diaphragm and dissipating rapidly.

Hurriedly Ben turned on the lights.

Franchino was slumped on his knees, holding his chest, gasping for breath.

"What is it?" Ben cried.

Confused, everyone started to move.

Franchino pointed toward a black purse he had left on the dining table. Max Woodbridge retrieved it. Inside was a vial. He took it out and handed it to Ben.

"This?" Ben asked.

Franchino nodded and fell on his side, rolling in agony.

Grace Woodbridge ran to the kitchen and returned with a glass of water.

Franchino's skin had started to discolor, shading toward blue; his body was racked by tremors.

Ben rolled him over and popped a pill onto his

tongue. Franchino jerked it in, Ben gripped him under the jaw, forced open his mouth, and poured in the water. Franchino coughed and swallowed, dribbling over himself.

"Get some air in here," Batille commanded.

The two secretaries opened the windows.

Gradually Franchino drew himself up onto his knees. Though he was still clutching his chest, Ben could tell that the pain was easing.

"Are you all right?" Grace Woodbridge asked.

Franchino balanced himself and etched a tentative smile. "Yes . . . angina . . . I've had it for years. It comes and goes. As long as I get the nitro, it can be controlled."

"Why don't you sit on the couch?" Ben suggested, as he moved toward the monsignor.

Franchino waved him off and struggled to his feet. "No . . . let's continue."

"Mr. Franchino," Grace Woodbridge said, "don't you think you should rest? The strain might—"

"I'm fine," Franchino protested. "Let's continue."

Sorrenson and Batille threatened to leave.

"I don't want anyone to go," Ben declared.

"Are you crazy, Ben?" Sorrenson asked.

"No," Ben replied. "But I want the ritual completed." He glanced at Franchino, searching for assurance. "And now!"

Ben maneuvered everyone back into the circle and lowered the lights again. Franchino raised the crucifix over his head and began to mutter and move. Suddenly Ben felt a twinge of frigid air touch his skin. Where had it come from? The air conditioner wasn't on, and besides, it felt like nothing he could remember; it was as if someone had placed a slab of frozen stone against his body.

Franchino stopped chanting.

Did anyone else feel it?

The feeling intensified. Ben started to shake. Franchino tried to continue but couldn't.

"It's freezing in here," one of the secretaries said.

Then, a sound. Pressure on their bodies, as if they'd contracted the bends. Franchino's cry. The sound of impact.

Someone hit the lights.

Franchino lay in the corner, toppled over the armchair, fighting a pair of imaginary hands that were tightening around his throat. He was bleeding from a cut over the right eye; his face was red from asphyxia.

Panicked, Ben fell to Franchino's side. "Franchino!"

"What's going on here?" Grace Woodbridge yelled from behind.

Franchino spurted saliva; his eyes rolled up. Ben loosened his collar and retrieved the crucifix from the floor.

Confusion.

"Call a doctor," Jenkins said.

"No!" Ben cried. "No doctors."

Crying, Faye was on her knees.

Then suddenly Franchino stopped writhing. He looked around the room and slowly rose to his feet once more.

Ben moved close to him. "What's going on?"

"Chazen won't let me do it!"

"Who's Chazen?" Sorrenson asked. Everyone had heard Franchino utter the name.

"Chazen?" Franchino asked blankly.

"Yes," said Faye. "You said Chazen won't let you do it."

Franchino looked at Ben.

"Who's Chazen?" Faye asked again.

"I don't know," Franchino replied, staring into space.

"Christ!" John Sorrenson declared, his mouth hanging open in amazement.

Ben looked around the room; it was a shambles. Franchino had just left. He had tried a third time, against everyone's objections, to conduct the ritual, nearly killing himself.

"He must be crazy!" Grace Woodbridge concluded as she held tightly to her husband's arm. At her feet was the stem of a broken lamp.

Ben glanced at Faye; she was ashen.

"You knew this man in college?" she asked.

Ben nodded.

"Why hadn't you ever mentioned him until tonight?"

Ben shrugged. "I just hadn't."

Jenkins breathed deeply. The lapel of his jacket was ripped. Franchino had done it when Jenkins had seized him during a fit, trying to keep him from swallowing his tongue. "What do you make of it?" he asked, staring at Ben.

Ben shook his head. "I've never seen anything like that before. Maybe he's sick. An epileptic. I don't know."

Sorrenson picked the crucifix off the rug and examined it. It was slick from Franchino's perspiration.

Ben took the crucifix and placed it back in the drawer. "I'm sorry this happened. I apologize."

"I think we should call it a night," Faye said cautiously. She bent down and righted the coffee table. "All right?"

There was no opposition; within minutes everyone had gone.

The floor was dry, a desiccant for his dripping body. He lay flat on his face, hands buried under his chest, eyes tightly shut, as if they had been welded together. His mind throbbed as he felt the taut pull of his arteries, the pain of angina.

He glanced ahead. The window frame was filled with darkness; the hem of Sister Therese's robe caught the corner of his eye; he could smell the acidic odor of her body.

And there was pain.

His limbs. Back. Hands. Face. All pinched by the claw of Charles Chazen's fury.

He had known beforehand that Chazen would not let him finish the ritual. But at least now he was certain. Chazen had been present!

Once again his mind picked at memory. He could see Allison Parker's face—what it had been—the night he had performed the transition, fifteen years before.

Was he reliving it once again, or was this Chazen's torture?

The images.

Michael Farmer, who had uncovered the transition files and vowed to alter Allison Parker's fate, had arrived at the brownstone just before midnight. Watching from the hidden recesses of the building, Franchino remembered the clutch of fear when he saw Farmer uncover the inscription over the entrance of the Gates of Hell: "ABANDON ALL HOPE, YE WHO ENTER HERE," and the dissevering jolt of expectation as Father Halliran descended the brownstone steps to the first floor, trying to warn Farmer of his impotence. But Farmer, who could not grasp Halliran's silent message, followed Father Halliran to his fifth-floor apartment, trying to make the mute divulge the truth, and, when failing, wrapping his hands around the cleric's throat and smashing the cleric's head against the hard wood floor. It was then that he had been forced to stop Farmer's interference. Hidden in the room, he raised the base of a metal lamp and smashed at Farmer's skull until Farmer was dead. And then there was silence.

Fighting the memories, he crawled to the base of Sister Therese's chair. He could see her face, bathed in the morbid light of a partial moon. Was there movement in her eyes? No, nothing but a flicker of what had been, of what she was, of the fragile woman he could remember entering the brownstone fifteen years before, half in a trance, searching for Michael Farmer, programmed by forces beyond her comprehension, programmed to respond, to appear, to obey, called to the brownstone to prepare for the transition.

Once again he had watched from the shadows as she searched the brownstone, finding only a trace of Michael Farmer's blood and one of Farmer's cufflinks that had fallen off when he had moved Farmer's body into one of the closed apartments. Panicky, she had sealed herself in her apartment, certain it was empty. But was it? Moments later she heard footsteps and hid in the bedroom closet. Although he was in Five-A with Father Halliran, he knew what had happened: Michael Farmer's soul had confronted her, Farmer having become a soldier in Satan's legions, condemned to eternal hell for having arranged the murder of his wife. And now Farmer had become Satan's instrument, the means to lead Allison Parker toward suicide. As he revealed his true self, she broke into the halls and raced to the ground floor. Charles Chazen, the Satan, stood at the main hall, waiting, beseeching her to strike at herself and rid herself of the eternal pestilence. She had retreated upward. The souls of Satan's armies—her neighbors, her father, and Michael Farmer—had surrounded her, condemned, vapid forms, rattling their armor. Trying to escape, she ran into apartment Four-B. In they came to torment her, led by Chazen. They bade her join them. Betray her God. At that moment he led Father Halliran into the hall. The armies of the night rebelled, rattling their spears and armor. Thousands challenged, throwing their formless bodies against the ancient priest. But on they went, he and Halliran. Amid the infernal outcry. On and on. Searching for Halliran's successor. Allison Parker. The chosen of God. The Sentinel!

They found her in Four-B, surrounded by the multitudes—Chazen, his arms raised, his armies singing, clanging armor, filling the room, the halls, the building with hell's own echo. She lay on the ground, shaking, losing control, wanting death, believing her fate was to damn herself with her own hand.

Even now Franchino remembered the terrors as he fought to transfer the crucifix. But beyond that there was little. Recollection swirled in a vortex. And so it had always been from the moment he kissed the ring of Father Halliran's hand, murmured the last rites over the lifeless priest, prayed for forgiveness for his own mortal sin, and hustled Allison Parker, now Sister Therese, from the building.

So it had been, and so it had ended, and so it had begun once again.

"Help me, God," he cried, grasping at the base of Sister Therese's chair. "Give me the strength. I beg you. Give me the strength."

He lowered his head on the floor as a trickle of salty sweat creased his lips, then curled into a ball and prayed for the sensuous caress of the sun.

Shortly after ten o'clock in the morning, Franchino entered his office at the archdiocese. He was exhausted. A brutal welt marked the crest of his cheekbone; dried blood colored the ridge of his upper lip.

Father McGuire was waiting.

"Are you all right?" McGuire asked.

"Yes," Franchino replied.

"Was Chazen in the room?"

"Yes."

"But it failed?"

"Yes."

McGuire sat down across from the desk. "Biroc completed his investigation." He handed a folder to Franchino.

Franchino opened it.

"He did as complete a job as he could. There are reports on Batille, Jenkins, Sorrenson, Max Woodbridge, and Lou Petrosevic. Everything matches our previous records except for the file on Jenkins. Biroc could not verify a single fact. Jenkins is our mystery man, perhaps even Satan." He waited for a response.

Franchino remained silent, reading Biroc's intelligence.

"But no matter what the conclusion, it still makes no sense. Even if Satan had murdered Jenkins and replaced him, Jenkins must have had an identity before."

Franchino nodded thoughtfully.

"What should I do?" McGuire asked.

Franchino looked up. "Have Biroc recheck Jenkins' past. And I want him to obtain the birth records for Joey Burdett!"

"The baby?"

Franchino nodded.

"Why? Chazen can't possibly be the child. The body found in the incinerator was a man's. And how could he influence the Sentinel's existence from a crib?"

Franchino turned on McGuire angrily. "You are to do as I say. I want the child checked, and all the facts about him verified. I want it done immediately. Do you understand?"

Shocked, McGuire nodded.

"I must determine why Charles Chazen embarked upon the charade in the basement . . . the beatings. Beyond everything, I must figure that out. It is in that act of terror that the trail to Satan's identity lies hidden."

Franchino returned his attention to the files.

McGuire waited momentarily, until he was convinced that Franchino had said all he was going to say, then walked out of the room.

16

The afternoon smog had begun to dissolve with the setting of the spring sun. It was half-past seven. Traffic was still bad. It had been three days since Monsignor Franchino had attempted the ritual. In the interim, Faye had returned to work, the building had recaptured a semblance of sanity, and Ben had not been contacted by Franchino—or anyone else, for that matter.

"I'm glad we decided to walk home," Faye said as she held tightly to his arm.

Ben smiled and kissed her.

They turned onto the Sheep Meadow bicycle path and headed across.

They had been in Central Park for an hour. Ben had met her in front of the General Motors Building on Sixtieth. From there they had walked through the zoo to the skating rink before turning uptown.

"It's the nicest night I can remember," she said, looking up through the trees. A hint of a cloud hung over the buildings on upper Fifth Avenue; the rest of the sky was clear, and a three-quarter moon had emerged, along with a solitary star at the base of the western horizon. "Don't you think?"

"Yes," he replied, walking slowly, his mind far away.

"Tonight reminds me of Chicago, Ben."

"It does?"

"You know. The clear nights. The walks we used to take around the Loop. The little apartment we had overlooking Lake Michigan."

"The lousy job I had with the airline."

She shook her head. "Our life-style probably wasn't the best, but we were so happy."

He ran his hand through her hair. "I know. But aren't we happy now?"

Her eyes flared, opening wide like gaping tunnels. "Happy? How could anyone be happy having gone through what we've been through? Oh, you know . . . I'm happy with you. I've always been, I always will be. But I'm so confused and frightened. Sounds scare me. Shadows. Almost anything. I just wish it was over."

"What?"

"Whatever's happening."

"There's nothing happening."

"Please, Ben. Don't treat me like a child. Something is happening. I'm involved and you're involved. And God knows who else. I don't understand why you're hiding the truth from me."

He stopped, wrapped his arms around her, and pressed his face against the wave of her hair. "Honey, I'm not hiding anything from you, because there's nothing to hide. And we've been through this before. Last week, remember?"

She looked at him blankly.

"Don't tell me you don't remember. The night you questioned me about Syracuse?"

She pushed away, walked under a bridge, and continued up a tree-lined path. He waited momentarily, then followed. It was getting dark; he did not want her to stray too far alone.

"There are other things," she said as he jogged up beside her.

"Like what?"

"Why didn't we call the police after we were beaten in the basement?"

"I explained that already," he said. "Neither of us could have described the boys accurately. It wouldn't have done any good. What would we have accomplished? Nothing. We would have wasted our time, and the police would have caught no one."

"All right. I grant that. But, Ben, there was no reason for us to shut ourselves in the apartment for ten days."

He gestured apologetically. "All right. Maybe there wasn't. But could you imagine if Sorrenson or any of the others had found out what had happened? There would have been panic. The whole place is still spooked by the compactor murder. One word about the beatings and the police phone lines would have been flooded! They would have driven us crazy. We would have had absolutely no peace."

She sat down on a gray boulder and looked off into the rapidly deepening darkness; he paused, then joined her, leaning back against a supporting hedge.

"Maybe the beatings were related to the murder. That's a possibility, isn't it?"

Ben shook his head. "A possibility. But not likely."

"But assuming there was a connection, it would be our duty to report it to the authorities."

"And your point is?"

She looked at him and fought to hold back the tears that were welling in her eyes. "I don't know what my point is. If I did, I wouldn't be so confused. I wouldn't be driving us both crazy."

He reached out for her, caressing her shoulders.

"I don't care what you say about that Franchino, what I saw in our apartment was abnormal."

"I never said it wasn't. Franchino's obviously a sick man."

"A sickness which surfaced right after the beatings which occurred right after the murder which took place during a whole series of other strange incidents."

He laughed. "It does sound ridiculous."

"See," she said, seizing even his partial agreement. "Even you think so."

"All right, I think so. But that's secondary. What's important is you. That you feel well. That your head is together. That you know you have a husband who loves you very much and is going to see that nothing else happens to you. And that you have a son who at this moment is probably crying for his mother and driving Grace Woodbridge crazy."

He ran his lips over the bridge of her eyebrows, softly tickling her skin with his tongue. She placed her hands on his knees and buried her body under his arms. There was no light in the alcove. The nearest lamp was fifty yards away, over toward the wall that fronted the sidewalk on Central Park West. They were isolated, perched like two statues, insensitive to the distant noise on the avenues. They sat that way for a quarter of an hour until the first strong puffs of wind from the Hudson spanked against their faces. Then they stood and started to walk along the path once more.

"You know, Ben," Faye said as they passed into an illuminated cul-de-sac, "when you hold me, I almost believe that none of this has happened. When you reassure me, I almost begin to feel that it will end. That we can go back to the way things were. But in the end, I have to admit that for the first time since I've known you, I don't believe you."

He stopped and stared.

"Ben, you're lying to me. I don't believe a word you're telling me. Not a word!"

"I don't hear anything," Ben said, holding tightly to her hand while he looked around at pulses of green and black, hulking trees and shadows crossed like rapiers.

"But I heard something!"

He glanced toward Central Park West; they were opposite Eighty-third Street, about a hundred yards inside the park. It was very dark along the path, which was overgrown with bushes. Although the brightly lit buildings of Central Park West were only a short distance away, it still seemed as if they were thousands of miles from civilization.

"Ben, I've heard footsteps for the last five minutes. Every time we've stopped, the footsteps have stopped."

"You're probably imagining it." But he wasn't so sure.

"I'm frightened. I want to get out of here."

"All right. The paths intersect just ahead, and we'll be on the street in a few minutes."

They started to walk. But this time they both heard the sounds.

He whirled around as she buried her mouth in the palms of her hands, stifling a scream.

More steps. Then silence.

He moved toward the edge of the path, disappearing into the shadows.

"Ben . . . don't leave me!" she said.

He returned. "Let's go. And quick!"

He grabbed her hand and pulled her toward the intersection that lay just ahead. He could see the terror in her eyes, the look that reflected the same fear he had felt in the basement before the beatings. And he was not immune either. He felt the pulse of his jugular beating against his throat, the damp ooze of panic seeping onto his clothes.

"Turn," he cried as he pushed her in the direction of the street.

She jerked to a halt. A man was standing ahead, planted on the side of the path, about sixty feet away, watching them, hiding something in his hand. Strangely, though, the footsteps continued.

Ben turned, confused. Where should they go?

Faye grasped at him. "Ben!" she cried, her face slick with perspiration.

He took a step toward the figure and squinted. Should he call out?

The figure's right arm was swinging, though the rest of his body was rigid. And the footsteps tapped out of the bushes, so soft that they seemed to be carried by the wind. Whoever it was, was circling. And the figure ahead? Were they connected? Ben felt disoriented, frightened. Why had they walked through the park at night? Didn't he know better?

"This way. The bushes!"

They ran across the path, through a row of hedges. She fell. He picked her up, looking around, and forced her to continue through the thorns and barbs.

"Over there!"

The footsteps were still audible.

But there was light. Windows in the towering buildings. Streetlamps. Traveling beams from cars.

They followed the stone wall to the Eighty-sixth Street exit and ran out onto the concrete sidewalk of Central Park West. Faye fell, lacerating her knee. Blood poured down her leg. Neither noticed.

Exhausted, Ben placed her on a sidewalk bench and told her to wait. Then he walked back along the wall to a point opposite the path; he could still see the figure standing there. He waved down a patrol car, and two policemen climbed out. He told them what had happened. One of them produced a flashlight and sprayed the beam down the path, catching what Ben and Faye had thought was a man. It was an inoperative lamppost. Someone had draped a coat over it and tied a stick to one of the sleeves. The officers laughed. Ben thanked them, returned to Faye and told her about the lamppost. Still stunned, she hugged him.

"Would you believe it?" he asked.

She shook her head.

But what about the footsteps? Those had been real. No one could convince him that he and Faye were not being followed.

He walked several paces back into the park, listened, and peered into the darkness. Whoever was there had gone.

Returning to Faye, he helped her to her feet. But as they started to walk to the corner, he saw someone far down the walk racing to the curb and hailing a taxi, someone who might easily have just come out of the park, having climbed the wall.

The man was a long way off, and it was night. But Ben was sure: it was Father McGuire!

He said nothing. They waited for the light to change. Then they crossed the street and walked up Central Park West to Eighty-ninth, Ben trying to sort out the pieces of intrigue. And digest the new element—one he had not expected, but should have.

Father James McGuire was part of it.

Joe Biroc opened the building's front door. "Is anything wrong, Mrs. Burdett?"

"No, Joe," Faye said.

"She just feels faint," Ben added, holding her by the arm. "Do you have any water?"

"Of course. Just a second."

Biroc retreated into the doorman's office and returned moments later with a paper cup brimming over.

Ben took it, placed Faye's purse on the counter, and held the cup to her lips, coaxing her to sip.

"We were in the park," Ben said, "walking up from Central Park South. It was a dumb thing to do."

Biroc nodded. "You have to be crazy to go in there after dark. What with the muggings and other things."

"You're right," Ben said. "Anyway, we heard footsteps, which frightened Faye. Just down the street, she began to feel dizzy."

"Please don't make a big thing about this and

worry Joe," Faye said, trying to support herself. "I'm all right."

"Now, mind you, Mrs. Burdett," Biroc said, "if there's any worrying that has to be done, I'd just as soon be the one to do it."

Faye smiled. Ben patted Biroc's shoulder affectionately. Biroc walked ahead of them and pressed the call button.

"If you have a problem up there, Mr. Burdett," he advised, "call down. I'll be right up."

"Thanks, Joe," Ben said.

The elevator arrived. Ben helped Faye inside as Biroc retreated to the front entrance.

"Could you hit twenty please?" Ben asked the man who was standing by the control board.

The man leaned forward and pressed the twenty button. The elevator started to move. Ben propped Faye against the wall and stood next to her, facing the other rider.

Instinctively, Ben knew something was wrong.

The man seemed to be looking right through them. He was tall, slim, his eyes luminous, deep brown, almost hypnotic, his features sharp, olive-toned. He was wearing a blue blazer and a white shirt, the sleeves of which were held together with gold cufflinks initialed MSF. His shirt was open; there was a small stain just beneath the right collar.

"How are you?" Ben said.

The man nodded and stared.

"Is anything wrong?" Faye whispered. She had felt Ben's body tense.

"I don't know," Ben whispered back, aware that the incident in Central Park might have colored his impression of everyone.

The car continued upward, gently rocking back and forth.

"You forgot to press your floor," Ben pointed out.

The man looked at the board. Only twenty was lit. He smiled and closed his eyes.

Ben glanced quickly at Faye; she was puzzled, starting to feel uncomfortable herself.

"Who are you visiting on twenty?" Ben asked.

The man looked at him, cleared his throat brusquely, smiled once more, revealing a set of perfect teeth, and again said nothing.

Ben drew closer to Faye. Could this possibly be the killer? he thought. No . . . Franchino had insisted that Charles Chazen had committed the murder and substituted himself for the victim—a victim familiar to everyone in the building. And this man was a stranger. But still . . . there was something wrong.

The elevator started to slow, then stopped; Ben and Faye entered the hall. Ben took out the key to their apartment, two doors away. The man also stepped out, but remained near the elevator, staring at them.

"Can we help you?" Faye asked.

The man shook his head.

Faye grabbed Ben's hand; he could feel her fingers trembling.

The man moved toward them, then stopped as the service-elevator door opened and Biroc emerged, announcing they had left Faye's purse downstairs.

The man quickly stepped behind Biroc, moved past Sister Therese's apartment, drew out a key, opened John Sorrenson's door, and entered.

"Who was that man?" Faye asked after thanking Biroc.

"I don't know," Biroc replied. "He must be a friend of Mr. Sorrenson's."

"Did you see him enter the building?" Ben was very disturbed.

"No . . . but he might have come in before I went on my shift. Where did he get into the elevator?"

Ben and Faye exchanged rapid glances.

"Where?" Faye asked. "He was inside the elevator when Ben and I got in."

"He was?"

"Joe . . . are you feeling all right?" Faye touched his

hand. "He was right in front of your eyes, standing next to the call board."

"I'm sorry, Mrs. Burdett . . . but I didn't see him. Maybe I didn't look inside. I might have been thinking of something and . . . I don't know . . . my mind must have been elsewhere."

Ben felt a surge of nausea.

Biroc advanced to Sorrenson's door and rang the bell. After the tenth ring, he turned back. "No one's there!" he said.

"That's impossible!" Ben knocked angrily on the door. "Get a passkey. Open it up!"

"Mr. Burdette . . . I can't do that unless it's an emergency."

"Well, dammit," cried Faye, "this is. Something might have happened to Sorrenson."

Biroc shook his head. "Oh, no. Sorrenson left the building no more than five minutes before you arrived. He took that car of his, and I know he didn't come back."

"Are you sure?"

Biroc nodded. "Of course."

Frustrated, Ben rammed his fist into Sorrenson's door; it shook, barking an echo down the hallway, but again no one responded.

"It will have to wait until Sorrenson returns," Biroc declared. "But if you hear anything up here or see the man again, call me, please."

Ben nodded and walked to his door. Faye wrapped her arms around his waist and held him tight. Behind them Biroc entered the service elevator.

Ben rubbed his hands across his face. "What a night!" He turned and caressed her gently.

"That man had something to do with all this, didn't he?"

"I don't know," Ben replied. "I just don't know!"

Shortly after three o'clock in the morning Ben climbed out of bed, opened the draperies on the bedroom window, and looked up at the moon, which was even more prominent than it had been earlier that evening. He had been tossing and turning for the last hour, reviewing his impressions of the man they had seen in the elevator. There was something, something he sensed. But he couldn't identify it—at least not while he had remained between the covers.

He yawned and pressed his face against the glass. Tall, dark, slim, olive-skinned. Blue blazer, white shirt.

He grabbed a cigar off the night table, stuffed it into his mouth, chewing deeply into the end, leaving it unlit. He looked down at Faye, his thought hopelessly winding down a maze of dead ends.

And then it hit him like a bolt of lightning.

He remembered the cufflinks. Gold. Round. And initialed MSF. Michael Spencer Farmer!

"I told you not to attempt to contact me!" Franchino screamed as he bolted the office door.

Ben restrained himself and looked around.

The office was large and lavishly furnished, befitting a man of the monsignor's stature. A carved crucifix hung on the wall. On one side was a picture of the Pope, on the other the Cardinal. The resemblance was remarkable, as if by some grand design God had chiseled the features of his disciples from the same pattern. Even Franchino's face was vaguely similar.

"What do you want?"

"Some words with you!"

Franchino sat down and stared.

"Father McGuire is involved, isn't he?"

Franchino continued to stare, then said, "Yes!"

"He followed Faye and me in the park. Why?"

"Because I told him to."

"Why?"

"That's none of your business. But I'll answer your question anyway. He was there to protect you from Chazen."

"Why didn't you tell me?"

"Because I didn't want to."

"You miserable bastard."

"Shut up and sit down, Mr. Burdett!"

Ben trembled and dropped into Franchino's armchair.

"Are you finished?" Franchino asked.

"No. Last night Faye and I were followed in the building, too. But not by McGuire."

"Then who?"

"A man who wore gold cufflinks initialed MSF."

Franchino remained calm. He nodded and smiled. "That wasn't a man, Mr. Burdett. That was a soul! A member of Chazen's legions."

"What was he doing there?"

"I don't know."

"Now, look, Franchino, I—"

"You are not to come here again," Franchino shouted, his face flushing, his voice exploding. "You are not to contact me. You are to stay in your apartment, or else!"

Ben looked up, his eyes bulging.

"I cannot afford your interference. Not now! Tonight is the crossroads, Mr. Burdett. Your piddling complaints are but a nuisance. And I will not hear any more of them."

Franchino grabbed Ben under the arm, snapped him to his feet, hurled him toward the door, then followed. "I have discovered the identity of Charles Chazen! Tonight I must move against him!"

"Who is he?"

Franchino opened the door. "Get out!"

Ben hesitated, staring at the stone mask of Franchino's face. The monsignor repeated, "Get out!" then placed his hands in the small of Ben's back, pushed him out into the hall, and slammed and locked the door.

"Hey!" Sorrenson cried as he rushed from his apartment, holding a cello bow in his hand.

Ben, who had ridden up the elevator with Daniel Batille, turned and stared blankly, the confrontation with Franchino having obliterated his awareness of his surroundings. "What's the matter?" he asked coldly.

"The matter?" Sorrenson smiled. "Nothing. Nothing bad, that is. Didn't Faye tell you?"

"I've been gone . . . and tell me what?"

"They found Lou Petrosevic!"

Batille tightened his grip on his law books. "Where?" he asked, obviously pleased.

"Well, I just spoke to him. I was practicing in the apartment, and he called. He had no idea what had happened here. He phoned his secretary yesterday to apologize for his behavior and absence, and she told him the police were looking for him—and that he was suspected of either having committed a murder or having been the victim."

"That's a pleasant choice," Batille said as he chewed into a stalk of licorice.

"So where was he?" Ben asked.

"Well . . . I always told you that Petrosevic's eye would get him in trouble. The client Petrosevic went to see the day he disappeared happens to have been a very charming young lady, so I'm told, and Petrosevic just up and disappeared with her into the mountains for . . . well, let's call it a rendezvous."

"And he didn't call his secretary?" Ben asked.

"Guess not."

"Must have had a good time!" Batille said, laughing.

Sorrenson admonished the young law student with a pointed glance, then waved his arms enthusiastically. "Anyway, he spoke to the police and they have tentatively cleared him of any complicity in the murder, and I just think it's great."

Ben grabbed the bow. "You'll poke out my eye, John."

Sorrenson giggled, apologized, and placed the bow

behind his back. "You don't look overjoyed," he said, staring at Ben.

"Overjoyed? No . . . let's just say I'm happy for Lou. When's he coming back?"

"In a couple of days."

Batille excused himself and entered his apartment. Sorrenson moved closer to Ben, his expression deepening. "By the way," he said, "Biroc told me about last night."

"Did you know the man?"

Sorrenson shook his head, looking puzzled. "I don't understand it. I checked the apartment. Nothing was taken. Other than a broken cello string, which must have snapped by itself, there was nothing out of place. So I didn't call the police." He flipped his lip with his finger, thinking. "What do you make of it, Ben?"

"I don't know," Ben replied, placing his key in his door. "Best forget about it." He turned the lock. "Oh . . . and if you talk to Petrosevic again, give him my regards and tell him I was pleased to hear he was safe."

"Of course, Ben."

"See you later, John."

"Ben," Sorrenson said, stopping, disturbed by Ben's grave expression, "are you all right."

"I'm fine," Ben said, closing the door.

17

It was 3:14 A.M.

The air was warm, choked with a heavy shroud of humidity. The sky was overcast. It would soon rain. The streets were empty, though an occasional taxi or police car could be heard rumbling nearby. All the parking spaces on Eighty-ninth Street were taken. The wood fence surrounding the foundation of St. Simon's had been sealed. The main door to 68 West was locked; the night doorman was seated in the office, drinking a cup of coffee, watching the late-night movie on a portable TV.

Nothing unusual.

Joe Biroc snapped open his eyes and stood.

Knocking!

He quickly shut off the light in the janitor's room, closed the door, shuffled down the dimly lit corridor, past the compactor chamber and laundry room, and opened the rear basement entrance.

Monsignor Franchino and Father McGuire stepped inside. Both carried Bibles.

Biroc bowed, kissed the ring on Franchino's right hand, then led the two priests through the cinderblock corridor to the elevator.

"Take us to nineteen!" Franchino ordered.

Biroc turned the key on the operating board and pressed the nineteen button; the elevator started to rise. Franchino and McGuire opened the Bibles and began to pray. Biroc listened, but kept his eyes on the elevator door.

Seconds later the car jerked to a stop; the door opened. Franchino and McGuire got out.

"Pray for us, my son," Franchino said.

"Yes, Father," Biroc replied.

Biroc turned the key and stood back; the elevator door closed.

McGuire drew a watch from his pocket. "Three-thirty."

Franchino walked to the stairwell; McGuire followed, listening to the hypnotic cadence of their footsteps.

They entered the stairwell, climbed to the twentieth floor, and stopped at the fire door.

Franchino prayed softly once more and reached for the knob. "May God protect us!"

McGuire grabbed his arm. "Who is Charles Chazen?"

Franchino shook his head; McGuire could feel Franchino's hands trembling, see his lips shaking.

McGuire fought off a wave of fear. "You must tell me," he demanded. "I must be told, if I am expected to face him!"

"You will soon know," Franchino declared.

Franchino slowly turned the knob; McGuire wiped the perspiration from his hands; all the blood had fled the capillaries of his face, leaving behind a hue of death.

The door swung back; Franchino eased himself into the hall.

"Father!" he called, beckoning McGuire to follow.

McGuire hesitated, then stepped to Franchino's side. The door creaked back into its setting.

They were situated at the extreme east portion of

the hall. All the apartments were located to their left. At the far end was a window that framed part of the building to the west and a portion of the night sky. The hall itself was empty, shorn of everything but a rug and a waste receptacle near the elevator. One of the overhead lights was out; the others filtered a flat, iridescent glow over the freshly painted walls.

"Chazen is here," Franchino declared, eyes darting as he crossed himself.

McGuire did likewise, then blotted a drop of sweat off his lips.

Franchino maneuvered himself into the center of the hall, then walked forward slowly, warily, sensing the presence of evil.

"Monsignor!" McGuire whispered as he felt the first snap against his face. He steadied himself and brushed away the strand of hair that had been blown in front of his eyes. He listened; the shrill scream of wind? Yes! But from where? "There's something!"

Franchino stopped and waited.

Again it came, pounding them. It moved straight down the hall from the direction of the window. But the window was closed!

McGuire fell to his knees.

Another blast! This one from behind, almost as if it had sifted through the wall. Franchino stumbled. McGuire lurched forward, breaking his fall with his hands, his Bible falling to the floor.

"Chazen!" Franchino said, his voice a whisper.

A shrill whistle began to rise, accompanied by the whoosh of churning air; it seemed to hang away from them, building like the approach of a tornado. Then it came from all sides, like the explosion of water through a broken dam, a torrent of violent wind. Instantly the hall was blanketed with swirling dust and debris. The sound was unbearable.

Franchino spun into a door frame; a laceration ripped from his forehead to his cheek. Suddenly there was no up, no down. Just the monsoon of air and dirt, beating, raging.

Franchino looked through the blood that covered his face. "We must get out of here. We cannot—"

Again he was slammed into the wall.

"What must I do?" McGuire asked, screaming to be heard over the crescendo.

Franchino pointed at the staircase door. McGuire grabbed him and hauled him toward it, their bodies buffeted between the walls, their faces red and blistered from the attack of the windstorm.

Someone else had to hear this, McGuire thought. Someone!

They reached the door and fought the knob. It was frozen in place.

They turned back into the holocaust, their faces flattened by the pressure; they could hardly move.

"The elevator!" McGuire cried.

Franchino fell to the floor. McGuire grabbed the collar of Franchino's coat and inched him along toward the midpoint in the hall. Almost there, McGuire covered his ears, leaning forward to shield his face from the piercing dust particles. "I can't stand it," he cried, his cheeks bloated like a balloon.

Franchino pressed the elevator button and rolled against the elevator door, fighting to breathe. The wind was hot, scalding; it bit at them like a thousand tiny blades.

The elevator door slid open; they dragged themselves inside, and the door slid shut. Suddenly it was deadly silent.

They lay on the floor, exhausted, Franchino dabbed at the cut on his head. Dazed, McGuire struggled to his feet and pressed the button for the first floor.

Nothing happened.

McGuire pressed again.

Nothing!

"He won't let us go!" McGuire cried, terrified.

Franchino hauled himself up and carefully turned

around the tiny car, clicking his tongue against the bridge of his mouth, listening to the echo.

"It is too quiet," he said, expecting the worst. "Too quiet."

McGuire moved; he felt something. And so did Franchino. They looked around. The car started to vibrate, heaving from side to side, throwing them off the narrow walls.

The overhead light broke. Darkness!

Hearing the sound of shattering wood, McGuire felt the walls. "They're coming apart!"

Franchino surged for the control board and rapidly pressed the buttons. "Back into the hall!" he yelled.

The floor was splintering beneath them, the walls tearing apart, the cable supporting the car chattering more violently with each sideward surge. Desperate, Franchino continued to press, as McGuire dug his hands into the seam of the door and tried to pull it back.

A slab of floorboard tore through Franchino's leg, chewing into the bone and cartilage. McGuire reached for him, secured him against the wall, and continued to pry at the door, trying to ward off the flying wood with his body.

Suddenly the door slid back. McGuire fell into the corridor and pulled Franchino out. Behind them, the car was splintering, the violence increasing until in one massive paroxysm it shattered and fell down the shaft.

The wind died; the hall was silent.

Franchino stood up; his legs were shaking, almost incapable of holding him erect. McGuire watched from the floor.

"I defy you!" Franchino cried. "I know who you are, Charles Chazen! And I defy you!"

A thunderous explosion of wind caromed down the hall, lifting Franchino off his feet, carrying him backward into the wall at the end of the corridor. The priest's body shuddered on impact.

The torrent continued, growing fiercer.

Once again Franchino tried to open the staircase

door, his hands slipping from the accumulated blood. He grabbed the fire box for support. The glass shattered; the hose flopped out. He smashed at the door with his fists. McGuire joined him as he fell to his knees, bracing himself against the wall. Suddenly the hose shot upward and wrapped itself around Franchino's throat, squeezing the flesh into blotches of red and blue. He gnashed his teeth and cried, trying to loosen the coil, which was tightening like a hungry python.

Blood spurted from his lips.

McGuire pulled at the hose, trying to free it. Around them the gale continued, joined by a horrible rumble from the floor. Pieces of concrete and linoleum burst into the air; the walls shattered. McGuire screamed his agony as his flesh began to sting. Turning blue, Franchino vomited.

Fires erupted; glass fell from the exploding light fixtures.

"I defy you, Chazen!" Franchino screamed as McGuire freed him from the noose.

Franchino's sleeves were burning. So were McGuire's pants. They rolled, trying to extinguish the fire; the flames on McGuire flickered out; those on Franchino increased, nearly enveloping him.

His face and arms singed, Franchino stood, cried, cursed, and stumbled to the middle of the hall.

"I defy you, Chazen!"

The hall imploded, raging inward, engulfing Franchino in a hail of glass, wood, concrete, and fire. McGuire fell on his face, shielding himself. Franchino raised his hands, a martyr against the power of Satan, his body dripping blood.

"Chazen!"

A rush of wind and noise.

"Chazen!"

A mushroom cloud of debris gathering near the wall behind the priest.

"Chazen!"

And an enormous explosion like the thrust of a rocket engine that blew down the hallway, carrying Franchino headlong through the hall window and out into the night sky.

McGuire forced his blistered eyes in the direction of Franchino's last cry and crawled down the hall, barely conscious. Reaching the window, he pulled himself up and looked down at the alley. Franchino's body lay spread-eagled below.

He stood, stared down the hall, and grabbed his face as his eyesight clouded over, seeping black where there had been flashes of everything unholy.

And there was darkness.

Detective Wausau knelt next to Franchino's body, his knees sinking into one of the puddles that had gathered beneath the light-falling rain.

"Any marks, signs of violence?" he asked.

The technician shook his head. "No. Not a one. I doubt it's homicide, but we'll have to wait for an autopsy."

"An accident?"

The technician looked up at the twentieth floor window. The first substantial thrust of daylight had invaded the sky. It was almost six o'clock. He shrugged. "Or a suicide."

Wausau frowned. "A priest? Never!"

He glanced over the alley; it was clean and uncluttered, separated from the street by a fence. Above him he faced a blank wall of the building, interrupted only by the perpendicular row of hall windows.

He walked to the fence and scanned the street. Several police cars were bunched near the building. A small crowd of spectators shielded under umbrellas had gathered nearby. It was very quiet.

"Jacobelli!" he called.

Jacobelli looked over the dashboard of the nearest squad car, spoke into the car radio, then jumped out and approached.

"We contacted the archdiocese. They'll have someone here in a couple of minutes."

"All right. They should be able to identify him.
That is, assuming he's a priest."

Jacobelli narrowed his eyes, puzzled.

"He might have just come from a costume party,"
Wausau suggested, smirking.

Jacobelli nodded. "We covered the building."

"Anyone see anything?"

"Not that we know of yet."

"You speak to the doorman?"

"Yes. He didn't hear or see anything either."

Wausau unwrapped a stick of gum, rolled it up
like a rug, and popped it into his mouth. "How'd you
like to live in this building?"

Jacobelli laughed and scratched his shock of black
hair. "Not a chance."

Wausau walked back toward the corpse. The rain
had just about stopped, though the sky was still
threatening. It was cold and uncomfortable.

"If you find anything, I'll be upstairs," Wausau
said, drawing the attention of the technician, who had
been joined by a second member of the team.

The technician nodded.

Wausau ambled to the open entrance, climbed the
ramp, and stopped. He looked back at the body, then
straight up above him at the point where the window
had shattered. The man had fallen more than one hundred and fifty feet. No wonder his neck had snapped.
Could it have been an accident? Unlikely.

Shaking his head, he walked inside.

"Does anyone recognize this man?" Wausau asked
as he passed a Polaroid of Franchino's body around
the room.

Everyone nodded as the clock on the mantel
struck nine.

John Sorrenson stood and cleared his throat. The
police had gathered everyone in Sorrenson's apartment,

so it seemed appropriate for Sorrenson to be the spokesman.

"His name is Franchino," Sorrenson said, glancing at Ben. "He was a friend of Mr. Burdett's. He was at Mr. Burdett's party two nights ago."

Wausau veered his stare to Ben, who was seated on the couch, supporting Faye. Her eyes were half-closed, her hair tousled and her face drawn; the baby was in her arms.

"Yes . . . he was a friend of mine," Ben offered hesitantly.

"Well, that's very good, Mr. Burdett. Then maybe you can tell me why Monsignor Franchino was walking around the halls in the middle of the night!"

The word "monsignor" drew surprised looks from everyone.

"I don't know," Ben replied.

Wausau began to pace over the red-and-brown Persian rug.

"Okay . . . Mr. Burdett. Then tell me what you *do* know."

"I don't know much," Ben began, trying to hold together the lies as convincingly as possible. "We met in college. At the University of Chicago. I was taking graduate courses. He was teaching history. We became friendly. But we've only spoken to each other one or two times over the years."

"Excuse me, Inspector," Daniel Batille said. "Did you say that Franchino was a priest?"

"That's exactly what I said."

An exchange of questioning glances.

"Didn't you people know that?"

"No," said Max Woodbridge.

"But you knew that, didn't you, Mr. Burdett?"

Ben looked at Jenkins, who was standing next to the living-room window, dressed in a satin bathrobe. "Yes . . . I knew he was a priest."

Jenkins interceded. "But didn't you say he had a wife, Ben?"

"Yes."

"And you never said he was a priest."

"I know. But I didn't know his wife. He just told me about her. I assumed he was married before he entered the priesthood." Oh, God, Ben thought. What was going to happen? His only remaining contact was Father McGuire.

"Assuming Monsignor Franchino wasn't married, which seems the logical conclusion, why do you think he would have made up such a story?"

"I don't know."

"I see. Did Franchino ask you not to say that he was a priest?"

"Yes."

"Why?"

"I don't know."

"You don't know very much this morning, Mr. Burdett. Now, do you?"

Ben nodded and took the baby in his arms. Faye rubbed her eyes, then sat back once again.

Wausau unwrapped another piece of gum and shoved it into his mouth next to the old piece that he had nearly chewed into oblivion.

"Why was he at your party?"

"He called me a few days ago and said he was in town and that he'd like to see me. I told him that my wife and I were having a party that evening and he was welcome to come by. He said he would, and he did."

"He said he was in town?"

"Yes."

"But he lived here!"

"All he said was that he had come into town."

Wausau blew a bubble, sucked the gum back into his mouth, and began to chew again.

"And all of you saw him at Mr. Burdett's party?"

Batille, the two secretaries, the Woodbridges, Jenkins, and Sorrenson nodded.

"Did he say anything to suggest that he was suicidal? Did he do anything to make you suspect that he might be unbalanced?"

Silence.

"I asked a question, and I want an answer!"

Jenkins stepped forward, drew a handkerchief from his pocket, which he used to wipe his face, then coughed uncomfortably. "Mr. Franchino—or Monsignor Franchino, as the case may be—was a very disturbed man."

Wausau sat on the arm of the couch, facing Jenkins directly. He placed his hands on his knees and condescendingly asked, "How so?"

. Jenkins described everything that had happened at the party—the ritual, the seizure, the violence—everything. Wausau watched the antique collector carefully, betraying his growing interest, then asked what Jenkins thought Franchino's behavior indicated.

"Well . . ." Jenkins postured eruditely. "I'd say he either was an epileptic or he had deep-seated religious psychoses. If I may, Inspector . . . based on what I saw in Ben Burdett's apartment, there is no doubt in my mind that this Franchino was capable of killing himself either consciously or during one of his seizures."

Wausau sat next to Ben and placed his arm over the back of the couch. "Tell me what you think of this, Mr. Burdett. A body is found in the building compactor by your wife. She goes into shock. Inspector Burstein investigates and becomes upset when he learns that an old blind and paralyzed nun lives next door to you. He asks me to investigate a series of murders that occurred in an old building that used to stand where this building now stands. I find that the files on those murders are missing. Burstein then gets in touch with Gatz, the detective who was in charge of the investigation into those murders. Gatz contacts you. He wants to talk. You go up to his house and discover his body—murdered. You then go to speak to Burstein, who we learn has just died in an arsonous fire. Then out of the blue pops a priest named Franchino, who throws a seizure during a religious ritual in your apartment and tosses himself out the window on your floor one night later. Now, this is very interesting, isn't it?"

"Yes," Ben replied. "The story belongs in a detective magazine."

Wausau smiled facetiously. "Or in a bill of particulars before a grand jury."

Nobody moved. No one said anything for several minutes.

Then Wausau stood and walked to the door.

"I want you all to think about what I've just said. Especially you, Mr. Burdett! Then we'll talk again."

He smiled, donned his hat, and left.

18

The room focused into his field of vision like a time lapse after a dissolve in an old thirties movie. It was small, maybe fifteen feet square, its white ceiling and walls eroded and dotted by swatches of brown. He was lying on an old mattress surrounded by a rusted iron bed frame. The dresser to his right, stationed beneath a cracked, imitation Chippendale mirror, had lost its knobs. In the corner was a chair submerged under dresses, bras, and soiled undergarments. Overhead burned a solitary white bulb. The only window was boarded with slats.

He wet his lips and tried to place himself. He remembered something—yes, the holocaust in the hall . . . Franchino falling out the window . . . the pain . . . blackness . . . but nothing else. How had he gotten here? And where was here?

He pulled himself up on his elbows. The place reeked of perfume. It nauseated him. He wet his fingertips with saliva and wiped the grit from his eyes. He heard something, someone moving about in another room.

"You stay right in bed, you hear!"

The voice was female and heavily inflected.

"Where am I?" Father McGuire called weakly.

"Where are you? You're in a room and in bed."

He pulled the tattered bedspread off his body; he was covered with bruises.

"Can I speak to you?" he asked.

"Of course. What kinda nigger do you think I am? But you hold on for a minute, Father. I got to clean the rest of your clothes and take the tea off the stove, and then I'll be in faster than you can kick a horsefly in the ass."

McGuire lay back into a stack of silk-covered pillows. On the floor next to the bed were several newspapers and a plastic cylinder shaped like a man's penis.

Seconds later a tall, moderately attractive black woman, about thirty, dressed in a white nightgown, walked into the bedroom, carrying his clothes over her arms and a tray of tea and crackers in her hands. "Well . . . don't you look a sight, Father? I tried to clean you up—you know, get all the grime off you, but it weren't easy. I wouldn't even want to guess at what you've been up to. No, sir."

"What am I doing here, my child?"

The woman laughed. "Child. Shit! I ain't never been no child. And if by some chance I was, I don't remember it now. You know?"

"Did someone bring me here?"

"Shit no . . . and don't take no offense at my language. I'll try to keep it clean, but you know, you can't teach an old dog new tricks."

McGuire relaxed. He felt secure with this woman. Though she was heavily made up and had a jagged scar running from her upper lip to the base of her eye, there was something in her manner that was reassuring.

"Now, to answer your question," she said as she placed the tray on the bedspread and laid his clothes over the iron posts. "You found this place all by yourself. You see, I was returning home after a night in the streets, and there you was, flat on your face, lying on the stoop, not looking very happy. Shit no. Now, I don't know how you got here, but that ain't none of my business. And of course I wasn't going to leave you. So I called my friend Jose, the best damn pimp in Manhattan, who came right over, and we hauled your holy ass up the steps and put you into the bed." She stopped, took a cigarette from the nightgown, lit it with an expensive-looking lighter, and puffed deeply. "You know, Father, you're the first priest I ever did have in my apartment. In fact, it's been a long time since I've seen one up close in any way or place. You dig?"

"Of course," McGuire said, rolling into a more comfortable position. "But God is with you."

The woman laughed, baring a mouth of stains and cavities. "Father, if God is with me, he's done seen one hell of a show. I bet he's done turned blue in the face—that's assuming he's got a face and ain't just some cloud in the air."

McGuire smiled. "Where are we?"

"Oh, Second Avenue and 121st Street. In Spanish Harlem."

He tried to sit up.

"Now, you be careful, Father. And before you go asking, I'll tell you that my name is Florence. Now, I know you ain't too interested, but I also got to tell you that I'm a prostitute . . . and the best one there is. You just ask any of them jiving pimps and they'll tell you about old Florence's ass. You bet! But I ain't looking for no trick from you. God would really bend my ass if I even had thoughts like that."

"I'm sure you don't, my child. And I'm sure that God has a warm spot in his heart for you and will forgive you your sins."

"Amen." She broke up laughing, one of those high-pitched, gospel-sounding chortles that can pierce eardrums. "And hallelujah."

"What time is it?" he asked.

"Oh, about ten in the morning," she replied. "Now, you have some of this tea. It will make you feel better. If you don't like the smell of smoke, I'll put out the weed."

"I don't mind the smoke," McGuire said as he reached for one of the cups, which, strangely, were expensive china. They were probably one of Florence's indulgences, and he quickly complimented her.

"Well, now, I appreciate that, Father. I do got good taste, though I got to admit that the dishes belong to my ex-boyfriend."

"Ex?"

"Well . . . I guess so. . . . He got his hairy ass locked in the joint for twenty years for dealing dope. But he had taste, too. He ripped them cups off this rich broad on Fifth Avenue. And don't go thinking it was a whitey, 'cause it weren't. It was a rich old nigger woman who made her money owning land."

"God has a lot of forgiving to do around here," McGuire said with an amused laugh.

Florence nodded and sipped the tea.

"If it's only ten o'clock," McGuire observed, stretching his legs, "I couldn't have slept very long."

"Are you crazy, man? This ain't ten o'clock the morning after. You've been out for two days. I done shucked me a lot of bread in the time you been getting the Z's. And it ain't been easy. If any of my regular customers find out that old Florence's been keeping a priest in her bed, it would ruin my business."

McGuire's eyes were wide open. "Two days?"

"You heard me. And it weren't no peaceful two days. You should have heard yourself. Moaning and groaning and talking in your sleep."

He grabbed her hand and lifted his head. "What was I talking about?"

"I'm not sure. But it scared me awful. You were sweating and cussing and talking about the devil and some guys named Franchino and Chazen. You kept telling the air that the devil was among us—which I'm sure he is—and that he was killing a lot of people— which I'm sure he does. But it was the way you said it. And the way you screamed that he was trying to get you next. Now, I don't want no devil to get you, 'cause you look like a good man, but I 'specially don't want him to do it when you're in my bed and I ain't too far away. I'm gonna meet him sooner or later, but I want it to be as later as I can make it!"

"I'm sure God will see to it that you will achieve salvation."

"After I repent?"

"Yes . . . my child."

"That's all well and good, Father. But I don't got no time to repent. I hardly got time to stop and take a shit." She covered her mouth, embarrassed.

McGuire laughed. "The salt of the earth never killed anyone." He tried to get up again; his legs were wobbly. "You're going to have to help me, my child. I must get back to the archdiocese."

"You should rest another day. You're not well yet."

"I've got to get back, no matter what," McGuire protested.

"Well . . . of course . . . sure I'll help you. But it won't look too good if your friends see me lugging your ass all over the place."

"You let me worry about that, Florence. There are many of them that would be blessed if they possessed as much goodness as you seem to possess."

"Oh, Father, if that ain't the darnedest thing I ever did hear. Me? Goodness? Wait till I tell them other pussies on the street."

"Please help me dress and get a taxi."

Florence nodded.

He touched her cheek gently. "When this is all over, I will say a prayer for you."

"A prayer? Father, that's well and good. But I never did know no prayer that put food in the mouth."

He reached for his pants and started to put them on. "I suppose you're right," he said.

"You bet your ass I am."

He stopped and stared. Thank God she had found him and sheltered him and nursed him. He owed her much. He dug into his pants, removed a twenty-dollar bill, folded it, and placed it in her hand.

He nodded.

And she nodded back.

Father McGuire stepped onto the curb and watched Florence's smile fade with the retreat of the taxi. He had never met anyone quite like her, a street philosopher, brimming with aphorisms culled from the gutter, surprisingly sophisticated in her perception of the world, the real world rather than the pristine surroundings of ecclesiastical consciousness.

"Take care of yourself, Father" had been her last words.

He had promised her that he would; hopefully they would meet again. At worst he would pray for her, asking Christ to forgive her sins.

Immediately before him was the entrance to the seminary rectory.

He walked through the door, climbing onto a staircase that led to the third-floor dormitory.

What would happen now? he asked himself. Whom should he contact? And why hadn't Franchino revealed the identity of Chazen before his death? He prayed for Franchino's salvation, yet he cursed him for his discretion!

Reaching the third landing, he walked down a long colorless corridor. His cell was near the fire door, about fifty feet away. The dormitory was deserted; the only sound of life was footsteps on the floor above.

He entered his room.

Three men were waiting for him, two seated on the bed, one in the desk chair. He had never seen them before.

"Father McGuire?" Father Tepper asked, rising from the desk chair.

"Yes," McGuire answered, puzzled.

"May Monsignor Franchino rest in peace."

McGuire nodded.

Father Tepper stepped forward; he was slim, about forty, black-haired and pink-skinned. "We have been asked to bring you."

McGuire glanced at the two men on the bed. "To where?" he asked with growing uncertainty.

Tepper said nothing as he walked to the door and opened it.

"What is this about?"

"I'm sorry, but we cannot tell you."

McGuire looked squarely at all three men, one at a time, then stepped into the hall.

After climbing into a limousine at the rectory, they traveled downtown on the East Side Highway, crossing the East River on the Brooklyn Bridge. From there the car slipped onto the side streets for a convoluted journey through slum neighborhoods along the waterfront. Past the nub of Manhattan, it turned east, crossing a predominantly black neighborhood and finally pulling to a stop in front of an old Gothic church.

In silence they left the car.

Slowly following his escorts, McGuire looked toward the corner, hoping to catch a glimpse of the street sign. But it was too dark. He scanned the residential neighborhood. There were several people walking; all were white. They were probably in south Brooklyn, near Flatbush, though he couldn't be certain.

Father Tepper opened the front door of the church and led them through the hallway.

Heading toward a staircase at the end of the corridor, McGuire glanced inside the chapel. It was empty, and the lights were muted, giving ascendance to the burning candles near the confessionals.

They descended three flights of stairs into a subbasement, stopping in front of a large oak door. Tepper opened it and motioned them inside. They entered an anteroom with ten rows of pews set before a second door. Two candles on a shoulder-height candelabra provided illumination. A man was seated in the first pew. McGuire looked down at him; it was Biroc.

Tepper opened the second door and ushered McGuire into a small chapel. The other two priests remained outside.

Inside the chapel—a bare room made of cinder blocks—another priest, whose head was shielded by a hood, stood alone. A simple crucifix hung on the wall. On the altar was a coffin. The body inside was raised. McGuire gasped as he approached and realized that the body was Franchino's. Below the coffin was a second altar. On it were two books, one open, one closed.

The hooded priest led McGuire to the books. He pointed to a page and whispered.

The direction given, McGuire started to read out loud, his lips quivering as part of his attention focused on the dead man's face. The readings, consisting of Latin prayers for forgiveness, oaths of fealty to Christ, and chants for the dead, continued for more than an hour, until he reached the last page of the open book. Then, closing the book, he turned toward Tepper and the hooded priest, who had been standing in the rear.

"God help you, my son," the hooded man said. "Your trial is about to begin."

McGuire crossed himself. The hooded priest escorted Tepper out of the room and shut the door.

McGuire flinched as he heard the door shut. Then he was alone—alone with the corpse of Monsignor Franchino, alone to face an unknown ordeal for which the protection of the Almighty had been invoked.

19

"Now, Faye," Ralph Jenkins said vehemently, "all I want is some sugar."

"That's no problem," Faye said as she popped two pieces of toast, well done, out of the hopper. "But I won't have you racing in here without staying for coffee."

Jenkins shrugged.

Ben lifted his head out of the *New York Times* and smiled. "Don't look at me, Ralph. She's the boss. Argue with her."

"Now, come on! You take your coffee with half a teaspoon of sugar, right?"

Jenkins dropped into one of the chairs. "Yes . . . and light cream."

Faye opened the refrigerator. "I wish I could convince you to use an artificial sweetener. Too much sugar is bad for the teeth. And it feeds the bacteria in the body."

"Yes, I know. But I'd rather pollute myself with natural products than an amalgam of chemicals produced in a laboratory."

Shaking her head, she poured the coffee, pulled four boiled eggs from a pot on the stove, and placed them in egg cups on the table. That done, she removed her apron and straightened the chamois skirt that tightly hugged her waist and the white taffeta blouse that billowed like a jib sail about her broad shoulders and small breasts. She looked rested. She'd taken the day off from work after the discovery of Franchino's body, and after sitting in the apartment listening to Ben bang at the typewriter for six hours during the afternoon and then another two at night, seemed eager to get back to her job.

She left the room, returned moments later with the baby and placed him in his high chair, then offered one of the eggs to Jenkins—he refused, too much cholesterol—and poured herself a cup of coffee, black.

"Everything fine at work?" Jenkins asked.

Faye nodded and smiled. Behind her, bright unfiltered sunlight burst through the open kitchen window.

"I've been assigned to an interesting project," she said, turning toward Jenkins. "A television campaign for a pleasure-boat manufacturer."

Jenkins listened attentively, lifting the coffeecup to his lips.

Faye looked at Ben. "I may do some traveling for the client, honey."

"Oh . . ." Ben mumbled, his attention still focused on the paper.

"Their offices are in San Diego."

"That's great."

Faye pulled down the corner of the newspaper. "Are you with us?"

Ben peered over the top. "Sure. I hear everything you say. I'm just reading some—"

"Well, you can read it later," she snapped. "Ralph is here. A guest. And all you've been doing is crumpling the pages and ignoring us. You're being rude."

Ben looked up. "All right. What do you want me to do, honey? Sing and dance?"

"Very funny."

Uncomfortable, Jenkins started to rise. "Listen, why don't I talk to you later?"

"Ralph, sit down. We're only kidding. Come on. We'll talk and make Faye happy."

Faye leered at him. "Sometimes you make me so angry."

"I'm just kidding." He pointed through the kitchen doorway toward the typing table near the living-room window, and the stacks of white sheets piled to the side. "And I'm trying to keep my mind off that."

"Why?" Jenkins asked.

"I'm starting to hate it. Every time I get a plot line going, an inconsistency pops up and I either have to reroute the narrative or tear up the pages and start over again. . . . Ralph, this may be my first and only novel."

Jenkins nodded sympathetically.

Ben looked back into the newspaper, forcing himself to maintain as pleasant an attitude as possible. The only reality that mattered was the whereabouts of Father McGuire. He'd started searching for him as soon as the police had left, the morning of Franchino's death, but had not been able to find a trace. McGuire's office at the seminary was locked, and the janitor told him that he had not seen McGuire in days. The manager of the seminary's rectory said the same. No McGuire. No messages. No contact. He placed several calls to the archdiocese, but the people he spoke to had either never heard of McGuire or, if they had, could not locate him. Certainly McGuire knew about Franchino's death. Most likely he would be involved in the contingencies. And he would eventually appear. But would it be soon enough?

The wait was excruciating.

The baby giggled and patted his hands on the surface of his chair tray. Faye leaned over, kissed him, then smiled warmly at Jenkins.

"See, Ralph?" she said. "You come over and everyone is happy."

"You're being overly kind, Faye, but maybe the enthusiasm is infectious."

"Enthusiasm?" Ben asked. "About what?"

"I just received a shipment from Europe. It's in my apartment. Both of you must come and see."

"See what?" Ben asked.

"Two rare pieces of Biedermeier furniture—designed by Karl Friedrich Schinkel for Queen Louise of Prussia. They're here for a private exhibition, and they've been entrusted to my care. They're very rare and very valuable. Yes . . . you must see them."

Faye stood. "I'll stop by after work, if you'll be home."

"After seven."

"Good."

Jenkins looked at Ben, who was skimming the last page of the first section. "And you . . . Ben?"

Ben glanced up, preoccupied. "Sometime this afternoon. I have some writing to do, then I'll buzz."

Jenkins nodded approvingly and stood as Faye looked at her watch and grimaced; she was late.

As she cleaned away the remnants of breakfast, Ben sank his entire attention into the paper. Then he folded it, cleared his throat, and leaned back, tilting the chair.

"Here's an interesting piece," he said, "Obituary. Monsignor Guglielmo Franchino. Born Turin, Italy. Died New York City. Entered the priesthood on June

11, 1939." He laughed—Faye and Jenkins watching —then threw the paper on the table and picked the baby out of the high chair.

"May he rest in peace," he said.

Shortly before noon, after a walk in the park, Ben returned to the apartment with Joey, placed him in his playpen, and sat down at the typing table. After Jenkins and Faye had left the apartment, Ben had tried once more to locate McGuire, and that failure, coupled with the unproductive walk, had left him with the book as his only means to keep his mind off Faye's fate and McGuire's whereabouts.

He sat thinking about the beginning of a new chapter. Then he banged away at the typewriter keys. The more he typed, the more manic he became, pounding out his frustrations and anger. He continued, faster, breathing deeply, until he pulled the last page from the carriage, and after reviewing the material, tossed it into the trash. Then he fell on the couch and held his head, overcome by the hopelessness. And then what? Another walk? More time at the typewriter? Or the continued introspection, the relentless battering he'd been giving his mind and body?

He picked up the baby, rocked him in his arms, walked to the door, and stepped into the hall. Jenkins had asked him to come over and look at the antiques. And that was precisely what he would do to occupy his mind.

He rang the bell to Jenkins' apartment. He heard the shuffling of feet, then the click of the doorknob.

"Ben," Jenkins said as he pulled back the door.

Ben smiled. "I came over to look at the shipment."

"I've been expecting you. And Joey, too, though I'm sure he's not old enough to appreciate Biedermeier."

Ben laughed. "I may not be old enough either!"

"Nonsense," Jenkins said as he ushered them into the living room.

Jenkins' living room appeared to be cropped from an eclectic exhibit at a museum. Apart from several pieces of useful furniture, the apartment contained mostly French-provincial furnishings that were decorative, untouched, and according to Jenkins, very valuable.

"I don't think you've ever seen anything quite like these," Jenkins declared as he maneuvered Ben across the room and lifted the coverings from the two recent deliveries. "This is a bed, designed for Queen Louise. The veneer is pearwood."

Ben leaned over. The bed looked like a large crib. It didn't appeal to him; it was too delicate and without a distinctive line.

"And this is a collector's cabinet," Jenkins continued. "Circa 1835. The veneer is bird's-eye maple and the decorations are transfers in the form of mezzotints of German scenes. Inside are a number of shallow drawers." He demonstrated. "Cabinets of this sort were often made as masterworks by craftsmen, for they lent themselves to veneering and carving and were an excellent test of an artist's abilities. Beautiful, isn't it?"

Ben nodded, appraising the piece. It looked like a rectangular box set on its side, mounted on four legs. But it was ornate and pretty and far more striking than the bed.

Jenkins covered the objects once again. Ben sat on one of the two facing sofas, wiped the baby's chin—he was drooling—and listened to Jenkins explain the nature of the forthcoming exhibit while fetching some coffee and cakes.

"So what do you think?" Jenkins asked in conclusion, sitting across from Ben.

"They're beautiful," Ben replied, admitting that he didn't respond personally to the pieces, although he could recognize their intrinsic value.

Jenkins laughed, forgave him his ignorance, patted his lips with a handkerchief, and placed his cup of coffee on the table. "I'm glad you came over for another reason, Ben. There's something I want to discuss with you. Something I did not want to bring up with Faye in the room."

"What?" Ben asked, puzzled.

"I have a friend at the police department, who's assigned to the office of the chief medical examiner. I called him this morning to find out whether the medical examiner had made a determination on Mr. Franchino. He told me they hadn't, because they had lost the body!"

"What?" Ben cried, leaning forward, almost dropping the baby.

"The morgue was robbed. The body was taken. Can you imagine?"

Yes, Ben thought. But he said "I don't believe it" for Jenkins' benefit.

"Why do you think anyone would want the man's body?"

Ben shrugged. "I don't know."

"But I do," Jenkins declared.

Ben looked up. "You do?"

Jenkins lifted the cup of coffee and swallowed a mouthful. "Of course, Ben. . . . Let's talk about good and evil." He stared, waited; then: "Would you believe this building has been a battlefield between opposing forces? Good versus Evil. God versus Satan."

Ben stood, a descending curtain of fear on his face. He strained his expression, gaped at Jenkins awkwardly, and tightened his grip on the baby.

"I don't understand," he said.

"Yes, you do. You understand very well. You know that the Sentinel sits at the behest of God. Of course you know that, don't you, Benjamin Burdett? Detective Gatz did a very good job. So did Monsignor Franchino. You're very well-versed."

"How do you know this?" Ben asked in panic.

Jenkins started to laugh, rising from the sofa like a leviathan, turning toward Ben and straightening his three-piece suit. "You're frightened, Ben," he said, adjusting his glasses. "As well you should be. But after you and I have had a long talk, you won't be frightened anymore."

Ben started to move toward the door, a violent shock of tremors pulsing through his body. Ralph Jenkins' expression had molded itself into a visor of steel; it was obdurate, lifeless.

"Leave me alone!" Ben said.

"I can't, Ben!"

Ben frantically grabbed the doorknob; the knob didn't turn.

He fought it, holding the baby in one hand as he kicked and scraped at the door; but it was sealed, as if it had been soldered in place.

He looked back toward Jenkins.

Jenkins was gone!

"My God," he screamed, rocking the baby in his arms, shielding Joey from whatever inhabited the apartment.

He walked wildly around the room. What should he do? He raced to the wall and banged as hard as he could. If the Woodbridges were home, they would hear him. But, no, he remembered, the Woodbridges had left for the day. And banging the other walls would do no good, since they faced the open side of the building.

He pulled the cover off the Biedermeier bed, placed the baby on the couch, and smashed the bed into the door, trying to break it down. The Biedermeier shattered; the door remained intact.

He heard movement. "Jenkins," he cried, grabbing the baby once more.

Footsteps.

He grabbed the phone; it was dead. He attempted to lift the living-room windows. Impossible. He tried the intercom. Nothing.

"What do you want from me?" he screamed.

Suddenly Jenkins reappeared, moving into the living room through the bedroom doorway.

Ben glared, incredulous. What was Jenkins wearing? And what had Jenkins become?

Jenkins pointed at the couch. "Sit down, Ben," he commanded.

In terror Ben fell onto the sofa, the baby buried tightly in his arms. Jenkins walked to him, looking down through eyes sculptured in granite—hypnotic eyes that riveted Ben in place, paralyzed him, froze his will.

"Pray, Ben Burdett. Pray to your Almighty God."

20

Buried in silence, Father McGuire ran his hands across the Florentine etchings, as if they were braille, then opened the book. The print was large, the words Latin. This, then, was the means by which he would learn of Franchino's duties, now his own. He wiped the drops of perspiration from his face and glanced at the death mask of his predecessor, which glistened like freshly poured wax beneath the flickering lights of the room's candles. Why was Franchino's corpse there? he asked himself, revolted by the presence of death. Could he not have read the volumes without seeing the reminder of his guilt?—that it had been Franchino alone who had died at the hands of Satan.

His fingers trembling, he began to scan the lines, reading slowly, realizing he was reliving the dawn of iniquity, the confrontation between God and the fallen Archangel.

The liturgy spoke of God's summons to his angels, who came from the ends of heaven to hear the Almighty reveal the existence of a Son to whom all power would be bestowed.

> Hear, all ye angels
> This day I have begot an only Son
> To him shall bow all knees in heaven.
> And him who disobeys me
> Will be cast into darkness

And it spoke of Satan, the first Archangel, whose envy and jealousy rose against this pronouncement, and who, thinking himself impaired, resolved to dislodge the Almighty throne.

> Meanwhile the Almighty, whose sight
> Discerns all thoughts, saw
> Rebellion rising, saw what multitudes
> Were banded to oppose his high decree.

And the Almighty charged his Son to protect the mighty throne, which charge the Son of God gladly accepted. And the Almighty sent his angels Michael and Gabriel to battle Satan and his legions and drive them to their place of punishment, the Gulf of Tartarus.

> Now storming fury rose, and clamor
> Arms on armor clashing, horrible discord
> Dire was the noise of conflict
> All heaven resounded, as
> Millions of fierce angels
> Fought on either side.

McGuire stopped reading. He listened; the silence continued unabated. Avoiding Franchino's face, he tried to insulate himself from the urge to panic that had been growing inside him. For the last few hours he had been part of it all, the words transformed into vivid images, an incredible, penetrating flash through his mind. And yet there was more to come, hundreds of pages more. He found his place and delved into the primordial war.

> Two days are passed since Michael went
> Forth to tame these disobedient.
> The third day is Thine, Son, and
> The glory of ending this great war is thine.
> Go, then, ascend my chariot,
> Pursue these sons of darkness,
> Drive them into the utter deep.

And the Son of God did as his Father commanded, driving Satan from heaven.

> He drove them from the bounds of heaven
> And into the wasteful deep.
> Hell received them and on them closed
> Hell, fraught with fire
> The house of woe and pain.

McGuire read of the Son's triumphant return to heaven. Then, despite a wave of exhaustion, he released the ties that held the next ten score of pages together. When they opened, he read of the perversion of man by Satan, man's fall, and God's subsequent charge to man, creating the Sentinel. He fought to keep himself awake, his body sagging under the hours of strain. He prayed for an end to the torment. But there was more, page after page of detailed instructions, the nature of the transition, the entire sweep of numbing truth. And at last he knew everything Franchino had known.

Pounded by vertigo, he closed the volume, stood, walked back to the door, rapped on the wood, and waited. The door remained shut, the room silent. He pounded again, fighting a strange sensation of terror, then returned to his seat, laid his head on the books, and closed his eyes. He was so tired. He wanted sleep.

He heard movement. He looked up, back at the

door, listening, trying to identify the sound. It intensified, waned, then burst on him like a storm of emotion. He grabbed for his ears, holding his head, then stood and backed away. Franchino's body had risen. Amid a howl of sounds, it hovered over him. Terrified, he fell to his knees, his eyes slammed shut to ward off the vision, his ears pressed close to exorcise the sound. He felt afire, as if touched by the breath of Satan, and then he was transported away, carried back in time to what had been before. He heard the clanging, saw the swish of soul's, their bodies bedecked in armor, their leader, Charles Chazen, beseeching them onward, their prey, Allison Parker, helpless on the floor of the brownstone apartment, their foe, the Father, Matthew Halliran, the Sentinel, moving forward, aided by Franchino, attempting to transfer the crucifix and send Chazen, the Satan, back into the throes of Tartarus, the eternal hell, to bathe and writhe in the molten fires. Exploded through time to moments immortal, yet still in the room, he witnessed the transition and the imposition of penance upon the mortal soul of Allison Parker. Then the vision of Sister Therese diffused and was gone, dissolved from his mind, replaced with a shattering headache and a loud ring in his ears. He opened his eyes, his senses raped by the sight of Franchino's mortal body, the flesh withered, standing before him. Again he flashed to blackness. He sensed the thing trying to become one with him. And he knew! This was not mortal flesh, for Franchino's mortal form still lay in the box. No . . . Franchino's soul was imparting itself. This was his true ordeal, a transmigration, the succession of not only the Sentinel, but of the mortal seraphim conscripted to serve the Almighty, to ensure the continuation of the line of succession.

Delirious, he dropped to his knees. A presence had entered his body, reinforcing his will. He stiffened, feeling a myriad of sensations, until, drenched in a clinging sweat, he fell unconscious onto the floor.

Father Tepper entered the room and walked to the chapel door. He had changed clothes; he was clean-shaven, though he carried the same grim expression that had marked his face since the start of Father McGuire's ordeal.

He grabbed the metal door bolt and drew it back.

Moments later Father McGuire walked out.

Biroc looked up, appalled at the sight. Yes, it was Father McGuire, but he had aged, unbelievably advancing through time in the past forty-eight hours. His hair had turned white; his face was deeply etched; his eyes had grown cold and distant.

McGuire and Father Tepper embraced.

Biroc stood, fearful and intimidated.

McGuire approached and placed his hand on Biroc's shoulder. "My son!" McGuire said, his expression comforting, yet commanding.

"Are you all right, Father?" Biroc asked.

McGuire nodded. "There is much to do."

"I am your servant, Father."

McGuire moved the Slav toward the door. "I want to know everything there is to know about the Burdetts' child and Faye and Ben Burdett, too. I want you to use your considerable resources to accomplish this as quickly as possible. There is little time, and we must use that time expeditiously."

Biroc nodded. "I will start immediately."

McGuire smiled. "Good," he said, opening the door to the anteroom.

They walked upstairs. A limousine was waiting. McGuire assisted the Slav into the car, then stepped back as it started down the street.

Then McGuire turned and reentered the church.

21

Four days later Joe Biroc called Father McGuire at the seminary and told him that his attempt to gather information about the Burdett baby had proven far more complicated than expected. Notwithstanding their previous information, which fixed the baby's birthplace as Presbyterian Hospital in Manhattan, a check of the Presbyterian files contained no references to the Burdetts whatsoever. In fact, he had been unable to locate any record of the child's birth anywhere.

Puzzled, McGuire instructed him to continue the search. Then he called the Burdetts and talked to Faye, who told him that Ben had gone to the Knickerbocker Athletic Club and that if he called within the next hour he could reach Ben there.

Rather than calling, McGuire left the seminary, taxied to the athletic club, and located Ben on the squash courts. Climbing to the third floor, ten feet above the playing area, he pressed close to the glass of the court-two observation window. Moments later, Ben saw him.

Father McGuire walked away from the glass and descended the steps to the squash court; Ben was waiting.

"I want to talk to you!" Ben said contemptuously,

while staring at McGuire's hair. What had happened to the priest?

"And I with you," McGuire responded. "Where can we be alone?"

Ben wiped his face with a towel and led the priest into an empty card room.

They sat down across from each other at a poker table. Ben took a cigar from the pocket of his warm-up jacket and offered one to McGuire, who declined.

"I want you to answer some questions," McGuire began after gruffly clearing his throat.

Ben rapped his fists on the table. "No! You're going to answer the questions. If not, you can go paddle your wares elsewhere."

"Ben—"

"Forget the bullshit, Father."

McGuire sat back, tugging at the sleeves of his jacket.

"You've been part of this damn thing since the beginning!" Ben declared.

"Yes," McGuire replied.

"That's why you were on the ship."

"Yes."

"And why you arranged for the table change?"

"Yes."

Ben leaned across the table, staring icily. "You left the crucifix!"

"Yes."

"And if Franchino hadn't died, you would not have come forward."

"I can't answer that. I did what I was told. I took no initiatives."

Ben leaned on his elbows. "I saw you outside the park. Hailing a taxi."

"I know," McGuire said stoically. "Franchino told me."

Ben puffed deeply on the cigar, blowing a billow of smoke up toward the ceiling. "How did Franchino die?"

"I don't know."

"Bullshit! I repeat: How did Franchino die?"

McGuire's expression changed. "Don't overreact, Ben," he said curtly. "I'm answering your questions because I want to. I'm trying to show good faith, to gain your confidence. I am no longer a pawn in Franchino's hands. Nor do I have the luxury of Franchino's presence. His duties are my duties. And I will execute them without fear for my life, and without countenancing any interference."

Ben was dumbstruck. He swallowed hard, then continued, though less aggressively. "Where have you been? Why didn't you contact me after Franchino's death?"

"I was unable to. There were things that had to be done. But it matters little. Other than my ascension to Franchino's role, nothing has changed."

"Then Faye is still to be the next Sentinel."

"Yes."

"But Franchino told me there was an alternative—a way to alter her fate."

McGuire nodded. "And I'm sure he told you that in order to accomplish that, you would have to do as he—and now I—say. Without question. Without regard for the consequences."

"Yes . . . I understood that."

"Good," McGuire said, standing. He walked to the window, then turned. "Where was Joey Burdett born?"

"I don't—"

"Where was your son born?"

Ben looked off into a void of space. McGuire watched the reaction; he had hit a chord. He waited.

"In Manhattan," Ben replied.

"In which hospital?"

"Presbyterian. At the Columbia Medical Center."

"Who was the obstetrician'?"

"Dr. Herb Raefelson."

"How can I contact him?"

"You can't. He died of a heart attack three months ago."

Very clever, McGuire thought. "And his files?"

Ben threw his cigar on the floor. "How would I know? I wasn't his secretary." He stood and approached the priest. "Look, Father. I don't know what you're after. But I have nothing to hide. My son was born in Presbyterian Hospital; Raefelson delivered him."

McGuire smiled. "We checked the hospital records. There's no trace of a Joey Burdett. Or an admission record for Faye Burdett. Or a payment receipt in your name or your wife's."

"Then that's the hospital's fault. I'm not responsible for their inefficiency. The baby was born there, and that's all there is to it!"

McGuire nodded ever so slightly. "Ben . . . are you telling me the truth?"

Ben exploded. "You're goddamn right I am. And what of it? What does it matter where the baby was born? And why are you wasting your time, when my wife's life is in danger?"

McGuire grabbed Ben by the shoulder. "Why am I wasting my time?" he asked. "I think you know the answer to that!"

"There's no way that Chazen can be the baby!"

"Perhaps. But there's a reason why you're lying to me." He released his grip, then walked to the door and turned, staring angrily. "Call me if you intend to tell me the truth. If not, I'm going to find out for myself. Then God help you!"

Consumed by an increasing spiral of frustration, McGuire went to the archdiocese, secluding himself behind the locked doors of what had been Monsignor Franchino's office. Fortunately, though, he had Biroc. If anyone could unravel the truth and discover the reason for Ben Burdett's intransigence, it was the giant

Slav. But that might take time, and there was little to spare. The transition was to take place on Friday, six days away.

He adjusted the desk lamp and rubbed his eyes. The windows behind him were closed, covered by a corroded venetian blind, admitting no light.

Turning, he opened a small double-locked cabinet that stood behind the left wing of the desk. Inside were files, arranged chronologically, each partitioned into two sections and marked along the borders.

He pulled out the first two, Allison Parker/Sister Therese and William O'Rourke/Father Halliran. The O'Rourke file contained the résumé of the man Father Halliran had been before he was conscripted. Then it segued into a second file, containing the manufactured identity of Father Halliran, attributing to him the pastorship of the Church of Heaven's Angels in Flushing, Queens, a congregation disbanded more than two decades before.

He read the file, then examined the Allison Parker/Sister Therese material—the detailed treatment of Allison Parker's life, the bogus background to support her assumed ecclesiastic identity.

And then it began to grip him—that sense of horror wrought by the unbelievable charade of which he was a part.

He replaced both files and removed a third double-sectioned envelope, which he placed under the light. Turning over the flap of the first, he reviewed the documents, focusing finally on a psychiatrist's report, written by Dr. Martin Abrams. It described his patient's psychoses, delving into the death of the patient's mother and the eventual attempted suicide of the patient, concluding with a detailed analysis of the patient's repression.

This was the most significant document, the key to the selection of the patient as the next Sentinel, the explanation of why the next Sentinel had no knowledge of his past.

McGuire flipped over both sections, the first labeled Father Bellofontaine, the second Ben Burdett.

Ben Burdett—the next Sentinel.

Had it really made it easier for them that Burdett, through a sequence of unbelievable coincidences, had become convinced that Faye was the chosen?

In retrospect, he was sure that it had. Certainly it had allowed them to manipulate Ben Burdett more completely.

Shutting off the desk light, he replaced the files and left the office.

On Monday morning Biroc called Father McGuire, told him that he had uncovered additional information and that it was imperative that they meet at once.

McGuire arrived at 81 West Eighty-ninth shortly before ten o'clock. Biroc appeared ten minutes later.

"What is it?" McGuire asked, his pulse already racing.

Biroc sat on the basement couch and rolled the pipe that Ben and Faye had given him between his fingers. McGuire sat next to him.

"I double-checked the information I'd received from Presbyterian," Biroc began, speaking soberly. "All of it was accurate. The child was not born there. I also followed up on Raefelson. He did treat Faye Burdett, although the nature of the treatments were unspecified. Nevertheless, he wasn't an obstetrician, and there's no indication he delivered their baby. I started to check every hospital in New York and up the New England coast. And I found what we wanted."

McGuire tensed, his curiosity nourished by the morbid train of events.

"Joey Burdett was born in Massachusetts General Hospital in Boston," Biroc continued. "And Faye Burdett is not his natural mother. The real mother lives in Concord, New Hampshire. Her name is Burrero. The baby was put up for adoption two days after its birth by the hospital service, and was claimed by Ben and Faye Burdett on July 22."

McGuire wove the venomous information through his mind.

"As you requested," Biroc continued, "I also verified our information on Ben Burdett. In my opinion his entire background was fabricated."

"What do you mean?" McGuire asked.

"The file is wrong about his whole childhood. More important, both his parents died of coronary heart disease. There was never a case of cancer in the immediate family, and certainly his mother did not die of the disease. Likewise, there is not even the slightest doubt that the mother died of natural causes. Ben Burdett did not kill her, and he never attempted suicide."

McGuire was stunned. "That's impossible. Franchino could not have made such mistakes."

"Franchino or no Franchino, the mistakes were made. I have never been so sure about anything in my life. . . ."

"Is there anything else?" McGuire asked, so confused he could hardly think clearly.

"Yes," Biroc said. "There's a lead. I kept coming across the name Arthur Seligson. Arthur Seligson had something to do with Ben Burdett. I checked further and found a man named Charlie Kellerman. I haven't spoken to Kellerman, but I have his address."

"Can he help us?"

"I don't know. But he's the only lead we have."

McGuire nodded. "Where can I find this man?"

"In the Village," Biroc answered. He handed McGuire a slip of paper with the address.

McGuire glanced at the paper, folded it in quarters, and placed it in his pocket.

Charlie Kellerman looked up from the cot and laughed—a peculiar chortle interspersed with strident wheezes and rasps.

"Sit down, Father," he said, forming the sounds

with his lips, tongue, and palate. "I ain't got no voice box, so it ain't easy to talk, and it's none too easy for people to understand. They had to remove it. Cancer." He pointed. "There . . . pull up the seat."

McGuire grabbed the chicken crate that Kellerman had indicated; it creaked under his weight.

"So you want to talk to me, eh?" Kellerman asked.

"Yes," McGuire replied. "But first I'd like to put on a light . . . perhaps open the windows."

"I'd appreciate it if you don't. Light hurts my eyes, and sunglasses don't do no good no more. You know what I mean?"

McGuire looked at the man's body. The veins on his forearms were crusted with scabs. His right wrist looked gangrenous. His pupils were hugely dilated, and his ankles, which extended beyond the base of his djellaba, were bloated with water and discolored. Not only was Kellerman a mainliner, but he'd obviously been one for a very long time.

"You like my place?" Kellerman asked, sweeping his arms across the expanse of the one-room garret.

"Yes," McGuire said, trying to remain cheerful by ignoring the stench, piles of clothes and broken dishes, and the inch-deep layer of dust that covered everything in sight.

"I've lived here about five years," Kellerman said. "Since my gay club, the Soiree, closed. I was making a lot of bread then. I had a big duplex on Third Avenue and Twentieth. All the drugs I needed. Broads. Fags. Orgies. It was happening. But that was a long time ago. So now I'm in SoHo. There ain't no money no more. Blew it on coke and heroin. And couldn't get a new club open. The SLA wouldn't give me a liquor license because I'd been busted for selling dope." He wet his lips and shifted into a more comfortable position. "Yeah . . . but I dig the way things turned out. I'm easy, man. I live on a cloud. Way up in the sky in the shadow of God. I got my astral self. Even the Big C couldn't beat me."

McGuire shook his head, pitying the man, his emaciated body, his distorted view of the world, wrought by his heavy doses of narcotics.

"Is there anything I can do for you, Mr. Kellerman?"

"Well, now that you ask. Yeah. You want something from me? Information? Okay. Then I need something from you."

"What?"

"The green. I need cash to make my connections. I can't deal no more. And I can't scam the streets. So I got to hope that the good fairy comes to visit me." He paused, juggling the many moods of his face, then beamed. "And here you are . . . Mr. Fairy."

McGuire took a fifty-dollar bill from his pocket and laid it on the edge of Kellerman's pillow.

"That ain't enough," Kellerman warned.

McGuire placed another fifty on top of the first.

Kellerman grabbed the bills and stuffed them under the blanket. "The next fix is on Jesus, Father."

McGuire waited while the addict convulsed with laughter, rising and falling on the bed, rapidly exhausting himself.

"Might we talk?" McGuire finally suggested.

"Of course, Father," Kellerman replied, brushing a cockroach off his blanket. "You want to ask questions? I got this urge to answer."

"Does the name Arthur Seligson mean anything to you?"

Kellerman strained to remember. "I'm not sure," he said. "The name sounds familiar."

"It should," the priest prompted.

Kellerman withdrew into himself, mumbling incoherently, moving his festered arms to his sides. Several times he started to say something, then stopped, rejecting the thought, moving elsewhere in time and place. McGuire sat rigid, watching him struggle with himself, trying to resurrect memories.

After ten minutes of silence, Kellerman hoisted himself up on his pillow. He asked McGuire to get him a cigarette from a nearby ashtray. The priest fetched it—it was only a butt—and stuck it into the man's mouth, lighting it.

The tobacco was stale; the odor made McGuire wince.

"Yeah, I remember him," Kellerman said, proud of his accomplishment. "He used to come into the Soiree. Became kind of a regular. Once or twice a week. He was attractive. Sexy."

"Describe him!"

"Dark hair. Medium height. Good-sized jewels."

"Jewels?"

Kellerman giggled. "You know. Jewels. Cock and balls. I'd give them a squeeze every once in a while, though I did it on the Q.T., 'cause Seligson's lover was a jealous bastard."

"Who was his lover?"

"A queen named Jack Cooper."

McGuire pulled a notepad from his pocket and jotted the name.

"So as I was sayin'," Kellerman continued, "he used to come in a couple of times a week to see Cooper, who worked for me."

"How long did this continue?"

"About a year or so. Then suddenly Seligson disappeared. Never came in again. Never saw him again."

"Is that all you know about him?"

"Yes. But what's there to know? Listen, Father, back in the mid-sixties, most queens had not come into the open. Some were still hanging in closets. Others just laid low, inhabiting the bars and bath houses. A lot of guys had two identities. The false one they showed the real world. The real one they showed the gay world. You dig? So if you wanted to operate a successful joint, you didn't ask no questions. As long as the customers paid their tabs, I didn't give a flying fuck. Sure, I knew about my friends, but the general customers, like Arthur Seligson—no way. They came and went. Sooner or later, every one of them disappeared. Some moved into new territory. Some left town. Some straightened out and got married, though I can tell you, the ones that did were few and far between. Some hit the mainline. And others just died. There's hardly a one that I know anything about anymore. And who cares! Fuck 'em. They were all a bunch of assholes anyway."

"What happened to Jack Cooper?"

Kellerman lay back in the pillow, puffing the butt. "I don't know. He came to me in 1968 and said he was leaving town. I didn't ask where he was going."

"Where was Arthur Seligson when Cooper left?"

"God knows. Seligson had already been gone over a year. In fact, Jack told me he had lost track of Seligson also. You see . . . Seligson was bisexual. All the time he was getting it on with Jack, he was living with a girl. Most likely he decided he'd had it with the gay trip and married the broad. He's probably got five kids now, a nine-to-five job, lots of bills, and the trauma of ten years of connubial bliss to massage the piles in his ass."

"And Jack Cooper?"

"He's probably dead—the callous bastard—and it wouldn't bother me none."

"Do you know the name of the girl Seligson lived with?"

Kellerman laughed. "Father, you got to be kidding. It took me long enough to remember Seligson's name and who he was. How the hell do you expect me to remember the moniker of a broad years later, especially since I'd maybe only heard her mentioned by name once or twice."

McGuire straightened. "Of course."

Kellerman shrugged, constricting his gaunt, emaciated frame.

McGuire stood and balanced himself against one of the garret's open rafters. "You're sure that's all you remember?"

"As sure as I need a fix."

McGuire took out the notepad and scrawled a phone number, which he handed to Kellerman.

"If you think of anything else in the next day or so, call me. It's important."

Kellerman smiled. "Be happy to do that."

McGuire buttoned his coat. "Thank you again," he said, turning to the door.

"My pleasure."

"By the way," McGuire added, almost as an after-thought. "What did Jack Cooper do for you?"

"Old Jack . . . well, he tended bar part of the time."

"And the other part?"

Kellerman broke out laughing again. McGuire turned fully around, at once curious.

"Well?"

Kellerman pointed to the corner, toward a card-board box tied together with twine. He asked McGuire to bring it over and undo the knot. That accomplished, Kellerman opened the top. Inside were hundreds of photographs. He started to sift them. McGuire moved in close.

Suddenly Kellerman stopped, closed the top of the box, laughed again, and looked closely at the picture in his hand. "Yes, sir," he said. "This is Jack Cooper. And you want to know what he did for me?"

McGuire nodded once more. Kellerman handed him the picture. McGuire walked to the shuttered window, opened the slats, and examined the eight-by-ten.

Seconds later he turned back to Kellerman, hands and body shaking.

He knew!

22

The wheels of the black sedan gouged through the potholes, shaking the chassis and jostling Father McGuire against the rear passenger door. Joe Biroc was seated next to him, holding a notepad and flashlight in hand, the tenacious lines of his face etched deeper than ever. There was a third man in the rear, another in the shotgun seat, and one behind the wheel—all dressed in soiled black coveralls and dark hats. Outside, it was overcast. Ahead, the road reached into the distance, unlit and unmarked. They were not far from New York, somewhere in Westchester, along a stretch of quaggy, uninhabited land—a strange place to have buried a murder victim, disposed under the auspices of the chief medical examiner of the city of New York. But it was here, according to Biroc, that the compactor body had been buried in an unmarked grave.

"How much longer?" McGuire asked.

The driver glanced at an unfolded map. "Not long," he said. "Maybe three or four miles . . . ten minutes at most."

McGuire looked at his watch and nodded as the car kicked onto a stretch of newly laid macadam. The holes and ruts behind them, the driver accelerated, drove several miles to a river crossing, then turned off onto a dirt road that curved past an abandoned mill. Reaching the crossroad immediately beyond, he slowed the car, carefully scanned the roadside, then stopped.

"There!" he said, pointing.

Just ahead was a high fence fronted by two heavy gates padlocked together with a chain. The area was deserted, shrouded in darkness. McGuire rolled down a window. The air was heavy with the odor of sewage, and the surroundings were strangely silent—devoid of cricket beats and the movement of foraging night animals.

The driver maneuvered the car into a bank of trees, where it would be hidden from the road.

"Don't slam the doors!" McGuire warned. "And if you have to talk, make it a whisper."

They climbed out. Biroc opened the trunk, took out a black satchel, then turned the flashlight on the fence.

"Let's go," McGuire said.

They started to walk. The ground was loose, jelled together with a clay composition that stuck to the bottom of their shoes. Reaching the fence, Biroc took a wire cutter from the bag, snapped the chain, pulled the gates open, waited until everyone was inside, then closed the gates and placed the chain back in position, so if anyone happened by, the barrier would appear unmolested.

Leading the group beneath a line of old maples, Biroc carefully examined the area. The cemetery was overgrown and cluttered, unmarked by signposts and covered with the same red clay that bordered the road. There were no lights and no roadways.

Stopping, Biroc pulled a schematic drawing of the cemetery from his pocket, showed it to McGuire, and indicated the route to the victim's grave. McGuire asked Biroc to lead. Biroc pointed to get his bearings, then walked down a cobblestone path to the top of a hill and turned off to the right into the rows of tombs and sepulchers.

McGuire was last in the procession, acutely attuned to the myriad of lifeless stones, of knee-high tombs eaten away and covered with vines. Biroc and the three men walked ahead, unaware of the magnitude, the implication of what they were about to do.

"Are we okay?" McGuire asked after Biroc had spoken to the driver, altered their path, and continued ahead.

Biroc turned and nodded. "We're doing fine."

Suddenly Biroc stopped, consulted the schematic, turned off the path, and knelt next to a stone marked only by a number. "This is it," he said.

McGuire wiped the perspiration from his face, leaving a smudge of clay. "All right," he ordered, "get it out."

The three men took folded shovels from the satchel, snapped them open, and tore into the ground.

"According to the medical records," Biroc said softly to McGuire, "there's a pin holding the patella in place. We'll break the kneecap. The pin should be visible. We can also look for a hairline fracture on the fourth rib."

McGuire nodded.

The sound of the shovels echoed, dropping dirt, sliding earth. Grunts, minute after minute—and then the impact of metal on wood.

"We have it," the driver said, his body extended from the hole.

McGuire looked inside the grave. The top of a plain wooden box was visible beneath the remaining crust.

"Open it!" he commanded.

The men lifted the coffin, eased it onto the mound of dirt, took chisels from the satchel, jammed them under the lip of the coffin top, and pried the nails from the wood. Father McGuire stood back, watching, his mind picking up light strains of music and the whisper of choral voices, all plucked from the recesses of his memory, the vestige of a Hollywood horror movie seen as a child—the association so vivid it hurt.

The men removed the coffin top.

McGuire looked down at the clump of burned and decayed flesh. A wave of nausea mushroomed up his esophagus. "Get it over with," he said.

Biroc grabbed the corpse's right knee. Pieces of ash, that has been flesh, decomposed in his hand. He grimaced, but moved closer.

A massive rip of thunder exploded above them.

"What is it?" Biroc cried, looking up, terrified.

"Quiet!" McGuire warned, staring at the sky.

The air settled, recapturing its tranquillity.

The gravediggers backed off, shielding themselves under a tree. McGuire glanced at them, then turned to Biroc.

"Quickly!" he whispered.

Biroc reached into the coffin.

Again it came, bursting against their ears. Biroc buried his face in his hands. McGuire grabbed him and forced him to look inside.

"If you're not going to do it, I will."

"I'm sorry, Father," Biroc said, struggling with his will.

A shattering bolt of lightning surged across the sky. They waited for the clap of thunder, but none came.

Once more Biroc grabbed the leg.

Suddenly McGuire's eyes fused shut from the ignition, the hideous flash of lightning that bore down on them from above, its heat searing his face and burning the edges of his clothes.

The lightning had struck the coffin, incinerating it. Biroc was frozen in position. Burned beyond recognition, cremated.

Chazen knew! He could not let them inspect the remains!

"God!" McGuire cried, answered by a wild crash of thunder.

The gravediggers ran toward the cemetery exit. Half in shock, McGuire trailed behind, rushing along the dirt path and out into the road. Hearing the whine of the car engine, he ran toward it, then moved out of the way as the car backed furiously into the clearing. He screamed for help. Whipped with panic, the men ignored him.

The sky blackened; a roar of thunder began to build once more, illuminated by intermittent streaks of lightning. He turned dizzily in place, covering his eyes, hunched in pain. The sound increased; so did the frequency of the flashes. Then they joined, focusing into a laser of energy.

It came—like the whoosh of wind and fire that had claimed Franchino—shooting downward, enveloping the car in a fission of heat and fire. The car exploded. A terrible concussion pitted his ears, the burning pieces of metal spiraling through the air. And then the thunder and lightning were spent. Within minutes it was dark again, and silent.

He stumbled forward, his eyes fastened catatonically on the road. He was alive. He had been spared.

Tears streaming down his face, his clothes ripped and hanging off his body, he started up the road, licking parched lips, wiping his black-streaked face, praying for the morning.

23

"That's the doorbell, honey," Faye said as she wrapped a large towel around her bustline and sat on the bed. She had just gotten out of the shower and was still wet. "Could you get it?"

Ben popped out of the bathroom. "What?"

"The door."

He nodded, disappeared into the bathroom again, then emerged moments later wearing a terry-cloth robe.

"I told Sorrenson not to come over so early," he said, glancing at the bedroom clock. "It's not even eight."

He walked out of the bedroom, across the living room, and into the foyer to the door.

"Who is it?" he asked.

"Father McGuire."

"McGuire?" Ben mumbled as he snapped the latch, removed the chain guard, and opened the door.

"Good morning, Ben," McGuire said. "Can I come in?"

"Yes . . . of course," Ben stuttered. He moved back, staring at the priest.

McGuire pulled his bloody hands from the door frame and entered. His feet were covered with red clay; his face was smeared with blotches of blood. The unmistakable smell of smoke reeked from his clothes. "Where is the child?" he asked as he stepped into the living room.

"In the bedroom."

"With Faye?"

"Yes."

"Bring them to me."

Ben hesitated. "What happened to you, Father?"

"Do as I say!"

Ben shrugged, loped into the bedroom, and reappeared moments later with Faye and the baby.

"Father McGuire!" Faye cried the moment she saw the priest. She embraced him, ignoring his appearance. Ben had warned her in the bedroom that something was wrong. "Oh . . . am I happy to see you. I was so angry when Ben didn't tell me you had called. But now, well . . ." She stared. "I just hope you're all right."

McGuire took her hand. "Sit on the couch. I want to talk to you and Ben."

Faye stroked her lips with her tongue. "Of course, Father."

She back-stepped to the couch and sat. Ben gave her the baby.

"Several days ago," McGuire said, staring at Ben, "I asked you about your son." He took the baby from Faye, kissed the child on the cheek, and brushed back the strands of blond hair that flopped over his ears. "Do you still maintain he was born in the Presbyterian Hospital?"

"What's this about?" Faye asked, alarmed.

"Was he?" McGuire prompted.

Ben nodded. "Yes."

McGuire turned toward Faye. "Where was the child born, Mrs. Burdett?"

"At Presbyterian Hospital."

McGuire advanced to the couch and placed the baby's face next to Faye's, then Ben's. He examined their curious reactions and returned the child to his mother.

"There's not much of a resemblance, is there?"

"I don't know what you're getting at," Faye snapped, "but there's a damn good resemblance—Joey looks just like me. And he has his father's nose."

McGuire smiled sardonically. "He may well have his father's nose, but not Ben's. And if he looks like you, it's solely a coincidence of nature. Now, tell me the truth!" Silence. "Then I'll tell it to you. The child was born in Massachusetts General Hospital. His natural mother lives in New Hampshire, and his father lives in the Midwest. Joey Burdett was adopted! You were never pregnant, Faye. Your pregnancy was a charade. You did not have a baby. Nor could you ever!"

McGuire swallowed hard, the first vestige of fear

trickling into his voice, an onslaught of terror eroding the ambivalent expression he had carried into the apartment.

Faye held the child close. Ben stood and caressed Faye's shoulders.

"So what?" he said. "So the baby was adopted. What does it matter?"

"What does it matter?" McGuire raged, the muscles in his neck tightening like thongs of leather. "Faye Burdett could not have had the baby . . . because Faye Burdett is a man! A man whose name used to be Jack Cooper—a transvestite and female impersonator, perhaps the most convincing the world has ever known—a sinner against God and Christ!"

McGuire threw the picture Charlie Kellerman had given him into Faye's lap.

"Look at it!"

Faye glanced at the photo.

"Jack Cooper, now known as Faye Burdett, dressed as a woman in 1966 at the Club Soiree, just prior to going onstage."

Ben stared at the priest, hate and fear warring in his face.

"Jack Cooper . . . Faye Burdett!" McGuire repeated, easing closer to Ben. "Do you deny it?"

"They'll take the baby from us if they know!" Faye cried.

"Do you deny it?"

"No."

"You met at the Soiree in 1966. Ben called himself Arthur Seligson—a fictitious name he utilized when prowling the gay bars to protect his otherwise normal way of life. You spent time together, first occasionally, then more often, until the relationship grew into a love affair. During the courtship, Jack Cooper remained at the Soiree tending bar and performing in the cast of a transvestite revue. After a year, Arthur Seligson disappeared. Later, Jack Cooper vanished." He grabbed Ben. "You are Arthur Seligson."

He looked at Faye. "And you are Jack Cooper. Or at least you were!"

Ben stood, his face drained of color. Finally it had come out. They had known that someday it might. But so what? They would find a way to keep the baby!

Ben walked to the window, leaving Faye behind, crying on the couch. The morning sunlight struck his face. He turned.

"All right. You know everything. Yes, Faye is Jack Cooper. Yes, we adopted the baby. But for all purposes, Faye is a woman. And has always been. But what were we supposed to do—announce it to the world? If the authorities had known, they would never have allowed the adoption, and if they find out now, they'll take Joey away! Father, what does it all matter? We've been happy. She's my wife. We'll raise the baby like any other. Joey will be a fine, normal boy. What does it all matter?"

"What does it matter?" McGuire screamed, his body rearing. "Besides being a sin against God and Christ, this perfidy has fooled everyone—endangered all of mankind, possibly ended all hope, and *certainly* would have, had it not been for Joe Biroc, may he rest in peace."

Ben soundlessly mouthed the name "Biroc."

"The compactor victim was a man. Thus Franchino and I concluded that Chazen, who took the victim's place, had to be a man. When the Sentinel identified Chazen's presence on the twentieth floor, it narrowed the possibilities. Chazen had to be Sorrenson, Jenkins, Batille, Max Woodbridge, or Ben Burdett! Caught by the charade, Franchino and I were blinded from the truth, and further misled by Chazen's cleverly orchestrated rape sequence in the basement, designed to camouflage the truth—to allay any suspicions we might have had." He moved toward Faye, who stood, meeting his accusatory stare. "The real Faye Burdett or Jack Cooper was killed in the compactor room by

Charles Chazen. The body in the compactor was Faye Burdett's. Her soul has since been condemned to eternal hell—joining the very legions she was to oppose." He braced himself. "You are Charles Chazen. You are Satan!" He waited, then pointed. "I curse you. Anathematize you. Execrate your existence. You are the eternal malediction. The scourge, plague, affliction of humanity. The nefarious, noxious essence of hell. I curse you. And defy you!"

Faye said nothing; she did nothing.

The mantel clock ticked forward with the cadence of a metronome. Once again McGuire hurled invectives at the figure who maintained the appearance of Faye Burdett.

Ben moved between them, reaching for Faye's hand. His face was wet, sopped by perspiration. He questioned himself. Could this be true? Oh . . . but it was. . . . It had come down to this. He knew it. "Is this so?" he asked, abhorring the sudden mannequinlike texture of Faye's skin and the dispossessed look in her eyes.

She pulled away her hand and faced McGuire.

"I defy you!" McGuire cried.

Faye laughed, the decibels of sound increasing. Ben and McGuire grabbed for their ears. The baby wailed in agony. Faye moved toward them, her expression ebbing and flowing like hot wax, her features slithering from one pose to another, the movement accompanied by the loathsome laughter that kept getting louder, more revolting. And the air began to smell foul, as if a piece of carrion had been flung into their midst.

"Faye!" Ben cried, not at this thing, but for his wife, who had died in the compactor. He fell to his knees and buried his head in his hands.

The discreet outline of Faye's body began to disengage. Slowly her skin became thin and brittle, fading in and out of the dimension, altering her female form, materializing the image of the Charles Chazen Franchino had met fifteen years before.

The air rang with an invasion of wind. Papers began to fly . . . the ashtrays emptied . . . pictures fell . . . the fury of the wind increased. McGuire grabbed the mantel for support. Ben shielded the baby.

Chazen continued to laugh as he backed to the door, reveling in their terror.

The air blackened. Everything whirled; furniture toppled. McGuire and Ben looked up. Chazen was leaning against the wall. And then, as quickly as the wind and sound had come, they were gone, and so was Chazen—vanished like the fade-out of a desert mirage.

Ben cradled the baby in his arms, trying to stop his body from shaking.

"Ben," McGuire said accusingly, "because of you, this has happened. Because of you, we were not given time to deal with Chazen."

"The hell with Chazen. I don't give a damn what happens."

"That's not true, Ben."

"No?"

"Not if you love your God."

"There is no God."

"There is Satan. That, you know. And I can assure you, there is God."

"Faye is dead. If she was to be the Sentinel, then there will be no Sentinel."

McGuire moved to Ben. "You have a fine son. He should be given the chance to live a full life. There is still a chance for him. There is an alternative."

"What?"

"You must trust me!"

"Like I trusted Franchino?"

"I am not Franchino. And you have no choice. You must listen to me and do as I say."

Ben stared.

"Tomorrow night at twelve o'clock, you are to be in this apartment. You will leave with me now. Find a place to stay. Send the baby to relatives. Then re-

turn here at midnight tomorrow. Do you understand?"

"Yes . . . but you must give me a reason."

McGuire smiled. "A reason? If you're not here, and
if Satan does not destroy you, I will! You *and* your
son! Do you understand?"

Ben nodded slowly.

McGuire stared silently. "Good" was the last thing
he said.

24

Dreams came quickly that night. Several times he
woke, writhing between the bedcovers, trying to sep-
arate reality from the manifestations of terror and discover the answers to the questions that Biroc had
posed about Ben Burdett's background. He was convinced that Biroc had unearthed a precise chronology
of Ben Burdett's life and had accurately described the
shocking failure of Franchino's research. But how?
Franchino had not been one for errors. How could he
possibly have compiled something so erroneous? And
where was the missing piece—the suicide attempt,
the key that had to exist somewhere in Ben Burdett's
background to have precipitated his elevation to the
role of Sentinel? No easy questions, especially in the
depth of the night, facing the specter of the upcoming
confrontation and the vivid recollection of the scene

in Ben Burdett's apartment, the incredible vision of Faye Burdett's transformation and the horror of staring at the image and essence of Satan himself.

The alarm buzzed at ten.

Father McGuire jumped out of bed, showered quickly, dressed, left the dormitory, walked across the street to his office, opened the office door, and stopped abruptly, facing the three men who were already inside.

"Good morning, Father," Detective Wausau said.

"Yes . . . good morning," McGuire replied, puzzled. "Who are you? And what are you doing in my office?"

Wausau rose from McGuire's desk chair, held up a badge, then pointed to the two other officers and identified them: detectives Jacobelli and Dellamare. Sitting once more, he invited the priest to have a chair, stay awhile, and answer some questions.

Indignant, McGuire grabbed one of the armchairs. "What is this about?"

Wausau popped a stick of gum into his mouth. "Murder."

"Murder?"

"You've heard the word before, haven't you, Father?"

McGuire glanced at the other men, then nodded, squinting into the halo of light thrown by the desk lamp that Wausau had turned in his direction. "But why do you wish to talk to me?"

Wausau pulled a picture from his coat pocket and tossed it onto the desk. "The dead man in the picture is Guglielmo Franchino. Monsignor Franchino. Several nights ago he fell through the twentieth-floor hall window at 68 West Eighty-ninth Street. Apparently it was a suicide, though you and I both know that it would have been highly unlikely for a priest to have taken his life. And Monsignor Franchino was certainly a priest, according to the Archdiocese of New York. Did you know the man?"

McGuire looked at the picture. Had Ben Burdett said anything? Impossible. "No. I'm sorry."

"I see," Wausau said, nodding smugly. "Do you know a man named Ben Burdett?"

McGuire tried to remain composed; he shook his head.

"Or Faye Burdett?"

"No."

"Or anyone at 68 West Eighty-ninth Street?"

Again McGuire shook his head.

Wausau smirked and rubbed his hands nervously together. "Have you ever been in the building at 68 West Eighty-ninth Street?"

"No. I should think that would be obvious by now."

"Obvious, Father?" Wausau walked around the desk and sat on the edge. "Did you know a man named Tom Gatz?"

"No."

"An Inspector Burstein?"

McGuire shook his head.

Wausau laughed. "Have you ever been accused of lying, Father?"

McGuire sat up in the chair, the focus of his stare narrowing. "No."

"That's unfortunate. Because I'm going to be the first to do so. We have reason to believe that you know every one of the people I've named. Not only know them, but are actively involved in their lives—and possibly, in the case of Gatz, Burstein, and Franchino, their deaths. Father? Weren't you with Monsignor Franchino the night he died?"

McGuire surged to his feet. "I told you I've never heard of or met the man."

"Yes, I know." Wausau paused, his eyes meandering. "Didn't you and Franchino have an argument in the hall the night Franchino was murdered? Didn't Franchino threaten to report some of your very un-Catholic activities to the archdiocese? Didn't you hit him with a pipe you had secreted under your robe? Didn't you take the monsignor, who was unconscious, and throw him through the hall window to his death?"

McGuire blistered with rage, as he again denied knowing any of the people or having been involved in any of their lives or deaths.

Wausau listened, then pulled a pair of handcuffs from his pocket and tossed them to Jacobelli. "Read him his rights."

"There must be some mistake!" McGuire cried.

"I'm sorry, Father," Wausau said. "But you're under arrest."

"On what charge?"

"The murder of Monsignor Franchino."

"But how? Why? I never——"

"Save it for the jury," Wausau said, interrupting. "You're going to need lots of help. There was a witness, Father, who has just come forward. Unfortunately, the witness waited, afraid to be implicated, afraid of retaliation. The witness saw you in the hall. The witness saw you strike Franchino and then toss him out the window. The witness also took a picture." He reached into his pocket once more and tossed a photo onto the desk. Astonished, McGuire picked it up—a glossy of Franchino lying on the hall floor, bleeding, and McGuire standing over him holding a pipe.

Angrily McGuire threw the picture on the blotter. "This is a sham! A fraud!"

The detectives laughed and shook their heads. Jacobelli read the Miranda rights from a small note card and clamped the cuffs on McGuire's wrists.

"Who was the witness?" the priest asked.

Wausau walked to the office door and opened it. "A woman named Faye Burdett!" he answered.

The pounding at the base of his skull had nearly obliterated his senses. It had started shortly after his arrest and had continued to aggravate in the confines of his tiny cell, which was located in a midtown precinct, somewhere on the second floor at the end of a barren corridor.

All he could do was wait. Prior to being booked, he had phoned the archdiocese and had spoken to Father Tepper. Tepper had cautioned him to remain calm and had advised that the archdiocese would send counsel to try to arrange for bail, but so far—it was nearing seven o'clock—no one had arrived. Certainly, someone had to come. The transition was scheduled for midnight.

He felt like crying out. But who would hear him? The old man who lay prone on the cot behind? The other prisoners in the cellblock? No, his frustrations would find meaning only in his own ears. Only he could appreciate what Chazen had done—reappearing as Faye Burdett, manufacturing the pictures of him and Franchino, placing him in an impossible situation.

At eight o'clock he contacted the archdiocese again and asked for Tepper; he was told that the priest had left. He tried to find someone else who might be able to help, but there was no one in authority at the archdiocese. He called the Cardinal's residence but was told that the Cardinal was out of town and that he would have to contact one of the Cardinal's subordinates in the morning. Disgusted, he returned to the cell and fell on his cot—the headache continuing—and lay, eyes open, sensing a growing desperation whittling at his self-control. The old man was still asleep. He could hear voices in the other cells; one prisoner was whistling. Every few minutes an obese guard inspected the area. After the guard's tenth passage, he again looked at his watch. Almost nine o'clock. The window above his head was already dark. And still no one from the archdiocese. No word or message. His patience worn, he rose from the cot and started to pace, sweating heavily, his heart beating like the slap of a hammer. Then suddenly the cellblock door opened, and the obese guard entered.

"Your attorney's here," the guard said, pointing at him.

"My attorney?" McGuire asked.

The guard retreated. McGuire sat down on his cot, glanced at the old man once again, looked at his watch, then stood, responding to the encroaching echo of footsteps.

The guard opened the gate and admitted Ralph Jenkins.

"Please sit down," Jenkins said, removing his hat.

McGuire was astonished. What in the world was Ralph Jenkins doing here?

"I've been asked to help you," Jenkins said. "I assume you know who I am."

"Ralph Jenkins."

Jenkins nodded. "And Ralph Jenkins will do for the moment." He smiled. "I will have you out of here before midnight."

"How?"

Jenkins angled his brow. "Preliminary bail was denied, pending your arraignment, which is to be held tomorrow morning."

"But that will be—"

"Too late? Yes."

"Then how?"

"Arrangements have been made."

"What kind of arrangements?"

Jenkins glanced over his shoulder. The hall was empty. He looked at the old prisoner. McGuire assured him that the man was asleep.

"We are going to break you out," Jenkins whispered.

"You can't be serious," McGuire said.

"Just remain calm and quiet, Father, and do not ask questions."

McGuire wiped his expression clean. Jenkins again cautioned him to remain calm, then called for the guard, who opened the gate.

"You're all talked out?" the guard asked.

"Yes," Jenkins replied. He stepped out the door and

turned to McGuire. "I'll see you in the morning, Father."

The guard locked the gate.

"Thank you, Mr. Jenkins," McGuire said, joining the charade.

Seconds later he heard the main cell door close and lock. He took off his watch and placed it on the pillow, where he could consult it easily. Then he leaned back against the cold slab of wall and closed his eyes, ready to wait.

Thrown onto the floor, he grabbed the leg of the cot and held it tightly. The roar had momentarily deafened him. The entire building was shaking. There had been an explosion below, somewhere on the first floor, perhaps in the basement. He could smell smoke. Soot was belching out of the exhaust and air-conditioning ducts at each end of the corridor. There was pandemonium in the cellblock, cries for help, the sound of chairs and beds being smashed against bars. Next to him, the old man had woken and was screaming for the guards.

Desperate, he ripped the pillowcase from the pillow and folding it in half, pressed it against his mouth to keep his lungs free from smoke.

"We're gonna die," the old man cried as he retreated to the rear of the cell and grabbed the priest.

"No one's going to die, my son," McGuire said assuringly.

The building's alarm sounded.

McGuire pulled the old man to the floor as another explosion pounded the building.

"Down here," he said. "There's less smoke."

The man nodded, his eyes flashing terror.

McGuire waited. The cries continued, growing more frantic. Was this his means of escape? It seemed impossible. Would they endanger the lives of everyone in the building just to get him out? Unlikely. But yet . . . if he did not reach freedom, all their lives and many more besides would be imperiled. Pressing the cloth harder against his face, he prayed. Then he looked at the watch—10:43. For all he knew, everyone had fled, abandoning the prisoners, leaving them to die in flames.

Suddenly he heard a sound down the hall. Starting to cough, he crawled to the gate and looked out. Two guards wearing gas masks had entered the cellblock door and were racing between the cells, opening the gates and releasing the prisoners, who were surging ahead, trying to get to the main staircase before being overcome by smoke.

The obese guard opened McGuire's cell. "Let's go," he screamed.

"Come," McGuire said, helping the old man through the gate.

Stumbling, they exited the cellblock. There was less smoke in the hall, though there was little reason to feel secure. The guard told them that the basement boiler had exploded, the entire basement and part of the first floor were in flames, and that flames had advanced through the ducts to other parts of the building as well.

"Then where do we go?" the old man asked.

"Down the staircase!" the guard screamed.

The old man looked over the railing; the base of the staircase was clogged with flames.

"It's impossible."

The guard grabbed the man and pushed him onto the steps. "You have no choice. Get going."

"Please!"

"And pray."

The old man grabbed the guard's leg, holding it tight. The guard kicked him in the face and pushed him down the steps. McGuire tried to follow. The guard jammed him against the banister.

"He'll die!" McGuire screamed.

"Too bad." The guard pulled his gun and placed it next to McGuire's temple. "You make one move down those steps and I blow out your brains!"

McGuire looked down the hall. Flames were shooting up the walls. The ceiling had started to buckle.

"We've got to get out of here!" the guard screamed. "But not this way."

"Then where do we go?" McGuire asked, holding the guard's arm while looking after the old man, who had already disappeared.

"Shut up!" the guard shouted as he grabbed McGuire by the shirt collar and pulled him back into the cellblock.

"Are you crazy?" McGuire cried.

"Shut up!" the guard warned again.

"We'll die in here!"

The guard took a second mask from his jacket and placed it over McGuire's head. Then he moved McGuire to the rear exit, the one that had always remained locked, and opened the door with a key.

Beyond was a concrete stairwell, free from smoke. The guard pointed downward. McGuire descended several steps, then stopped, turned, and looked up. The guard was gone; the door was closed once more, probably locked. Having no alternative, he started down, reaching the first floor. The exit door was closed too. He fought the hot bolt, finally snapping it open. Pushing the door aside, he emerged into the alley behind the station. Above, flames were shooting from the building. Pieces of wood and concrete were showering down; the alley was strewn with debris. There was a gaping hole in the lower wall, probably at the point where the boiler had blown.

One alley exit led to the street in front of the precinct station, while another, directly across, stretched in the opposite direction.

He moved forward, toward the second, still choked by smoke inhalation. Behind him he could hear the arrival of fire engines. Ahead was darkness.

Halfway down the alley a figure leaned out of a doorway and pulled him inside. In the hallway were three men. One was Ralph Jenkins. Another was Father Tepper. The third man, whom he had never seen before, picked up a bottle of oxygen and applied it to McGuire's mouth. After several seconds he pulled it away and set it down again.

"You blew the building!"

Jenkins nodded.

"People may have died in there!"

"We pray that that is not so."

McGuire started to cough. Jenkins applied the oxygen once more. Then, placing the bottle on the floor, he grabbed McGuire by the arm and pointed toward the staircase. "This way, Father McGuire," he said.

25

"Who are you?" Father McGuire asked.

"I am your friend," Jenkins answered.

Father Tepper, who was seated in the front seat, his attention riveted on the circuitous journey of the car, looked at his watch. "Eleven-twenty-one," he announced.

"We'll let you off on Ninety-fifth and Amsterdam Avenue," Jenkins said, staring at McGuire's desperate eyes.

Moments later the car left the park at Seventy-second and Central Park West and started slowly uptown.

"You won't answer my question?" McGuire asked.

"There's no need for questions or answers," Jenkins

replied. "You are committed. You know your duties. When Sister Therese joins her God, Father Bellofontaine must be seated. That responsibility will not change, no matter what I reveal."

Nodding, McGuire focused on the hypnotic vibrations of the car. Of course, Jenkins' identity was superfluous. There was only one significance in his life: Sister Therese . . . Father Bellofontaine . . . Charles Chazen . . . Ben Burdett . . . the transition. He breathed deeply, sucking courage from his gut, carefully reviewing Father Tepper's tutelage, the instructions in the literature, the subliminal sensations of the death watch, realizing that Father Bellofontaine was not the only pawn in God's hand. He had become one too—the Almighty's instrument.

"This will do," Jenkins said suddenly as he leaned forward in the seat and tapped the driver's shoulder.

The driver pressed the brakes and stopped the car next to a hydrant.

Jenkins opened his door and stepped out. McGuire followed.

"May God be with you," Jenkins said, embracing him.

"May I be worthy of his love," McGuire replied.

McGuire stepped onto the sidewalk. Jenkins climbed back into the car; the driver executed a tight U-turn and peeled off into the distance.

McGuire walked to the corner of Amsterdam, south of Columbia University, and faced downtown, looking at a stretch of old stone apartments. To the east, several blocks of low-income housing extended to Central Park, towering over the older buildings. The streets themselves were dirty, covered with papers. There were a score of Irish pubs, alive with light. Most of the storefronts, though, were black, closed for the night. A smattering of people were on the street; there were few cars.

He buttoned his coat—it had gotten chilly—and started to walk, fighting off visions of Chazen and the gripping cold of fear inside him. A sweat broke on his forehead; his feet started to drag as the blocks melted away. He was flashing, losing his sense of time and space. At each intersection he glanced up at the street sign, marking his progress. And then, as if he had been there all along, he was standing by the excavation of St. Simon's, looking up at the form of Sister Therese sitting in the window on the twentieth floor of the building, the moonlight defining the outline of her head.

Crossing the street, he walked into the alley, entered the backyard ramp area, and climbed the ramp to the basement door, which had remained locked since the death of Monsignor Franchino, under orders from the building management—the Archdiocese of New York. He opened the door with a key and disappeared into the dark basement corridor.

Alone, he rode the elevator to the twentieth floor, the claustrophobic feeling in the car increasing, trapping him, the door mercifully sliding open long moments later, releasing him into the hall.

He looked around, sensing Chazen's presence, fearing death. Soon, though, it would be over.

He opened Burdett's apartment door with Biroc's passkey and turned on the lights.

"Ben," he called, wiping sweat off his palms.

The only reply was the chime of a clock.

He called again, and receiving no answer, searched the apartment.

Ben was not here!

But that was impossible. The man had to be here! If not by his own will, then by the power of the Almighty God.

Father McGuire looked at his watch—11:42.

Something was terribly wrong!

The bartender hesitantly filled the glass. "I think you've had enough," he said, arching his brow beneath a pair of hornrimmed bifocals.

Ben shook his head and tried to lift his eyelids. "I'll be all right," he declared, belching inebriatedly at his reflection in the bar mirror.

"Is that so? Hey, I don't mind if you have a good time, but I'm not going to have you keel over in my joint."

Ben laughed, lifted the glass, and slurped off the rim. "I'm not even drunk," he said, smiling, his expression slipping almost at once into one of confusion. The bartender looked blurred, and the place itself seemed like a surreal Chagall compilation of chairs, booths, and patrons. "Do you remember me?" Ben asked, lifting his head.

The bartender paused, glanced at another customer who had called his name, then shook his head.

"You've got to," Ben pleaded.

The bartender drew a tap beer for the other patron—there were only six people in the place—and turned back. "I'm sorry, but I don't."

"I came in a couple of weeks ago during the day. With a detective named Gatz."

"I only work the night shift."

"But you look familiar. I'm sure it was you."

The bartender shrugged, looked up at the television, which was angled down toward the patrons, then began to clean some mugs.

Ben placed a cigar in his mouth. "The guy I came in with was murdered."

"Is that so?"

"Yes . . . murdered. And so were a lot of other people."

"Look," the bartender said, "maybe you'd better go home and get some sleep."

Ben shook his head. "Please listen to me. My life has been destroyed. Everything."

The bartender leaned forward as Ben started to cry. "All right. You want to talk? Okay. I'll listen. Let's hear."

Ben wiped his eyes. "Not only was Gatz murdered, but so was a priest named Franchino. And a cop named Burstein. And my wife."

The bartender grimaced, adjusted his glasses, and filled a glass with beer for himself. "Is this on the level?"

Ben nodded and ran his hands over the brown portfolio that lay on the bar; protruding from it was the crucifix. Jenkins had told him to carry it, no matter where he went.

"Do the police know about this?"

Ben laughed, his face a mix of humor and indignation. "They know about some of them. In fact, all except my wife. But they have no idea who committed the murders."

The bartender blinked rapidly; he was curious. Sure, he heard a new story every night. But occasionally one came along that was particularly interesting, and this one had suddenly become so. "Do you?" he asked.

Ben nodded. "But I can't tell." He belched; his head swayed.

"Why not?"

"I was sworn to silence." He put his finger to his mouth to demonstrate.

"By whom?"

"Ralph Jenkins."

The bartender poked at his gold inlays with a toothpick. "Who's he?"

"My neighbor."

"What does he have to do with it?"

"I can't tell you."

"Look, mister, if there's been a murder, several murders, and you know the identity of the murderer, then you've got to go to the police."

Ben hiccuped. "It wouldn't do any good."

"Why not?"

"Because they're powerless. The church is involved. And God and Satan."

"God and Satan?" the bartender mumbled, shaking his head. "Are you crazy?"

"You can bet your life I'm not."

The bartender smirked. "I only bet on sure things. Look. I get all kinds of kooks in here talking about the end of the world or the coming of the Messiah." He placed a clean mug on the bar and filled it with beer. "I don't dig that crap. And I ain't got the time for it. So if you don't mind . . ."

Ben grabbed the bartender's wrist. "Look. It's not crap. It all happened. There's a plot."

The bartender ripped Ben's hand off his wrist. "You do that again and I'm gonna break your arm. Understand?"

Ben inched backward, wiped some saliva from his mouth, and looked at his watch—11:45. He had to get out of there. Jenkins had told him to be waiting for McGuire at midnight. And it was a five-minute walk back to the apartment.

"I better go," Ben said, pulling himself off the barstool.

"That's a good idea, mister. Go home. Get some sleep. Then, in the morning, when you're sober, all the dead bodies will be gone and you'll feel like a million bucks!"

Ben wobbled in place, dropped the cigar on the bartop, edged the portfolio under his arm, and turned to the door. Leaving a smudge track in the sawdust, he bumped through the exit, walked onto the street, and looked around, getting his bearings. Home was four blocks away, two east and two north. He walked to the corner and crossed the street. Except for the hum of a broken alarm ringing loudly in the still night air, the neighborhood was peculiarly quiet. He rubbed his face, trying to throw off the effects of the alcohol, assuring himself that it wasn't a dream, that he was actually awake and moving toward a rendezvous with terror.

He walked along the edge of the curb. Several cars passed, their headlights temporarily blinding. All his senses seemed enervated. His memory, too. He could see Faye standing before him, her image fading into a vision of Jack Cooper. He hadn't wanted to fall in love, certainly not with a transvestite. But it had happened. Oh . . . so many things had happened. And now this! And what would become of Joey, especially if he did not make it through the night, if he joined Gatz, Burstein, and Faye in death? A vivid possibility—and one that strangely did not frighten him. No, death was easy. Staying alive and continuing to face the horrors of his life was difficult.

Why had it all happened? he asked himself. He could have been happy forever. Faye was a fantastic woman, having developed a full-blown female personality over the years. When they had started together, he had doubted whether it would ever happen. But then it had —so suddenly. And it was strangely satisfying. At once, both his homosexual and heterosexual desires were being satisfied by one person.

Another car passed, another explosion of light, the sound of a grinding engine. He watched the car bounce over broken macadam, stop and switch gears, and arch a tight turn back in his direction, the beam from the headlights striking his face. He tried to identify the driver. But behind the wheel was a black hole. Was it possible? He looked behind him at the sheer wall of a building, then down at the corner, fifty feet away, then back at the car and the sway of its beams. Suddenly the car gained speed, angling toward him. He grabbed at his mouth, trying to hold his insides in, and started to move along the side of the building, heading for the corner. As the car neared, he began to run. The car cut steeply to the left, careening onto the sidewalk and into the wall, barely missing him. He looked inside again. There was a driver. Charles Chazen. Smiling. The car pulled back from the wall, bounced down the concrete, and bore down, hitting his shoulders. He cried, grabbing the lacerated flesh, stanching the flow of blood; part of his collarbone was exposed, the shoulder socket dislocated. He almost blacked out. Everything turned.

The car, engine raced again. Chazen's narrow features leered through the windshield. Ben jumped behind the rear of a pickup truck; the car smashed into the plate-glass window of a Chinese laundry.

Ben struggled across the street and ran into the stairwell of a subway station, falling down most of the steps, his free hand barely maintaining a grip on the banister. At the bottom, he located the change booth, ran to the window, bought a token, deposited it at the turnstile, descended the next staircase to the train platform, and fell to his knees, sweating heavily, eyes darting. The place was empty. He listened for sounds as he started to crawl toward the end of the platform, where he could hide in the darkness. He hauled himself along like an ape, one arm for balance, his body crouched low and bent at the hips. Then he stopped. Footsteps descended toward the platform—slow, chugging noises, deliberate in their indecision, calculated just for him. He tried to move faster, but couldn't. He looked back. There was still no one on this level. Suddenly, more sounds came from ahead—footsteps and laughter. Shadows moved across the wall. He hunched himself into a ball, stifling a cry of pain. A roar echoed out of the tunnel like the explosion of a Gatling gun, the rhythm of slowing wheels. Looking over the edge of the pit, he saw the beam of a train's lamp turning a bend a short way off.

The train raced into the station, its windows moving by like flying mirrors. The train stopped and its doors opened. He crawled into the last car. The doors closed. The car was empty; a conductor was riding on the coupler. He heard the brakes release and felt the first jerk of the car as the train gained speed and burrowed toward the black tunnel ahead.

As the train roared from the station, he saw Chazen

on the platform, staring. Then he fell on the passenger bench, still holding tightly to the portfolio, the crucifix inside. Dazed and breathless, white from fear, he buried his head in the palms of his hands, listening to the rhythmic grind of wheels on track. The train was moving very quickly, too quickly, the car bouncing furiously from side to side. He looked for the conductor; the man was no longer in sight. He walked to the door, pressing his face against the glass. The next station shot by; the train didn't stop, didn't slow. Something was wrong. He moved to the connecting door and left the car, moving toward the next forward one, holding the chain rail for safety. He tried the door. It was jammed. He reached behind him, taking the handle of the car he had just left. It too was frozen. The train's velocity increased. At any second he expected it to shoot off its track. He turned his face away from the fierce blast of wind that raged through the tunnel. Another station disappeared. He looked into the lead car. The conductor had returned, his back to the window. Ben pounded on the glass, screaming. The conductor remained frozen in position. Suddenly more speed. Tremendous vibrations. He grabbed the hold bars of the front car. The train lurched up and forward, throwing him to his face; the portfolio dropped below, under the wheels, the crucifix buried in the oily gravel. He looked back under the car into the rain of pebbles, then stood and banged once more on the door. The conductor moved, touching his hand to his cap, then turned, smiling.

Charles Chazen!

How?

Ben recoiled, the taste of bile surging into his mouth, as it had so many times during the last few weeks. His grip weakened as the train began to bang off the tunnel walls. They reached ninety, a hundred miles an hour —speeds that he knew New York subway trains were incapable of reaching.

Ahead he saw the gleam of station lights. He

grabbed a handbar and extended himself. The lights came closer as the train entered a station, hurtling by the platform. He let go, throwing himself onto the concrete. He felt an impact as he slammed against the station wall. His hands exploded with pain. Two of his fingers were broken. Blood spurted from deep lacerations on his scalp and legs. He fought to get up, responding to the squeal of the train's brakes. He heard the train stop, then start again, backing up.

"God," he cried, realizing that the crucifix was gone.

The train pulled into the station and sat silently, its doors closed. He glanced along the cars, looking for Chazen. A burst of steam and noise erupted from the brakes. Then silence again.

He crawled backward toward the platform gate. The train doors opened. He waited.

Seconds crept by.

Then something darted by one of the windows.

He inched closer to the gate, reaching for the handle.

"Ben Burdett!" Chazen cried.

Ben looked back at the train. Chazen was standing in front of the next-to-last car, laughing.

"God damn you!" Ben cried, his anger freezing his terror.

Chazen spread his arms; the station grew dark.

Chazen stepped toward him, then suddenly retreated into the car and disappeared behind closing doors.

Ben watched the train move out of the station and disappear, its red lights bleeding into the distance.

What had happened? he asked himself as he pulled himself to his feet, holding the gate for support. He looked around; there was no one in sight. Slowly, painfully, he staggered into a transit hallway that branched from the subway platform.

At twelve o'clock Father McGuire felt a charge of emotion rift his body, a sensation that warned of Chazen's presence. He had sensed Chazen's absence for the past twenty minutes, a feeling that had made him vaguely uncomfortable. But now Chazen had returned—there was no doubt about it—returned to prevent the transition between Sister Therese and Father Bellofontaine.

Father McGuire left the apartment and entered Sister Therese's.

He had never been inside before and had never seen the woman up close. And although he had been warned what he would find, the sight made his stomach turn. The apartment was empty, and there was no light. Sister Therese was seated in front of the open window, immobile, her body rigid, her face as revolting as ever. He felt a clutch of emotion as he looked at her, trying to comprehend. The years of devotion to her God had left their mark. Her body was covered with spiderwebs. Mice were clustered at her feet; her skin was pocked with sores.

"Father McGuire!"

He turned.

Chazen was standing at the door, dressed in a frayed, creaseless gray suit. The top two buttons of the jacket were missing, as were those from the sleeves, though the button threads still remained. In his lapel was a shriveled flower, on his shoulder a green-and-gold parakeet. "This is Mortimer," he said, indicating the bird. "And this is Jezebel." He held up a frazzled cat that had been cradled in his arms. "They're friends of Sister Therese—old friends. So I thought that I would bring them along to say good-bye to the good sister, who will be leaving us tonight. Isn't that true, Father?"

McGuire steeled himself against the vision.

"Now, come, Father. You're not afraid, are you?"

"I defy you, Chazen!" McGuire cried.

Chazen laughed. "You do? Where is Ben Burdett, Father?"

McGuire stared.

Chazen laughed again. "He's not coming, because he's dead!"

McGuire's body surged forward. "I defy you and your lies. You cannot destroy a chosen!"

"But he can destroy himself. And he has." Chazen smiled, enjoying the strange dialogue.

McGuire pointed to Sister Therese. "She would know!"

The cat spit at the holy sister. Chazen's eyes burned with hate. "Then where is he?" he asked.

McGuire moved close to Sister Therese and fell to his knees, praying to Christ. Chazen spit like the cat at the mention of the Son's name, then stood over the priest and raised his hands. The room shook. Behind them, near the apartment door, the air began to shimmer. McGuire looked up, appalled by the vision that appeared through the walls. Before him was a bed. In it was a woman of forty, her cheeks sunken, her skin colorless, her body invaded by wires and tubes attached to machines and bottles of plasma. She was breathing heavily. On her hands were clumps of blue liver spots; her feet were swollen.

McGuire tried vainly to shield his eyes.

"I shall stand before Father Bellofontaine," Chazen cried.

A second vision appeared, a child dressed in black shorts and a white T-shirt, who stood near the bed and held the woman's hand, speaking to her softly. The woman screamed, racked with pain. The boy began to cry. "Let me die," the woman said over and over. Confused, the boy held her tight. "Do you love me?" the woman asked. "Yes," the boy replied. "Then if you love me, disconnect the tubes and let me die." The boy continued to sob, then pulled out the needles. The woman closed her eyes and smiled. The boy left the room.

The vision of the woman remained.

"I shall appear before Father Bellofontaine," Chazen warned the priest, "and reveal his sin. He shall see what has been. And he shall know!"

The room exploded with a blast of cold wind. Sounds grew from nothing. Trembling, McGuire held his hands together and began to whimper, overcome by the horror.

The image of the woman faded, replaced by a room, a garage. Chazen stepped back, whipped by the wind, pointing. A boy entered the garage from the rear, the same boy who had appeared at the bedside of the dying woman, but several years older.

"And he shall know he is one with us!" Chazen cried, his voice as fierce as death.

As McGuire watched, the boy closed the garage door, climbed inside an old sedan, started the motor, and pressed hard on the accelerator. Within seconds the boy began to cough. Then he closed his eyes, trapped by the fumes.

The vision of the boy remained.

"Look!" Chazen cried.

McGuire battled his will, sweat streaming from his skin, his body shaking.

"Father Bellofontaine shall know. He shall see both his past and what would be his future."

The vision of the boy disappeared. The wind increased, tearing at Father McGuire's body and the frail form of Sister Therese. Again came the rush of sounds and the hideous bale of Chazen's laughter. The room grew dark and colder, then burst with an explosion of light, revealing the form of a man, seated, holding a crucifix—Father Bellofontaine, the next Sentinel—shriveled and decayed, his face rotted through to the bone and infested with maggots.

Father McGuire screamed.

Ralph Jenkins rolled down the car window and looked out toward the alley entrance. He could hear footsteps.

"She's coming," Father Tepper said.

Jenkins nodded and sat back, waiting.

The car was parked in the rear of the alley against a dead-end wall. Its lights were out. Except for the glow of streetlamps about fifty feet away, they were surrounded by darkness.

"Is it midnight?" Jenkins asked.

"Yes," Tepper replied. "We'll be late."

"May God forgive us."

A figure appeared in the alley entrance. It waited, staring, then moved slowly toward them, its footsteps lightly echoing between the buildings.

"Turn on the lights," Jenkins commanded.

The driver hit the switch; the headlights came alive.

The figure—a nun—stopped in front of the car and squinted, her features lightly filmed by perspiration. She was black, about thirty, and moderately attractive, marked by a jagged scar running from her upper lip to the base of her eye. The makeup that Father McGuire had seen covering her face was absent.

She climbed inside the car.

"Sister Florence," Jenkins said, taking her hand.

Sister Florence kissed the ring on Jenkins' hand. "Cardinal Reggiani," she replied.

"Are you all right, Mr. Burdett?" Mr. Vasquez, the superintendent, asked as he placed a glass of water to Ben's lips.

Ben nodded, sipped the water, and sat up, holding his head, trying to regain his equilibrium. Mr. Vasquez knelt; so did the doorman.

"I'm going to call a doctor, Mr. Burdett," Vasquez said as he applied some gauze to the cuts on Ben's head.

"*No!*" Ben said, pushing the superintendent away. "No doctors. I'll be fine."

Vasquez glanced at the doorman and shook his head. "You have some bad cuts, a couple of broken fingers, and a badly damaged shoulder."

Ben tried to stand. "I'm okay. Just leave me alone."

"But, Mr. Burdett—"

"What time is it?" Ben cut in.

The doorman glanced at his watch. "Twelve-thirty."

"God damn!"

Vasquez held Ben's arm as he struggled to the elevator. "You passed out as you came into the building. Please let me call a doctor. Your wife will be very upset."

"My wife?" Ben cried. "Upset?" He laughed hysterically.

Vasquez and the doorman exchanged curious glances.

Ben held the elevator frame and waited. Moments later the door opened and he stepped inside, leaving a trail of blood. He looked out at the two men and smiled. "I'm fine," he said, wincing. Then he pressed a button on the panel and stood back as the door closed.

The elevator started to rise, bumping gently; he slumped against the wall, dizzy, fighting to withstand the pain, trying to remember everything Jenkins had told him, hoping that Jenkins would be in the apartment as planned.

The elevator door opened, and he stepped into the hall. It was quiet. Jenkins had assured him that they would manage the removal of all the tenants on the twentieth floor; judging by the absence of sounds, Jenkins had been successful.

Ben walked to Sister Therese's door and listened. Nothing. He grabbed the doorknob and turned. The door was open. Closing his eyes and breathing deeply, he passed through the doorway.

26

"Father McGuire?" Ben called from the foyer.

No one answered.

He walked into the living room, stepped around Sister Therese's chair, and touched her face, caressing the rotted skin.

"Father McGuire!" he called again, holding his fractured shoulder.

A drop of blood fell onto the Sister's frock; he touched his scalp, which was still bleeding, and walked back toward the foyer.

Could McGuire be next door?

He heard a sound.

"Who's there?" he called, looking down the bedroom hallway.

The noise came again, a light tap.

Terrified, he walked into the darkness and moved along the wall.

"That's you, Father McGuire, isn't it?"

No answer.

"Mr. Jenkins?"

Footsteps.

At the doorway, he reached for the doorknob, then suddenly fell back.

Someone had turned the knob from the other side.

"Where have you been?" Father McGuire asked as he walked out of the room.

Cardinal Reggiani rang for the elevator again, but nothing happened.

"Chazen," Father Tepper said.

Reggiani nodded. "You are to stay here, Sister."

Sister Florence stepped away from them and retreated to the basement entrance.

Reggiani and Tepper turned toward the staircase and inspected their waistbands to ensure that their crucifixes were securely fastened. Reggiani opened the stairwell door and entered; Father Tepper moved in behind, closing the door.

"Franchino's soul walks with us!" Tepper said as they started to climb.

"May God grant our fate be better," Reggiani replied in a whisper.

They turned the bend, quietly moving up the steps, breathing heavily, close together, pouring sweat.

Reaching the twentieth floor, Reggiani tried the door; it was locked.

"Chazen is waiting," Tepper said.

"Yes," Reggiani replied, grabbing the banister. "We must go down. . . . Hurry!"

They descended, stumbling; the walls and floor were speckled with their perspiration. As they reached the third-floor landing, the lights went out. They were caught in the middle of a funnel, submerged in blackness.

Reggiani wrapped his hands about his crucifix as they continued to descend.

A terrible laugh echoed, accompanied by a blast of hot air. Reggiani heard his name called out of the blackness.

"Chazen's below us!" Tepper cried.

"Back up," Reggiani said.

They turned and frantically began to climb.

They heard the creak of pipes.

"We must break out!" Reggiani screamed, the vision of Franchino's death looming before him.

They stopped on the nineteenth floor and attacked the door, kicking, trying to dislodge the hinges.

Then Tepper drew back. "Something is near!" he whispered, his voice breaking. "I can feel the fires of hell."

Reggiani reached into the darkness; Tepper cried in pain. "Father!" Reggiani called.

No reply.

Above him, the pipes continued to groan. A drop of water hit his forehead. He heard a cry, then the sound of a falling body.

"Father Tepper!"

"I'm all right," Tepper called from the landing below. "I lost my footing."

Again Reggiani was splashed with water. The pipes creaked once more. He pushed close to the wall, listening to the sound of seepage, then the thud of a rupture. Water was running. The roar increased. His feet were wet; a stream was flowing down the steps. He moved to the edge of the landing. "Chazen is trying to drown us. We must get out!"

"I can't move," Tepper cried. "I think my leg is broken."

Reggiani grabbed the banister. "I'm coming," he yelled, shuddering at the sound of an explosion above. Looking into the darkness, he could feel a spray of water against his body, increasing in ferocity. The water pipes, perhaps even the water tank, had burst.

A tidal rush slammed against him, pulling his feet from under him. He held to the banister, sliding down the steps, spitting water, trying to breathe. He could hear Tepper choking and slapping with his arms.

Water surged in giant eddies, filling the concrete stairwell, carrying everything in its way down through the darkness.

Reggiani went under, then surged up into the air, frantically fighting the flood, slammed off the banisters, clutching, dropping from one landing to the next, reaching out blindly for Tepper, who had ceased screaming.

Over the horrible thunder of deluge he could hear Chazen laughing, shouting his contempt for God and Christ.

Reggiani swept around a landing, his mouth and lungs filled with water. He was submerged, drowning in a rapid descent. Trying to keep his head up, he turned over, fell headfirst, and was carried to the first landing, where he was heaved against the basement door under a crushing wave.

Father McGuire pointed at Ben. "You are the next Sentinel, Ben Burdett." Ben stared, unmoved. "You are the successor to the angel Gabriel and his successors. You are the one who must guard against the approach of Satan." He placed his hands on Sister Therese's shoulder. "Chazen will try to make you destroy yourself. Chazen will prey on the weaknesses of your past, which have been buried in your subconscious. Chazen will do so, unless the crucifix is successfully transferred." He fell to his knees and began to pray. Ben watched the incredible sight. Then McGuire extended his hand. "You are the chosen," he said.

Cardinal Reggiani opened his eyes; the staircase was a blur. Holding his head, he blinked, trying to clear his vision. He was cold, shaking, lying on his back in a deep pool of water. The runoff from above had nearly stopped; except for a hollow tinkle, the stairwell was dead silent.

He pulled himself to his knees, sliding on the slippery concrete, and dabbed at the deep gash on his arm. How long had he been unconscious? And where was Father Tepper?

Grabbing the banister, he wobbled up the steps. "Tepper!" he called, craning his neck to look up the staircase. He listened to the lifeless echo, then started to climb, barely able to cling to the handrail. Reaching the second-floor landing, he stopped, staring at a dull red stain carried by the thin film of flowing water. He knelt and ran his hands through it, the blood sticking to his palm. Something hit his shoulder. More blood. He glanced upward.

Father Tepper's body dangled above, his lifeless head wedged between the joining banisters, his body hanging as if he had been strung from a gallows.

"God have mercy!" Reggiani cried, his face frozen with anger.

He heard the clink of metal. He stepped up, nearing Tepper's body. Caught in the banister was Tepper's crucifix, held by its leather strap, banging against the iron rail.

Sister Therese surged out of the chair, grabbing her chest with her right hand. Father McGuire, who had been prone, completing his incantations, stood and held her. Ben backed off.

Sister Therese grabbed McGuire's arm. The blood vessels on her face exploded under the skin. Saliva dribbled from her mouth. Whatever color had remained in her flesh fled rapidly. Sickened, Father McGuire gagged.

"She's dying," he screamed.

Still silent, Ben just stared. Suddenly a flash of light exploded through the room, blinding them. Sounds grew. A violent wind tore at them.

"Chazen is here!" McGuire cried as plaster fell from the ceiling, the glass in the windows shattered, and fire erupted at the base of the draperies.

Mr. Vasquez raced out of his apartment into the hall. "Who called down?" he asked as he grabbed the house phone.

"Mr. Chupa in Eighteen-E!" the doorman said.

Vasquez rang back. "This is Vasquez," he said when the tenant had picked up the line.

Chupa reported a fire somewhere on the floors above. The odor of smoke had reached the eighteenth floor, and the ceiling was getting hot.

"Get the hell out of there!" Vasquez yelled. "If you can, alert the other people on the floor! And use the stairs. There may be fire in the elevator shaft." He slammed down the phone and grabbed the doorman by the arm. "Get this building evacuated!"

"Right away." The doorman sounded the building alarm and began to buzz apartments.

Vasquez ran down the hall, and raced around the bend to the staircase. Shocked, he stopped. The rugs were flooded; water was seeping under the door.

He grabbed the handle; the door was jammed.

Cardinal Reggiani looked up at the hole in the roof. Part of the water-tank superstructure extended down, and water still leaked over the edge. There was space to climb through, though, and since there was no other way out of the stairwell, he had no choice.

He glanced quickly below—smoke had started to sift under the door on the twentieth floor—and climbed up the roof ladder. Reaching the hole, he grabbed the metal tank support and pulled himself onto the roof.

He made his way to the edge of the building and looked down the perpendicular row of windows. Directly to the side was a drainage pipe, stretching to the alley below. He lowered himself over the edge and began to shimmy down, barely keeping his grip, fighting the wind and the dizzying height.

Reaching the twentieth floor hall window, he extended his foot and kicked in the glass, slashing his ankle. In pain, slivers embedded in his muscles, he extended his leg through the hole, the sharp broken edges cutting into his thigh. He released his grip on the pipe, grabbed the bottom frame, reached inside the window, and pulled himself through into the hall.

Father McGuire stood over Sister Therese's body, chanting the last rites, then looked up and stared at Ben Burdett, who was holding the crucifix in his hand. Ben didn't seem to be enveloped by the power of the Lord God. Nor had he aged.

"Father Bellofontaine!" McGuire called.

And Ben just smiled.

Fire was shooting out the windows on the upper floors by the time most of the tenants had been evacuated. The lower floors were still untouched, though the blaze was rapidly advancing down the side of the building. Vasquez and the doorman were at the intercom. A detachment of police was assisting the stragglers.

"Keep trying!" Vasquez yelled.

The doorman pressed the twentieth-floor buttons; no one responded. "If they're up there, they're finished."

Down the hall, the elevator arrived; three tenants ran out, holding whatever belongings they could salvage. Vasquez surged for the car, got inside, and pressed the button. The door started to close, then shorted out. Reentering the hall and hearing the sound of sirens, he grabbed an ax from the utility closet, hurried back to the stairwell door, and attacked the lock, shattering it. As he pulled back the door, he was thrust against the wall by the explosion of fumes. It was too late. He ran back to the building entrance and joined the doorman in the street as the first of the fire trucks turned off the corner of Central Park West and headed down Eighty-ninth. Moments later a violent explosion ripped the center section of the building.

Vasquez looked up and shook his head. "It's gone."

As the form of the dying mother and her son once again appeared through the walls, accompanied by the sound of Chazen's laughter, Cardinal Reggiani, bleeding badly, pointed across the room at McGuire, and through the rising wall of fire cried, "Take the crucifix, Father Bellofontaine!"

McGuire looked at Ben, who was standing nearby, buried in smoke, then back at Reggiani. "I don't understand!" he screamed.

Sister Florence walked through the dark shadows, her attention riveted on the top floors of the building. From her position, along the St. Simon's fencing, she could see the burning face of 68 West and the access alley to the rear of the building.

Reggiani and Tepper had not reemerged.

Chazen's horrible voice assaulted the room. "I call ye and declare ye now returned," it cried, nearly buried by the howl of wind that was churning through the apartment, holding the fires apart like the parted Red Sea. The armies of the night filled the room, arrayed to challenge the Almighty God and his chosen.

Choked by smoke, Ben stood silently by the lifeless body of Sister Therese. Cardinal Reggiani remained still, pointing at McGuire, who lay coiled on the floor, clutching his withering body, vomiting, attuned to the voice of Chazen, frozen in the nightmare of his past, the years of repression undone in an instant, his subconscious mind laid bare to his conscious self.

"It was me all the time!" McGuire shouted.

"All along!" Reggiani said. "You are Father Bellofontaine. You are the chosen."

And Chazen's voice echoed, "You are the chosen of the Lord God, the tyrant and our enemy. You are he who is to guard and protect the entrance to the earth. You are he who must take up the scepter of the Lord. You are the appointed one who must be destroyed if we are to be successful. Now is the hour of decision and action. The work will be done. Ye shall become one with us, and then we shall up and enter into full bliss to join Sin and Death! You shall damn yourself with your own hand—for you must!"

Inspector Wausau clicked on the light, blindly turning his head in the pillow.

"Fucking phone!"

He seized the receiver, placing it to his ear.

Damn clock said 3:14. The middle of the night. And he hadn't gotten to bed till late because of the precinct disaster. How much sleep? Forty minutes? God fucking damn!

"Yeah, who is it?"

Detective Jacobelli identified himself and reported the blaze at 68 West.

Wausau jumped up, shocked, losing his pajama bottoms. "What's the line on it?"

"Don't know," Jacobelli said. Connection was bad, hard to hear. "I'm at headquarters. It was called in."

"You stay there. I'm going."

He hung up and dressed quickly and ran out the apartment door, cursing.

An aurora of blue flames, white-tipped, furiously hot, framed the twentieth-floor hall. Shielding Father Bellofontaine, who held the crucifix in his hands, the transition complete, Reggiani looked back at the door to the Burdetts' apartment.

Ben was standing silently under the arch, an unwilling party to a nightmare, dying inside from the pain of loss.

"You must come!" Reggiani cried, cringing from the heat.

Ben looked into the void. The armies of the night had retreated, as had the essence of Charles Chazen. Ben said nothing. Nor did he move.

"God will forgive you, my son."

Reggiani entered the stairwell with Father Bellofontaine beneath a rain of wood and fire.

The death of the structure cried out; the sounds were deafening. He looked back at Ben, whose face was raining tears.

"My God!" Ben cried in agony.

And then he was gone, buried beneath the roof, hungrily devoured by the inferno.

Cardinal Reggiani grabbed Father Bellofontaine and started down into the pit of the blaze, the dancing coils to fire converging, engulfing them.

27

Detective Wausau angled the squad car to the curb, jumped out, shading his eyes from the blinding light, and looked up and down the street, trying to locate someone in authority. All he could see was confusion. The block was jammed with fire engines. Blockades at either cross avenue held back pedestrians, while patrolmen manned the alleys and doorways.

Above him the inferno, which had started less than an hour before, continued uncontrolled, surpassing the ferocity of any fire he had ever witnessed. What had once been 68 West Eighty-ninth Street was engulfed in flames, the heat so intense that Wausau had to cover his face with his hands to prevent the searing of his flesh.

He burrowed into the melee, avoiding the confused network of hoses that stretched from the hydrants and engines to the building, moving from one truck to the next, his eyes shifting from the burnished faces to the hulk of flaming wood and metal above, his thoughts wandering, sifting the improbabilities. Only several hours before, a precinct headquarters had blown up and burned to the ground, a building that had held Father McGuire, the man who had been arrested for the murder of another priest, Monsignor Franchino, who had died inside the very building that was rapidly decomposing only yards away. Surely both fires could have started from natural causes. It was illogical to draw a parallel. Yet, that was precisely what he was doing, and including for good measure the fact of Inspector Burstein's untimely death from arson. Fire seemed to be the implement of eradication, the means of destroying the people who knew and the facts that existed.

He located the fire captain near the largest of the trucks and identified himself; the two men slid into a nearby patrol car and closed the doors.

"She's completely out of control," the chief said, looking up at the building through the windshield.

"How long will it take to put it out?"

"Several hours at least." His voice was strained. "We're trying to contain it."

Wausau shook his head. "Any idea how it started?"

"No. We can only guess. We questioned some of the tenants. No clue there. Fortunately, most of the tenants escaped."

"You said 'most'?"

"The building employees helped us get a head count. There are fifteen people unaccounted for, including everyone on the twentieth floor."

Wausau's eyes stretched wide. "Are you sure of this?"

"Pretty much." He pointed toward a fireman standing near the command area. "He'd be the one to talk to. But there's no rush. No one's coming out of there alive. We can take a more accurate count later."

Wausau popped a piece of gum into his mouth and nodded. "Where did it start?"

The fire chief began to answer, then stopped as a violent explosion ripped through the frame. "We're not sure," he finally said, "though it probably began on one of the top floors. The doorman received a call from a tenant on eighteen, who reported smoke in the halls and heat along the ceiling. The doorman called the department and evacuated the building. By the time we got here, the fire was out of control." He paused, rubbing his hands through the stubble of a beard. "Until it's out and we've had enough time to investigate, there's no sure way to tell where and how it started and whether or not there's arson involved."

"I see," Wausau said as he watched a segment of the building's wall cave in.

He thanked the chief, left the car, approached the man the chief had indicated, identified himself once more, and reviewed the list of known survivors. No one from the twentieth floor was listed. Either none of them had been inside—unlikely; or they had fled the building and the area as quickly as possible—also unlikely; or they had all perished.

Wausau returned the list. It occurred to him that they might never uncover the truth about the compactor murder or discover the identity of the victim, much less unravel the peculiar sequence of recent events and its possible relationship, if one existed, to the series of deaths that had occurred in the old brownstone more than fifteen years ago. As he looked up at the fire, he realized that Father McGuire was his only hope. McGuire alone held the key to the mystery. And Father McGuire was still missing.

He looked at his watch. Soon it would be morning. Perhaps the detail in charge of the precinct disaster had found McGuire or had, at least, discovered a clue to his whereabouts.

Returning to his car, he climbed inside, popped

another piece of gum into his mouth, then drove off through the blockade into the night.

Two days later Detective Jacobelli entered Wausau's office and sat in the chair opposite the desk, holding a clipboard in his hand.

"You have the report?" Wausau asked, sipping from a can of Budweiser.

"You're not going to like it," Jacobelli warned.

Wausau nodded. "I know."

Jacobelli consulted the paper. "The precinct fire had one certified fatality—an old prisoner found in the stairwell, who died of smoke inhalation. Father McGuire is the only person in the building unaccounted for. He did not die in the flames, and we assume he escaped. How, we don't know."

"Okay," Wausau said, nodding.

"Sixty-eight West Eighty-ninth Street. All but four people survived. One victim was the nun, Sister Therese. She was found in her twentieth-floor apartment. A second victim was a priest, a Father Tepper, found in the stairwell. We're checking the archdiocese for additional information to help contact relatives. The third victim, found on twenty also, was Benjamin Burdett."

Wausau shook his head. "Was the fourth his wife?"

"No. There's no sign of her. The remaining body was a man's. Apparently Mrs. Burdett wasn't in the building at the time of the blaze. The people who were taking care of her baby contacted us; they haven't heard from her yet."

"I want her found!" Wausau said.

"I've already issued the orders."

Wausau nodded. "Who was the man?"

"We don't know. His body was discovered in the elevator shaft, so burned and decomposed that identification is impossible."

"Can the medical examiner's office make an intelligent guess?"

"They doubt it, but they're still trying."

Wausau leaned toward Jacobelli and took the clipboard. He looked over the report, shaking his head, then placed it on the desk, unwrapped a new stick of gum, and popped it into his mouth.

The 1956 DeSoto backfired as John Sorrenson pressed the accelerator and wheeled the car off Central Park West onto Eighty-ninth Street. The day was warm and humid. The tart smell of a recent rainshower remained. Sorrenson's jacket lay on the back seat next to an uncovered cello and a hastily packed suitcase that was losing its contents. His white shirt was soiled, stained by sweat, and his beard was heavy.

He abruptly stopped the car midblock and stared at the monument of twisted metal and wire that stood where 68 West used to be. "My God," he said, rubbing the deep stubble of beard, his eyes flared in shock, his body shaking.

He pulled the car quickly to the curb, jumped out, and leaned against the barrier that had been raised around the debris. The scent of fire still tainted the air, though no doubt it had been several days since the blaze. He read the notice posted by the New York Fire Department. Then he walked along the sidewalk, staring at the remains.

"What happened here?" he asked an elderly black woman who passed by.

"A fire," she said, swinging a hatbox in her chubby right hand. "A bad one, I hear. Killed some, too."

"When? How?" Sorrenson cried, confused.

The woman stopped, stared at the old man, then walked toward the corner.

"This was my home!" Sorrenson screamed, moving quickly behind her.

The woman ignored him; he shook his head and returned to the car. Leaning against the fender, he massaged his forehead, squinting into a splash of late-afternoon sunlight. Then he crossed the street and looked through a hole in the fence surrounding the construction site of St. Simon's. The area was empty, the excavation partially filled with water; all the trucks and heavy machinery were gone, and there were no workmen.

Confused, he climbed back into the car and started the engine. There was a police precinct on Columbus, two blocks downtown. Someone there could tell him what had happened, perhaps even suggest who he could contact to determine whether anything had been salvaged.

He disengaged the parking brake, pressed his foot nimbly on the accelerator, and maneuvered the car down the block.

The sun had descended beneath the roof lines when Sorrenson returned to the site of the disaster and parked his car alongside the remains of the building he had called his home. Wiping tears from his eyes, he placed his hands in his lap and stared at the foundation, trying desperately to harden himself against the terrible reality of what he had learned. A chill had replaced the afternoon's warmth. Starting to shiver, he grabbed his jacket off the back seat and draped it over his shoulders, handling the fabric carefully; it was all he had left. All his possessions had been housed in his twentieth-floor apartment, and according to the police, nothing had been salvaged. He had little faith in banks, so most of his savings, kept in a box under the kitchen sink, were gone too.

The sun had set by the time Sorrenson wrenched himself from his self-pity. He had no family, but he hoped one of the members of the philharmonic would house him temporarily—at least until he had settled his affairs and arranged a loan. He would go to Philharmonic Hall first.

As he started the car, a cab pulled in front of him. Max and Grace Woodbridge climbed out.

"Max!" Sorrenson called.

Grace Woodbridge started to scream, Max grabbed her and tried to console her.

Sorrenson got out of the car and rushed to their side. Grace was hysterical, trying to climb over the protective wall, grasping her husband, crying, pounding her fists against her side.

"There's nothing we can do," Max said as he watched her dab at her eyes with a handkerchief.

"Nothing at all," Sorrenson agreed, his own frustrations fraying his voice. "The fire happened. There's no way we can bring back the building or anything that was in it."

The two men helped Grace Woodbridge into Sorrenson's car.

"What happened, John?" Max asked as he leaned against the car's fender.

"I just spoke to the police. The place burned four days ago—in the middle of the night. They think the fire started on the twentieth floor. There was nothing the fire department could do."

"My God. Oh . . . my God," Grace moaned.

Max took her hand. "Was anyone hurt?"

Sorrenson nodded. "Yes," he said, his voice quavering. "The old nun died. So did . . . Ben Burdett."

"Oh no!" Max said, shaking his head in disbelief.

"And Faye?" Grace asked, crying brokenly.

"The police haven't been able to find her. Fortunately, the baby survived. Ben had sent little Joey to friends for the evening."

Max placed his arm around Sorrenson's shoulder. "It's incredible, John. Just unbelievable. How will we ever dig ourselves out of this?"

Sorrenson shrugged. "We'll just have to, that's all."

"We're lucky we went away," Max observed, swallowing heavily.

"Yes," Grace agreed. "So lucky."

Sorrenson turned and stared at them. "Yes . . . you were most fortunate. But where were you?"

"What do you mean, John?" Max was puzzled.

"Where were you? Where did you go? Why did you leave town?"

Max stared at his wife. His expression was blank. He rubbed his chin with his hand, then drew his fingers through the thinning gray-black hair on his head. "I don't know!" he said, overcome with confusion. "Do you, dear?"

Grace thought for a second, then shook her head.

"You must have gone somewhere."

"Of course, John," Max said, suddenly smiling. "We went to . . ." He stopped talking again, shaking his head, trying to remember, confused.

"Max," Sorrenson said, gripping his forearm, "something is very wrong."

"Because we don't remember where we were?"

"Yes. And because I don't either."

"You don't?"

Sorrenson shook his head. "The last four days are blank, and I didn't realize it until the police asked me the same question I just asked you."

Grace Woodbridge wiped her dripping mascara with a tissue. "I don't understand."

"Neither do I," said Sorrenson. "And neither do Daniel Batille or the two secretaries." He cleared his throat and buttoned his jacket. "They also returned here after being away for four days. They also went to the police and were asked about their whereabouts. None of them knew where they had been."

"And Jenkins?"

"No one knows where he is. The police found a man's body in the elevator shaft. It could be him."

Max Woodbridge shook his head. "Four days. Four dead days. It's impossible!"

Sorrenson glanced back at the remains of the building. A dog was rummaging through the toppled wood. Two children were playing with a window frame they had dragged over the barrier. The rest of the lot was deserted.

"Impossible?" he asked, smirking.

EPILOGUE

It was nearly noon. The temperature was just over eighty, the air dry and invigorating.

A Yellow Cab pulled to the curb on St. Ignacio Street in the barrio of East Los Angeles and deposited two passengers in front of a three-story Tudor house with a broken front stoop and boarded-up ground-floor windows. The house was seemingly abandoned, but a shadow behind a drawn beige curtain in the center third-floor window suggested the presence of an occupant.

Cardinal Reggiani looked at Sister Florence and smiled, pleased with the neighborhood; the decision to remove the Sentinel from New York had been wise, and he felt he had selected the right place.

They walked up to the front entrance. Reggiani opened the door with a key. They paused at the base of the main staircase, inspecting the interior. The walls and floors were bare. There was no furniture. The air was heavy with the smell of mildew.

The banister swayed as they started to climb. Sister Florence shivered, disturbed by the surroundings. Cardinal Reggiani reassured her, then led her up the final ascent to the third floor, which was as uninviting as the rest of the building.

Reggiani opened the nearest door with the key he had used to enter the building. They went in.

Inside, someone was seated on a wooden chair facing the center window. Reggiani moved slowly through the barren room. Sister Florence followed. It was very cold; a horrible odor of decayed flesh pervaded the air.

Reggiani walked around the chair. "Father Bellofontaine," he whispered, his voice choked with emotion. He looked back at Sister Florence and beckoned.

She moved to Reggiani's side and crossed herself. "May God have mercy on his soul!"

Reggiani stared at what had been Father James McGuire. Father Bellofontaine resembled his predecessors. He sat motionless, holding the gold crucifix. His face was shriveled and colorless, the skin wrinkled and pocked. His pupils were covered with cataracts. The hair on his head was matted together and strangely damp. His fingers were dry, spindly, tipped by long curled nails like the claws of a sloth. There was no detectable movement in his chest, no sign that he was actually alive.

Yet he was. Seated as had been intended from the beginning. Although they had nearly failed, Father Bellofontaine's salvation had been achieved.

Reggiani shook his head. The past months, with their achievements and failures, had nearly severed his sanity: the deaths of Sister Angelina and Biroc; the intervention of Ben Burdett, Gatz, and so many others; their manipulation of Burdett, once he had become convinced that Faye was the chosen; the sham of the death watch, perpetrated to continue McGuire's unknowing path and cover the nature of the aging process; the horrible revelation of Faye's identity; the transformation of Ben Burdett's opposition to allegiance; the miraculous escape from the burning building; and finally, Franchino's death, his sacrifice, the incredible courage of a man who had allowed himself to be destroyed by Satan so that Father McGuire would be further drawn along—unknowing.

So many things, so many moments.

"And so it ends," Reggiani said softly, though he knew that someday the process would start again—perhaps in his lifetime.

During Reggiani's two weeks in Los Angeles, he had made the necessary arrangements to protect Father Bellofontaine. Cardinal Willings of the Archdiocese of Los Angeles had been contacted, and, of necessity, included in the small circle of knowledgeable church officials. The land adjoining Father Bellofontaine's sanctuary had been purchased, and preliminary architectural plans had been commissioned for the construction of a modest church from which Father Bellofontaine could be unobtrusively observed and guarded. And a successor to Monsignor Franchino had been appointed from within the Archdiocese of Los Angeles, charged to oversee the building, secure the safety of Father Bellofontaine, and prepare for the day when a new Sentinel would be chosen.

"We must go," Reggiani said.

Sister Florence nodded, content. She had asked to see Father Bellofontaine, and Reggiani had granted the request.

They descended the staircase to the ground floor and emerged onto the lawn, where they paused to look up at the shaded outline of Father Bellofontaine. The focus of the midday sun was directed against the glass. They squinted, and back-stepped toward the walk, trying to frame the image for their memories. Then they turned to the north, walking up the block toward the corner.

Moments later Father Bellofontaine inched forward in his chair and lowered the cross, his hands seared along the palms. He did nothing for several minutes, then sat back, flashed a sardonic grin, and began to laugh, the sound emerging from a deep well of nonemotion, his body gradually losing its substance, reforming into that of Charles Chazen, eyes burning with fire, reveling in success. The entire room filled with shapeless forms waiting for a sign. Chazen smiled. The clamor began anew, the sound of clashing metal and baleful cries.

"I call ye and declare ye now returned," he cried. "Successful beyond hope to lead ye forth. Triumphant out of this infernal pit." How many times had he called his armies, to no avail? But now it was different. Prior to the transition, he had preyed upon Father James McGuire when there was no one to protect the priest. For the first time since the millennium, a chosen successor to the angel Gabriel had been perverted! Father James McGuire had taken his life and joined them. And Chazen had assumed McGuire's mortal form, to accomplish the charade for Cardinal Reggiani and Ben Burdett during the transition, his consummate powers also preventing the Almighty God from discovering the deception. And now he needed only time—moments to muster the armies of the night, the legions of hell. Brazen with defiance, he called again. "We move triumphant out of his infernal pit. Abominable, accursed, the house of woe, dungeon of our tyrant."

The building began to rumble; the clamor rose. Chazen stepped into the masses and stopped before the forms of Jack Cooper's and Ben Burdett's souls, both without substance, like wisps of air. And then into the doorway stepped his anointed, the soul of Father James McGuire, the chosen of the Lord God, the perverted instrument of the Almighty's powers—now one of them.

"Now possess, as Lords, a spacious world, to our native heaven little inferior, by my adventures hard with peril great achieved."

Amid a swarm of flashing light and vapors, hell's own echo filled the room, rocking the foundation with a tremor of cataclysm.

Chazen watched the dimensionless hordes, realizing that the next Messiah would be himself.

The outcry continuing, he inched back toward the seat, sat once again, and placed the cross in front of him, to perpetuate the deception until the time was right, to wait in the seemingly deserted building in a downtrodden neighborhood on the east side of Los Angeles.

Postscript

Two days after Cardinal Reggiani had returned to Rome, he was awakened by an aide at three o'clock in the morning and handed a telegram annotated "urgent." The telegram came from the offices of the Archdiocese of New York.

Sitting up on the edge of his bed, Reggiani turned on the table lamp and opened the message. He read:

REGGIANI. NEW YORK MEDICAL EXAMINER HAS COMPLETED WORK ON THE REMAINS FOUND IN THE 68 WEST 89TH STREET FIRE, BODY FOUND IN ELEVATOR SHAFT HAS BEEN POSITIVELY IDENTIFIED AS THAT OF FATHER JAMES MCGUIRE. PLEASE ADVISE.

Reggiani shot to his feet, looking out into the shadows of the room.

"Are you all right?" the aide asked.

Reggiani began to tremble and pale, saying nothing. Suddenly he grabbed for his chest, the realization of what had happened striking his body like a jolt of electricity. He stumbled. The aide grabbed him and laid him on the bed. He began to shake, to gasp, grabbing his chest again, convulsing. He arched high on the bed, then settled back onto the twisted sheets as the coronary overwhelmed his body.

He was dead.

ABOUT THE AUTHOR

Born in New York and educated at Cornell and the Columbia University School of Law, JEFFREY KONVITZ began his career in 1969 working for a Hollywood talent agency. His stay there was short. Living by his motto—The day you take a job, prepare for the day you are fired, which is tomorrow—he wrote a film script *Silent Night, Bloody Night* which he ultimately produced himself. The film has since gone on to immortality on late-night television fright shows. Subsequent to the film's release he was general counsel to a theater chain and a production executive at Metro-Goldwyn-Mayer studios. It was during this period that he wrote his first novel, *The Sentinel*. The book was sold to hardcover and then to paperback where it became a multi-million-copy bestseller. Universal Pictures produced the film version. Since then Jeffrey has gone into high gear. He sold screenplays to two studios, finished *The Guardian*, and is currently writing as well as producing the film *Summer Dreams* for American International Pictures and a television version of the off-Broadway hit *El Grande de Coca Cola* for Home Box Office Cable Television. He lives in Beverly Hills, California.

RELAX!
SIT DOWN
and Catch Up On Your Reading!

☐	11877	**HOLOCAUST** by Gerald Green	$2.25
☐	12836	**THE CHANCELLOR MANUSCRIPT** by Robert Ludlum	$2.75
☐	10077	**TRINITY** by Leon Uris	$2.75
☐	2300	**THE MONEYCHANGERS** by Arthur Hailey	$1.95
☐	12550	**THE MEDITERRANEAN CAPER** by Clive Cussler	$2.25
☐	11469	**AN EXCHANGE OF EAGLES** by Owen Sela	$2.25
☐	2600	**RAGTIME** by E. L. Doctorow	$2.25
☐	11428	**FAIRYTALES** by Cynthia Freeman	$2.25
☐	11966	**THE ODESSA FILE** by Frederick Forsyth	$2.25
☐	11557	**BLOOD RED ROSES** by Elizabeth B. Coker	$2.25
☐	11708	**JAWS 2** by Hank Searls	$2.25
☐	12490	**TINKER, TAILOR, SOLDIER, SPY** by John Le Carre	$2.50
☐	11929	**THE DOGS OF WAR** by Frederick Forsyth	$2.25
☐	10526	**INDIA ALLEN** by Elizabeth B. Coker	$1.95
☐	12489	**THE HARRAD EXPERIMENT** by Robert Rimmer	$2.25
☐	11767	**IMPERIAL 109** by Richard Doyle	$2.50
☐	10500	**DOLORES** by Jacqueline Susann	$1.95
☐	11601	**THE LOVE MACHINE** by Jacqueline Susann	$2.25
☐	11886	**PROFESSOR OF DESIRE** by Philip Roth	$2.50
☐	10857	**THE DAY OF THE JACKAL** by Frederick Forsyth	$1.95
☐	11952	**DRAGONARD** by Rupert Gilchrist	$1.95
☐	11331	**THE HAIGERLOCH PROJECT** by Ib Melchior	$2.25
☐	11330	**THE BEGGARS ARE COMING** by Mary Loos	$1.95

Buy them at your local bookstore or use this handy coupon for ordering:

DON'T MISS

THESE CURRENT

Bantam Bestsellers

☐	11708	**JAWS 2** Hank Searls	$2.25
☐	11150	**THE BOOK OF LISTS** Wallechinsky & Wallace	$2.50
☐	11001	**DR. ATKINS DIET REVOLUTION**	$2.25
☐	11161	**CHANGING** Liv Ullmann	$2.25
☐	12683	**EVEN COWGIRLS GET THE BLUES** Tom Robbins	$2.75
☐	10077	**TRINITY** Leon Uris	$2.75
☐	12250	**ALL CREATURES GREAT AND SMALL** James Herriot	$2.50
☐	12256	**ALL THINGS BRIGHT AND BEAUTIFUL** James Herriot	$2.50
☐	11770	**ONCE IS NOT ENOUGH** Jacqueline Susann	$2.25
☐	11470	**DELTA OF VENUS** Anais Nin	$2.50
☐	10150	**FUTURE SHOCK** Alvin Toffler	$2.25
☐	12196	**PASSAGES** Gail Sheehy	$2.75
☐	11255	**THE GUINNESS BOOK OF WORLD RECORDS** 16th Ed. The McWhirters	$2.25
☐	12220	**LIFE AFTER LIFE** Raymond Moody, Jr.	$2.25
☐	11917	**LINDA GOODMAN'S SUN SIGNS**	$2.50
☐	10310	**ZEN AND THE ART OF MOTORCYCLE MAINTENANCE** Pirsig	$2.50
☐	10888	**RAISE THE TITANIC!** Clive Cussler	$2.25
☐	11267	**AQUARIUS MISSION** Martin Caidin	$2.25
☐	11897	**FLESH AND BLOOD** Pete Hamill	$2.50

uy them at your local bookstore or use this handy coupon for ordering:

Bantam Books, Inc., Dept. FB, 414 East Golf Road, Des Plaines, Ill. 60016

Please send me the books I have checked above. I am enclosing $_____
(please add 75¢ to cover postage and handling). Send check or money order
—no cash or C.O.D.'s please

Mr/Mrs/Miss _____

Address _____

City _____ State/Zip _____

FB—1/79

Please allow four weeks for delivery. This offer expires 7/79.

Bantam Book Catalog

Here's your up-to-the-minute listing of over 1,400 titles by your favorite authors.

This illustrated, large format catalog gives a description of each title. For your convenience it is divided into categories in fiction and non-fiction—gothics, science fiction, westerns, mysteries, cookbooks, mysticism and occult, biographies, history, family living, health, psychology, art.

So don't delay—take advantage of this special opportunity to increase your reading pleasure.

Just send us your name and address and 50¢ (to help defray postage and handling costs).